IDRISTAN

IDRISTAN

by

Nick Weldon

published by Verge

Published by Verge 2009

ISBN 978-0-9561129-0-3

Copyright © Nick Weldon 2008

Nick Weldon has asserted his right under the Copyright, Designs and Patents Act 1988 to be identified as the author of this work

All rights reserved. No part of this book may be reproduced in any form or by any means without the prior written consent of the Publisher, excepting brief quotes used in reviews.

This novel is a work of fiction. Names, characters, places and incidents are either the product of the author's imagination, or are used fictitiously. Any resemblance to actual persons, living or dead, or events is entirely coincidental.

Verge
The Shoefactory
23b Fitzwilliam Street
Rushden
Northamptonshire
NN10 9YW
UK

comprising

ROYAL MUSICS
the first book

THE KING'S EAR
the second book

THE MABOOB MOB
the third book

these being the first three books of

IDRISTAN

in
ninety-five chaplets

to my good friends

JC and TT

ROYAL MUSICS

the first book

Chaplet 1

Fever

Weird dreams come with the ear infection; fever, and weird dreams. The phone is ringing but I don't want to answer it yet; it might just be cymbals anyway.

Chaplet 2

Play Pretty

As the last note died away, Spiff Abrahams allowed the mouthpiece of his solid gold saxophone to drift clear of his teeth, nudged from below by the insistent pressure of his large throbbing member on the bell of the horn. He smiled, a coy covered grin, as he realized how beautifully he had just played, and thanked God, as he did every day, that he was still able to be excited by himself.

The desk phone rang, a jarring tone and three cents sharp of the glorious saxophone note that lingered in the room. Spiff sighed and picked up the receiver.

"Your meeting is in fifteen. Don't be late". The voice belonged to the fiercely charming secretary of the Conservatory Principal.

"Thanks, Muff", said Spiff. "I'll be there".

Myfanwy Maboob was Muff to the world. She was a Welsh Essex girl, though her grandparents were from Pakistan, and Spiff was eager to fuck her.

For one thing, he mused, as he packed away the more controllable of his two horns, I need a friend in that office.

Indeed today was the date of his Annual Performance Review, which was the subject of his meeting with the Principal, and Spiff feared the homecoming of some nasty chickens.

For another thing, he mused, there are those amazing tits. He stroked himself gently and crooned the old tune, in the manner of a lullaby. "There'll be a welcome in the hillsides..."

Spiff heard a cough. Looking down he realized that there was still a student in the room. The young Japanese man knelt before him, his own saxophone still in its unopened case across the room.

"It is such great honour, Spiff sensai, to hear you play. Your tunes are always so mightily pretty. Perhaps in your wisdom one day you will hear me play, excellency, and advise me of my shortcomings. I know I am unworthy, but this is my final year. I must leave soon, and would know my unworthiness more completely".

Anger boiled up in Spiff's body and his member jerked wildly. He wanted to strike this oily-tongued oik, this insolent dog who dared to invoke even the possibility of remote comparison with his master. He knew he would enjoy the boy's pain. But he knew also that in his current position he must exercise restraint; especially today, the date of his Annual Performance Review.

"Pretty? Mmmm. Pretty, you say?". Spiff spoke in a deadly whisper.

"Oh yes, Spiff sensai. Mightily pretty", replied the boy, innocently, and his face, taking on a vacant, sentimental cast, began to produce a tuneless pentatonic hum.

"Was Wagner pretty?", Spiff barked. "Schoenberg? Did they call John Coltrane pretty?" . He was shouting now, banging his fist on the desk. His student covered his face in his hands and wept in gratitude as his master enlightened him.

"I am Professor Spiff Abrahams of the Royal English Conservatory of Music", he shrieked. "You have come here to receive excellence; I must therefore give you such. You cannot waste your time here listening to yourself play. After all..." His voice softened at this point, though paradoxically his dick grew hard.

"After all, you have your whole life in which to contemplate your own mediocrity. Here, you are here for something else, something else entirely".

His student now clasped him round the knees.

"Oh thank you Spiff sensai, thank you. I am so honoured". The professor bent down, reaching behind the boy's head to thread fingers through his cute ponytail and pull him upwards until their faces almost touched. He all but spat into the boy's mouth.

"Never say pretty to me!".

As he made his way from his tiny top floor room down through the bowels of the ancient buildings towards the throne of power, Spiff felt strangely calm and powerful. He reminded himself to remind himself, next time he needed reminding, what a bloody good teacher he really was.

The short Asian woman who followed him everywhere knew that the briefcase he carried was quite empty; she knew that he carried it partly to reassure his bosses of his seriousness but mainly to conceal the corduroy knob in his front.

She understood that his most reliable asset was also the one most likely to embarrass him.

Spiff Abrahams, after all, was a man who got a hard-on just thinking about himself.

Chaplet 3

The Puzzle Of Beauty

If Myfanwy Muff Maboob had amazing tits, she also had a brain to match. With the combination of the three of them, she should by rights have landed an amazing job, an amazing husband, and an amazing house as well.

That she worked as a lowly secretary, that she lived alone in a caravan on remote wasteland in Chigwell, that she was single and lonely, well, you see, these quite regrettable circumstances all flowed from the fact that Myfanwy was caught in a puzzle about the nature of beauty.

The voice of her father was warm and kind, and his touch at the piano singing and mellow; Muff was bathed in beauty from her first breath. Yet because she could not reproduce it herself, because the flow of beauty seemed to dry up as it entered her body, because her own piano playing was hard, harsh and brittle, and her own voice scratchy and ugly, beauty, the nature of beauty, became a problem for Muff, a conundrum that both distracted and distressed her.

Her brain was both capacious and rapacious. She read music easily, and early, and by the age of nine had memorized the complete piano works of Rachmaninov, Debussy, Busoni, Lizst and Ligeti. She could play them as well.

They called her a genius, at school. Why then, Muff had to ask herself, did her father's voice grow cool when he spoke of her musical ability? Did he not love her, she wondered? The answer came in her teens, one fateful morning at the Saturday School of the Royal English Conservatory of Music, from her piano teacher, a plain-speaking young American named Cornelius Brewster.

"Very impressive, Miss Maboob", he responded, as she fisted out the final frantic chords of Rachmaninov's Third Piano Concerto. "Now see if you can make it sound like music".

Muff could not make music; she knew this better than anybody. Perhaps this nice man could help her.

"Tell me how", she asked him.

"You have the brain, you have the muscle tone, the finger strength; you have the technique. Everything is in place. Yet...".

He paused, then sighed.

"You are not alone, you know", he said. "An extreme case, yes, but by no means an isolated one. Because the piano looks so complex, with all of its notes on display, you see, it tends to attract boys and girls who are busy and brainy".

He sighed again.

"Just as the other percussion, the drums and bells and so on, attract the violent ones, who like hitting things. But busy, brainy, violent doth not the musician make".

Muff nodded eagerly, sensing him to be close to an answer.

"It needs to sing, you see", he said, leaning over to play the opening phrase of the slow movement, lovingly, 'dah dah dah dah dah', and as his arm rubbed softly, unconsciously, against her breast, she recognized the beauty in his playing.

"The upper partials must be there, you see', he purred, sounding a high Db over and over again, "and the upper partials will only come out if coaxed; coaxed and caressed". He stroked a few times more at the Db.

"But if you bash it like this", he struck the note violently now, "it will shout back at you in anger. Ugly, sour".

Muff had no idea what an upper partial was, but understood that she needed to play higher up in order to make the piano sing. She began the piece again, but on a higher note, for her brain was easily strong enough to do the necessary calculations. Cornelius shook his head as she played, partly in awe of her powers of transposition, partly in despair at her sound. With each shake of his head, she transposed again. Higher, higher, she went, up through the twelve keys, and the higher she went, the harder she played.

When Muff finally ran out of notes at the top of the piano, Cornelius was holding his hands to his ears with the look of a tormented frog upon his face. She brought the lid crashing down over the keyboard and ran sobbing from the room, and never touched a piano again.

That evening her father told Muff that he loved her. He was relieved that someone else had been holding the mirror.

Myfanwy found her answer that day, but it was merely the

beginning of another question. Her father loved her, but she could not make music. She felt she had failed him, and the steadfastness of his love merely intensified her feeling of failing.

There was another interpretation, towards which skilled therapists might have pointed her, but these were thin on the ground in Shadwell Heath. She might have concluded that she must be a very good person indeed for her father to love her so, despite her lack of music; she might have used her father's love to empower rather than to undermine herself; she might have struck out into new territories and found there the amazing job, the amazing husband and the amazing house that her amazing tits deserved.

Instead she lived alone in her caravan in Essex, and commuted each weekday to her mundane job at the Royal English, and she did this in order to be close at all times to music and musicians, to be as close as possible to what she couldn't play, and what she couldn't be.

If this seems strange, even masochistic, psychotherapy tells us it is very normal, that we spend most of our adult lives recreating the trauma of our childhood. And this was the case for Muff. But there was something else with her, for she was not only busy and brainy, but also a very proud, a very curious, a very courageous girl. She could have sidestepped her lack of music and used her father's love to go on to great and easy things. But she knew by instinct that the door onto her true destiny lay hidden in the murky pit of her own failure, and that she must stay only in that place if she would see that door open.

So this was the plan of Myfanwy Muff Maboob, for she needed above all to understand her lack of music, and find her own place, as well, in the puzzle of beauty.

Chaplet 4

The Cutting Edge Of Bip-Bop

It was with a mixed set of feelings that Cornelius Coltrane Brewster, youngest ever Principal of the Royal English Conservatory of Music, now surveyed his youngest ever Head of Jazz in his grand office down on the coveted lower corridor of the basement floor. He found Spiff Abrahams to be an utter buffoon. Yet his buffoonery was so natural, so unforced, so artless, and so quintessentially English, that Cornelius actually envied him for it.

Cornelius was a Jewish African American with a hard-on for the English. A self-styled squire, he frequented Annabel's and Rules, hunted out in the shires at the weekends, was a member at MCC, where he also played Real Tennis, and in his work at the Conservatory, tirelessly championed the music of the great English composers; Elgar, Purcell, Arnold, McCartney. Above all he loathed blues and jazz, which he regarded as one regards demented shaming relatives from a forgotten era. His father had been a jazz musician, and he hated the ugly middle name he had inherited from him. His own preference in light music was for something more hummable; Neil Diamond, perhaps, or Barry Manilow. Cornelius had been mortified to learn that a condition of his appointment was the perceived expansion of the Royal English Jazz Faculty.

Fortunately for him, he had found rising young jazz star Spiff Abrahams. It was like striking gold! Spiff had quickly dismantled the entire Jazz Faculty, removing twenty years of cultural cohesion, professional solidarity and teaching expertise in the space of a few short months, and then brought in a random selection of impressionable firefly celebrities from the pop session world to plug the gaps. This led inevitably to a massive drop in applications from quality students, opening the door to a correspondingly massive increase in the intake of foreign students, at the higher fee rate. My how the coffers had swelled!

The beauty of it was, reflected Cornelius, that the young fool had done it by accident, while intending something else. Or so he seemed to be saying.

"...and above all my new collaborators will be cutting edge!".

Cornelius smiled encouragingly at Spiff and reflected that the man was just as delusional when it came to his playing. For while he talked of great forces of anarchy, spirit and social chromaticism in his solos, all that ever came out was the same old tritely diatonic English folk songs.

A great lump arose in Cornelius's throat as he confronted his own reality, that no matter how hard he tried, he would never achieve this level of sublime Englishness himself. His heart was suddenly full of rage as he listened to Spiff blither on.

"My strength is my vision; my artistic vision. And I suppose my improvisations, in which I bring together two worlds, ancient and contemporary, the one raw, visceral and unwieldy, the other brittle, convenient and free of hope".

"Yes, you cunt", thought Cornelius, "that's why everything you play sounds like Green Grow The Fuckin' Rushes O!". His spoken words were more moderate.

"Quite, quite, old chap. That's very good to hear", he intersposed. "But we're perhaps slightly concerned at the level of ethnic creep on the course". He paused and smirked at the felicity of his own phrase. Spiff looked bewildered as Cornelius continued.

"This chap you took on for the Rhythm Method weekend, for example. Ahmed Tom Tom McSplash. Obviously a very effective teacher. And completely cutting edge. And we were perhaps naive in scheduling your weekend against the Elgar. But our concertgoers were most alarmed to find their drinks interval taken over by a half-naked Drum Orchestra. We feel perhaps, some of us, that this establishment was in fact created as a defence against just this sort of tribal hokey-cokey. Lady Mount Sand Rogers-Gardener, who, I need not remind you, is one of our most generous benefactors, is still looking for her husband, whom she lost in the, ahem, pêle-mêle".

"Pall Mall", said Spiff, ever bewildered, "What was he doing down there?". Cornelius pressed on.

"The point is, dear boy. We love what you're doing, but simply urge temperance and caution. And especially patience! We're a long old boat here, you know. Takes us a while to change direction. Take this Bip-Bop thing of yours. It sounds very mysterious and new. Is it just for your saxophonium thingummy, or can it be played on musical instruments as well?". At last Spiff had an idea what Cornelius Brewster was talking about.

"I think you're confusing two things, Principal. There's bebop, which is African American music from the 1940s, and there's hiphop, which is African American music from, well, from now, I suppose".

Cornelius smiled brightly. "That's where you lose me, old boy. I still can't tell the difference. Makes more sense to put them together, don't you think? Bip-Bop!"

There was silence in the room while a great light came on in Spiff's dark and crowded mind. He suddenly saw far and clear into the future, to the birth of a new metaphysics, of a new shape of musical man, built in Spiff's own image.

"Of course, Principal. What an inspired idea. You are perfectly right", he breathed.

Cornelius reached forward across the desk and took Spiff's hands in his own.

"Now, my boy! If you could only do your Bip-Bop, but also bring some of those lovely English qualities of yours into the mix! Now look, I've had an idea. There are some people I'd like you to meet. Some very important, influential people. Friends of the Conservatory. Friends of the Nation. Friends, I believe, who can help you with your ideas".

Spiff left the Principal's office having promised to return there later the same day to meet his secret friends.

Cornelius sat back in his chair and smiled, pleased with his day's work. A great lump arose in his trousers, along with a wet, tickling sensation, and Cornelius realized with surprise that there was still a secretary in the room. It was Myfanwy Muff Maboob; she was under the table attending to the Principal's privates, and she had heard every word of the confidential meeting!

Chaplet 5

A Word To The Wise

Myfanwy rang the number by instinct, without quite knowing why. The words of her Principal had been alarmingly jingoistic, and Muff thought she might have stumbled across a right-wing cabal of the Great and the Good. Freemasons, maybe, or Druids.

Her piano, her beautiful piano that of course she no longer played, had come from a different kind of organisation, an association of benevolent Welsh Pakistanis from the valleys who called themselves the League of Idristan. The only condition of the gift had been to swear loyalty to the League and to promote the health and spiritual welfare of Idristanis everywhere.

Muff knew little about the League, other than that it had Red Dragons as an emblem, that it was linked to the cause of the Welsh Separatists, that its members were highly suspicious of the English Establishment, and that it was funded by weighty and powerful political and financial players unknown.

She rang the number on her League Membership Card,

and was connected to the small dusty bookshop in Greenford, on the outskirts of West London, from where the League of Idristan marshalled its international resources.

She rang because she was still choked up about her lack of music, and therefore somehow doubly grateful for the piano, for the League's faith in her.

She rang in innocence, speaking in Welsh, and set in motion a concatenation of events in which our world was changed.

Chaplet 6

The Toilet Empire

Mickey was cleaning the toilets as a favour for Steve, who had nipped off early to see his beloved Arsenal at the Emirates. Len was upstairs on the front desk, happy enough to watch the willowy string players waft out on to the London streets at the end of the day.

Even in the old days of the trio, first as residents at Ronnie Scott's, and then as inaugural Professors respectively of Jazz Piano, Double Bass and Percussion at the Royal English Conservatory, the dynamic had always been the same. Len got all the glory on piano, Steve went wherever he liked whenever he wanted on bass, and Mickey the drummer was somehow always up to his knees and elbows in shit.

It was a bit of a climb-down, from Professor of Percussion, in line for an OBE, at the very least, to toilet attendant, but in the face of Spiff Abraham's new broom, Mickey, like the others, had been grateful for a job. And the academic and rhythmic skills still came in useful.

"Oh yes", said Mickey to the empty toilets, "I've got you lot sussed!".

He had calculated that the room generated 793 possible placements, or mop-points, and knew exactly how long it would take him to achieve total cleanliness.

As he counted in the tempo and prepared for his first mop-strike, the door burst open and the large brooding figure of Victor, the Nigerian Head of Conservatory Security, hurtled into the room. Looking neither to the left or to the right, he crammed himself into the nearest cubicle, whence there immediately emanated a long squelching fart followed by a sigh of contentment and relief. Mickey twisted his vocal cords into a tight configuration and spoke in the exact likeness of Principal Cornelius Brewster.

"I say, old boy, that's one for England!"

A panicked thrumming ensued on the inside of the door.

"Who dat dere?" enquired Victor.

"It's your Principal, old boy, but don't worry about me", said Mickey, "you just carry on as though I'm not here. I suppose you want a smoke now?"

Victor grunted an affirmative and soon the room began to fill with the acrid smell of cheap tobacco. Mickey knew, like everyone in the building, that Victor was a highly effective Head of Security except in the event of something happening, when he invariably needed a big shit and a long smoke. Mickey disconnected the smoke alarm, locked the toilet door, and went along the corridor to see what was going on on Victor's screen.

A call was in progress that Victor had patched through to the Special Services Headquarters with the grading "Medium Terrorist Alert". Mickey picked up the headphones and held one side to his ear. He recognised Myfanwy Maboob's scratchy tenor immediately, but not the guttural language in which she spoke these words.

"All I know is that it's a meeting, and I think it may involve some quite high-up Establishment people. What do you want me to do? OK, I'll do what I can".

Mickey liked Muff, liked her a lot. Of course he had said goodbye to her fellatio along with all the other secretarial support services, when he had been kicked downstairs, but he didn't blame Muff for that. In fact, she could have abused the role reversal, taken advantage, but instead she carried on being the same sweet lovable girl, just without the blowjobs. Mickey went back to reclaim his toilet empire, and resolved to keep his eyes and ears open, because he had a feeling his girl Muff might need his help.

Chaplet 7

Old Bones

Myfanwy followed the two men down the service corridor and into a cupboard. Narrow stone stairs led down into the darkness; Myfanwy could hear the men chatting as they descended below her. She took off her clackety high-heeled shoes and padded down after them.

"Well, Principal, I'm intrigued. I never knew any of this existed. Where are we going, exactly?"

"This web of stairs and tunnels has been in existence for hundreds of years. It is our private route to the Palace."

"To the Palace?!!". exclaimed Spiff. "You mean?...Is that where we are going now?"

"Yes indeed, my boy", replied Cornelius Brewster, portentously. "Finally you have been called. In this hour, if you only conduct yourself well, you will receive the blessing of your Sovereign."

Myfanwy heard a curse followed by a rattling noise as objects scattered across the stone.

"Bloody Taffs!" shouted Cornelius. The men were no longer moving, and Myfanwy crept round a succession of corners

23

until she could hear the Principal's murmured explanation.

"All this, stairs, tunnels, passages, the whole caboodle, is the work of the Welsh miners. Oh, back in the 1300s, I should imagine. When the Welsh were so Welsh they were almost Jewish. They were given the Royal Decree for their pathetic little Music School in return, but it wasn't enough. They wanted Palace Rights, like the rest of us, and Guild Membership, yes and all the High Teas and Holidays. That was never going to happen. They were only ever a bunch of burrowers, after all. But there was a hunger strike, and an ugly confrontation here in the passageways, and the miners perished. Here, below ground, in their finest digging! The bones are everywhere. Bloody Taffs!".

Myfanwy trembled all over to hear the fate of her ancestors so coldly described. She vomited quietly into one of her shoes. The men were on the move again. In passing, Myfanwy swiftly gathered together the bones of her forbear and fashioned them into the semblance of a human shape. On an impulse she then removed a femur from the skeleton and tucked it inside her neat shiny red leather handbag.

Suddenly, with her hand round the human bone, Myfanwy lost all desire to carry on with the mission she had agreed to, and which was now starting to feel dangerous. She wanted to be at home, in her cosy little caravan in Chigwell.

"Let them have their stupid meeting", she told herself defiantly. Then she heard footsteps above her, two sets, coming in her direction. One set, she surmised, belonged to the short Asian woman who followed Spiff everywhere, the other, heavier, more deliberate, and further back, to Victor, the brutal and intimidating Nigerian Head of Security.

Muff knew she had no choice but to continue her descent. In front of her, Cornelius was dispensing advice.

"Above all, old boy", said the Principal, "keep banging on about Englishness. And don't mention the Welsh at all, if you can help it. They have some sort of weird obsession with the Welsh, especially the Nutter Prince. They will speak Welsh among themselves, you'll notice, even though they'll address us in English. Just pretend you think it's normal! You won't be on your own, anyway".

As he spoke he indicated the small groups of people who were now joining them in the great stone passageway leading underground to the heart of Buckingham Palace.

Spiff recognised Principals and Heads of Jazz from the other Royal Music Colleges of the City. He suddenly visualized the cutting contest to come, and saw his exhausted competitors lay down their instruments while he completed his marathon solo serenade of the Sovereign; with this beautiful thought his penis, symbol of his self-belief, twitched into life and uncurled, warm and throbbing along his inner thigh.

Chaplet 8

The Baptism

Spiff held forth about his vision while the Queen poured tea.

"My new department is completely cutting edge. We have devised a new fusion music that combines the very best of the old bebop with the best of the new hiphop, but with an unmistakeable stamp of Englishness. We call it Bip-Bop, ma'am".

Cornelius Brewster nodded approvingly. The Prince was munching some ginger cake.

"Sort of hey nonny nonny John Coltrane. What a splendid idea." His tone was playful. He began to sing in a lovely bass baritone.

"On yonder hill there stands a jazzman. Who he is I do not know. Will he ever end his solo? Is the answer yes or no?".
He gestured around him, and the Queen, King, and various little Royal people, all joined in for the chorus,

"Oh no John, no John, no John, no!".

Spiff blushed, sensing he had been the butt of a joke that he didn't quite understand. He picked up his horn and began to play, determined to reestablish his creative credentials. The other Heads of Jazz joined him and soon the cutting contest was under way.

The Royal Hosts chattered continuously among themselves during the performance, but it was only during the bass solo that Myfanwy could make out their words from her hiding place behind the immense heavy red curtains in the corner of the hall. To her astonishment they were speaking in Welsh.

"Who are these lame tossers?", said the Queen.

"They couldn't swing from the gallows!", said her husband.

"How they could take the joy of Louis Armstrong, the fire of Ornette Coleman, the passion of John Coltrane, the humour of Roland Kirk...." said the Queen,

"...and turn it into this anodyne pap!", continued her husband.

"This one scale per chord stuff is doing my pretty little head in", said one of the Royal nieces.

The Prince's glorious bass baritone cut in with authority, sending a shiver of sexual allegiance jolting through Muff's body.

"It's only what they've done with the country", he said.

"Now don't start that again, dear", said his mother, "you'll only get over excited and be sick".

"N'empêche, chère maman", replied the Nutter Prince, "they despoil the memory of the Ancient Briton, whose blood courses through our veins; their notion of English Heritage is fake and lame, with as much true history about it as the Great English Ploughman's Lunch! It is a monstrous deceit, foisted upon a gullible populace to ensure their continued complaisance, and to bleed them dry of their money, and of their true birthright".

The bass solo transmogrified into a loud drum solo; the Prince continued his declamation in time with the drums.

"Yet we are the Ancient Britons; we have never gone away, and one day we will rise again and lead our people from the dark tunnels of English Heritage into the light of Idristan!".
Muff was nearly fainting with excitement. Never had she imagined that she would hear her destiny in this place and in this way.

The drums subsided and the horns took up their bleating refrain again; Spiff, aiming for late Coltrane sheets of sound, seemed to be playing the melody of 'All Things Bright And Beautiful'.

Myfanwy felt a strong hand on her shoulder. A large man towered over her and spoke to her of her destiny. She durst not raise her eyes, but she recognised the commanding and loving bass baritone of the Nutter Prince.

"At last you have come among us", he said. He bent and sniffed her skin, savouring its spiced perfume.

"You are she whom we have awaited so patiently", he announced.

"Yes, my liege", Muff murmured, her voice charged with excitement. She heard a zip coming undone, raised her lips to accept with gratitude the member of her Lord, but saw only her open handbag and the Welsh femur now resting between the gnarled but lissom fingers of the Prince.

"How could he possibly have known to look for it there?", she asked herself in silent wonderment.

He touched her lightly on each shoulder with the yellowed bone.

"Arise, I name thee Muse of Idristan, and charge you now to begin your work to save this kingdom. The realm of the Ancient Briton is in your fair hands."

He kissed her forehead and was gone.

Chaplet 9

The Chase

Twenty minutes later, Myfanwy was running for her life, pursued down the stone corridors by a posse of Special Services Personnel and by the enormous and terrifying Victor, Nigerian Head of Conservatory Security. The short Asian woman was being chased as well, and was falling gradually further behind. Myfanwy heard her fall and scream as the chasing party finally caught up with her and began their punishment. Muff pushed herself harder, though her ample chest ached from so much sustained bouncing. There was only one set of footsteps following her now; she knew from his unhurried tread that it was Victor, and that he planned to take his time over his prey. She flung herself up the last flight of stairs and emerged in a heap on the coveted lower corridor of the Conservatory. She could hear Victor close behind her, and in desperation pushed open the nearest door.

Victor came onto the corridor just in time to see the toilet door closing. He smiled sadistically and followed his victim in. All the cubicle doors were ajar, save for one.
As he approached the door, his face set in the savage rictus

of the torturer, a long squelching fart ripped through the silence.

"Who dat dere?". Victor thumped on the door.

The Principal's voice replied,

"Ooooh, lovely, that one's for England. It's me, Victor, your Principal. Now run along, will you, and leave a chap in peace".

Inside the cubicle, Muff finally relaxed as she heard the external door close behind Victor. Mickey held her tight on his lap and kissed her neck affectionately.

"You've been a naughty girl, Myfanwy, I can tell. What have you been up to? It's a good job your Uncle Mickey's here to look after you".

Chaplet 10

Battle Lines

So are the lines of battle drawn. On the one side lie delusional purveyors of convention, commerciality, celebrity, snooping, torture and deceit. On the other side stand our troubadours and workers, fairies and knights of an ancient realm, noble and just, but in comparison with the forces that oppose them, weak and few in number.

The status quo is a rabble of shallow emotion, but it is always tough enough to withstand the good, or so history tells us.

But we have not yet met all our protagonists, nor have those we already know yet found their full range. Perhaps this once there is hope for our noble warriors in their eternal terrorism against the forces of bullshit, gratification and baloney.

Chaplet 11

Latin Music

Spiff's meeting with his Principal, about a visit to the Royal Welsh Music Conservatory for some examining and consultative work, had been interrupted by a phone call. Cornelius Brewster was looking flustered, and apparently talking about Cuban Bass music, which Spiff found both surprising and bizarre. To while away the time, he began a 2-3 clave with his left foot 'erm bap bap erm beeurm baaap bap' and congratulated himself on his groundbreaking work at the Conservatory.

"If I can get the message of World Music through to the Mozart specialists", he told himself proudly, "I'm really getting somewhere".

With his right foot he set up the characteristic Tumbao of the Cuban Bass 'eeurm boooom boom, eeurm boooom boom'. When the two feet were locked in together and the time was rocking forward in that beautiful clockwork Cuban groove, Spiff conjured up a wild Free Jazz solo he had once heard played at New York's Village Gate, and began tapping out its frantic polyrhythms on the large mahogany desk. As the three rhythms came together in a glorious medley, Spiff felt his penis spring joyfully to life.

Cornelius recognised the desk rhythm immediately, and the tune it came from. It was 'Onward Christian Soldiers'. He waved angrily at Spiff to shut up; Spiff's penis shrank back along his thigh, abashed by the censure.

"Yes Ambassador" said Cornelius into the phone. "It sounds very unlikely. I must say, but my Head of Jazz is with me now, as we speak, waiting to give me his account. Yes, looking forward to seeing you at four. Goodbye now".

He spoke to Spiff now.

"That was the American Ambassador. Can you confirm that you have a saxophone student named, named..". He shuffled through a pile of papers searching for a name.

"...named Ang Li?".

Spiff grimaced. The name was familiar, but he couldn't remember whether or not he had ever taught her.

"She's an Asian woman" continued Cornelius, "a short one, if that's any help". Spiff continued to look blankly inward.

"She claims to have been following you for the last six months, trying to get a lesson with you. Dingaling, dear boy? Ring any bells?".

"I do recall seeing someone like that", agreed Spiff. "I thought she might be a stalker, or some kind of secretary".

"Yes, all very likely, I'm sure", said Cornelius. "But a young woman was found in the secret passageway near the Palace and taken into custody by the Special Services. This was in the middle of a terrorist alert, raised incidentally because of a phone call made by an unknown person from this building, in an unknown Asian Language, so this unknown young woman was therefore handed on to the Americans. The point is, she claims to be the student Ang Li, whom we do have on the student roll, whose fees we have already accepted and indeed spent, and whom, moreover, you are supposed to be teaching. Of course we're denying she's one of ours, because the whole thing is preposterous, and could make us all appear in a very poor light, but she has since been rendered to Guantanomo for interrogation".

Spiff was unable to speak, though his feet were still locked in their clave tumbao embrace.

"You know, old boy", said Cornelius. "Guantanomo Bay. The Cuban base".

Chaplet 12

Three Little Words

Cornelius's next meeting was with the staff member who had instigated the terrorist alert, his Head of Security, Victor. Although he had never spoken to the man, having inherited him a mere few years ago from the previous administration, he had on several recent occasions become involved in a mysterious and worrying winking session with him near the gentleman's toilet on the coveted lower corridor.

"The man clearly thinks there is a bond between us", mused Cornelius ruefully. "Perhaps he thinks I'm black. Or gay". Cornelius resented this sort of pigeonholing from the depths of his soul. In truth his sexuality was not this specific; he was the sort of rampant male who was just interested in fucking as an end it itself.

He perused Victor's Human Resources file. His last job, he noticed, had been at the University of Lagos, where he had held the Chair of the Professor of Forensic Law. "That's a hell of a job" thought Cornelius, "Holding a chair all day".

He passed into a brief and very satisfying reverie in which a team of lissom young people of various sexes followed him around attending minutely to his quotidien needs. Then, sighing, he read on, and learned that Victor wasn't the crude lackey he appeared.

"My God", said Cornelius, "I've got this wrong. He was actually sitting in the Chair. He was the Professor!"
Cornelius was filled with curiosity; his curiosity was filled with panic. Like many in high positions, Cornelius was terrified of falling. He scanned down to the bottom of the report to catch the Human Resources Profile Summary.

"...one senses a sharp mind, but he has communication issues".

Indeed Victor, waiting outside his Principal's office for the exact hour of his meeting to strike, had very severe issues as they say, 'around' communication, for he suffered from Aphasia. That is, he no longer had the ability to form language. His mind functioned normally; in fact it functioned exceptionally well, due to his high intelligence, fashioning exquisitely well-balanced and finely focussed responses that tragically never reached the outside world. To compound his tragedy, he had no awareness of his condition; Victor never knew that his fine messages were not getting through, and that we only ever experienced his mind in one of three basic phrases, in a bellowed 'who dat dere?', in a coy knowing wink, or in a long squelching fart.

It was at two o'clock precisely that Victor knocked on his Principal's door, sighing sorrowfully inside, for he suspected that despite all his best and most intelligent efforts, he would once again be taken for a fool.

Chaplet 13

Transfixed And Transfigured

Myfanwy "Muff" Maboob was desperate to get back to Wales. Since her Palace adventure, since her revelatory baptism by the Nutter Prince, she felt called there by destiny. She had it in mind to accompany Spiff Abrahams, the irritating little chump now running down the Jazz Department, on his visit there as Examiner, and, cheekily, had already packed a bag for the trip. She now needed formal permission.

Cornelius was in a bit of a mood when Muff walked in. He was still mystified and vaguely annoyed by his recent meeting with Victor, his Head of Security. He had managed to retrieve no information whatsoever about the phone call at the bottom of the terrorist alert, and Victor's frequent farts and, even more, his intimate winks, had unsettled him. He felt strangely breached, as though an alien worm had wriggled into his skin and was now making a playground of his body.

"Professor Abrahams has asked me to go to Wales with him, for secretarial support", she lied effortlessly to Cornelius, lowering her shoulders slightly towards him and setting her breasts into a gentle quivering motion. She thought he was mainly gay, but randy enough to have a go at anything.

"Yes, 'cept you will, won't you? Dirty little beast", she told herself.

Cornelius was shaking his head, both clearing himself of lust and laying down the law, when Muff found the magic in her words.

"To Cardiff", she said, but in the Welsh manner, spinning out the syllables in a song. "Caerdydd...".

Cornelius was suddenly caught in the sound, entranced, entrapped, and then spreadeagled face down upon his desk. He felt the rough scratch of his tweeds as they were pulled across his thighs, then a sharp pain as his rectum was breached not, as formerly, by the worm of his anxious imagination, but now by a great and powerful snake, and then finally, a flood of relief and pleasure. Still spatchcocked, he turned to kiss the mouth that was biting into his ear lobe and stared into the dark brown eyes of Victor, his Head of Security. As he looked behind him the eyes became hazel, then green, and were suddenly in front of him again, in the face of his secretary, Myfanwy Maboob.

Muff now began to know the magic of which she was capable. Although Cornelius's up-the-body experience had lasted only minutes in contemporary time, Muff had just lived, with Cornelius, through an entire aeon of the Ancient Celtic Calendar. She watched him now as he shook his head again, this time to free himself of his trance. As his eyes refocussed he bellowed "who dat dere?", winked at her, then farted loudly.

"I take it I have your permission, Principal?", asked Myfanwy meekly.

"Of course, dear girl. Naturally you must go. Young Spiff needs all the support he can get. I think you must travel first class, don't you?".

When he had dispatched a smiling Myfanwy, Cornelius allowed himself a moment of relaxation, and sank back into the sore glow of his own benevolence. He found that he was rather looking forward to losing to the Ambassador in their Real Tennis rendezvous later that day.

Chaplet 14

The Saxophone Lesson

Spiff was relaxing too, exploring Myfanwy in his mind's eye. Her silk black hair was cut in a bob, and framed an oval face with a delicately pointed chin. Her eyes were a sea green. Her nose, large in proportion to the face, and hooked in the Hittite style, was the feature that saved her from being pretty. The skin of her face was dark and smooth, and spicy, like savoury milk chocolate. Spiff licked his lips as her breasts hove into his imagination, full, firm and round. He turned her round and bent her over the desk, the better to get a take on her from the rear. Her waist was high and narrow, while her thighs and calves, though tapering down well into a small ankle, were solid and heavy, all working muscle. A neat bottom floated among the thighs, shaped by long African angles and possessed of a delectable tremble.

In his mind Spiff now reached out to seize Muff by the haunches, only to be interrupted by a shriekingly sharp top F played on a soprano saxophone.

An image of his own young wife cooking for him now came into his mind and he was filled with fury. She was so slim, so loving, so supportive, so devoted, so tadpole. Yet she always managed to spoil his dreams.

Spiff opened his eyes and was amazed to see a saxophone student in front of him, eyes shining with eagerness.

"Was I sharp at the top?", the student asked respectfully. Spiff groaned and looked at his watch.

"Only another twenty minutes of hell to endure", he told himself.

"It's better to be sharp than out of tune", he advised his student.

"Now. Think of a note. G sharp, good. Now think of a mode. Locrian, good. Now pick an interval. Sixth, good. Now play me a G sharp Locrian mode in intervals of a sixth".

As the hapless student began clambering up over his horn, Spiff closed his eyes and ears and tried to recapture the outline of Myfanwy Maboob's hips between his hands.

Chaplet 15

The Audition

Len, Mickey and Steve were all on duty together at the front desks, and were reliving the trio communion of their distant playing days. Though each on a single and discrete path, they made together the same collective journey and held before them the same vision, the gurning face of the jazz chimp who had displaced them. It was a boyish face, underlined by a scraggy collection of wispy beardlings and topped by a mousy fringe. It was an open face, pleasant enough at first glance, but of a self-satisfied fleshiness that hinted at a capacity for acts of great foolishness. Yes, Spiff's was a face, as Mickey often used to say, "one could never tire of slapping".

A commotion arose outside in the street. As the Edwardian doors of the Conservatory swung round, the trio saw a bowler-hatted man sprinting out into the traffic, a briefcase in each pumping arm, and terror upon his face.

"Fokkin' merchant booombaclaaat!", said the dreadlocked white woman now facing the trio in the vestibule.

"E touch me foot so I jook 'im wid me machete!".

She pronounced the last word in the French style, with a long grave middle E and a silent final one.

The youth with her, his face hidden in a voluminous street hood, turned to the trio at an imploring angle and shrugged at them. The woman pulled a scrap of paper out of her bra and consulted it.

"Is this the Hoodie Menuhin School for Music?", she demanded. "Me worry 'bout me son Jamal". She pointed to the hooded youth now shuffling his feet in embarrassment.

"Wid me bein' babymovver, an so many gangsta ebbryweir me wan' me boy Jamal to do somm'ting wid 'is life. An den I hear 'bout dis special music place for hoodies!". The youth shrugged again and opened his hands to them, disowning his mother.

"Well", said Len, the diplomat of the piano, "this is actually the Royal English Conservatory of Music. But I suggest you have a word with our Head of Jazz, Professor Spiff Abrahams. He deals with all the World Music here. Isn't that right, fellas?". Mickey and Steve nodded in unison.

"Also the CSS, that's the Community Support Scheme", said Steve.

"And the DES, that's the Deeper Education Strand", added Mickey.

And it was true, for all of Spiff's natural shortcomings, that his burden as Head of Jazz was a heavy one, for the COG, that is the Conservatory Old Guard, viewed this department not just as a necessary nod of acknowledgement to the modern world, but as a convenient bin for everything else they needed but didn't really want.

"If you'll just wait here, Madam", said Len, "I'll see what I can do".

The woman smiled, showing a mouthful of gold fillings and rotting teeth.

Steve brought the Conservatory bus round to the front of the building. Mickey loaded in the bags and briefcases and then settled his darling Muff into her seat, squeezing her arm affectionately. Len explained the situation to Spiff.

"It's an audition, Professor Abrahams. For admission to the Jazz Programme, the BMus. Under the CSS and DES schemes. I know how busy you are, Professor", he added ingratiatingly, "so I've arranged for you to see the boy and his mother". He paused to indicate the couple now seated in the minibus, "On your way round to the train".

So it was, at the beginning of their fateful trip to Cymru, in the dawn of the recreation of the ancient kingdom of Idristan, that Spiff Abrahams found a place in the hallowed halls of the Royal English Conservatory of Music, for the total beginner named Jamal.

"Tell me Jamal", asked Spiff, as they pulled into the drop-off zone of Paddington Station, "do you play any instrument in particular?"

The hooded boy shrugged and his mother laughed widely again. "Dat what 'e com 'ere for, innit?".

Spiff and Muff were on the pavement now, bags and briefcases in hands, and Spiff gave Jamal his decision, his eyes locked with those of Steve.

"I think you'd be perfectly suited to the double bass".

Chaplet 16

Dream Of Love

It so happened that Cardiff was shortly to be hosting the Olympic Games, and on the evening that Professor Spiff Abrahams travelled there with his secretary Myfanwy Maboob, the city was full. Teams of consultants had descended into the city to verify that work on the stadium roof would be completed within the necessary frameworks of schedule, budget, health and safety, and political correctness, and they had in turn been followed by teams of consultants whose job it was to verify that these verifications themselves were being carried out within the necessary frameworks of schedule, budget, health and safety, political correctness and so on and so forth, with the result that every hotel room in the city was occupied by a consultant.

As they waited in the long line for a taxi, Spiff's vision of a suite at the opulent Angel Hotel, where he would first have wooed Myfanwy with sparkling wine and toasties then fucked her brains out, was clouding over; he felt powerless and panicky. But their turn finally came and as he watched the skirt tighten over Muff's arse as she scrambled into the cab, his mood suddenly lightened.

"Come on Spiff, be flexible", he urged himself. "Make it happen in a different way. Adapt. You're a Jazzer, aren't you? Improvise!".

They were bound for a small village some forty-seven miles from Cardiff, where Heidi Hyson, Head of Jazz at the Royal Welsh Conservatory of Music, had a spare chapel. The small roads leading west from the capital were clogged with stadium roofers searching for hotels, and as they waited in the traffic, Heidi spoke reassuringly to Myfanwy on the mobile.

"You'll be there soon enough, it's always bad round the 'Lympics, see. You'll be met by friend Nicky; he runs the garage just down by the chapel and he'll look after you, like. Now just plant your feet and breathe deeply. That's it, let the energy come from underneath, right up through those lovely chakras, see, right out of the top of your bonnet, like, connecting you with the flow of the universe, so you're part of a circle, see, the circle of love. Ouuuuuuoouummm!", she chanted. Muff put her on speakerphone and they all joined in, even the cabbie, and became calm.

Heidi Hyson could have been a celebrity, because of her previous life as a terrorist back in the nineteen seventies. But while in prison in her native Luxembourg she had finally dissociated herself from the Baader Meinhof group, repenting for the bombings, kidnappings and nasty words, and transforming herself into a devout and clever Buddhist. She eschewed all publicity, and tended now to the musical and spiritual wellbeing of her young students at the Royal Welsh;

she felt qualified to bring them to the light, having spent so long in the dark herself.

"They say she's helluva musician", said Muff, "...'Creadible, from what I year, like". Her natural accent and intonation always came back to her within minutes of stepping onto Welsh soil. Spiff sniffed at this, but acknowledged,

"She's OK for a woman. She's only a singer anyway." Muff turned her head angrily away; thenceforward the journey into the Welsh night was silent.

"Hello there. I'm Nicky. Welcome".

The voice came from the shadows of the graveyard, and dying away yet left a single soft sustained note in the air that came searching for companion pitch and timbre in Muff's body; the sound both reaffirmed and reshaped her. She now saw his deep blue eyes and felt his large hand gently cupping her shoulder, and in that instant Myfanwy Maboob experienced a complete translation of being. She saw now that her baptism by the Nutter Prince had been merely the first arc of a circle now completed by the blue-eyed bear stranger who had just come into her life; she understood now that her political and metaphysical place in the creation of Idristan was intimately bound up with her love for Nicky. Love! Already she was speaking of love, yet she had barely met the man she loved, nor yet even seen him fully. Instinctively she knew, in the trinity of his eyes, his sound and his touch, that she would love the rest of him as well.

That night Muff lay awake in her sleeping bag in the pulpit. Bats swooped hither and thither in their nocturnal playground above her, while Spiff Abrahams turned from side to side, moaning his love for her, lost in the delusional sex dream that she projected upon him from a free corner of her mind. As he began thrusting his hips and thrashing about, she noticed a large bat fastened into his groin.

Muff slowly revisited each overtone of Nicky's voice, luxuriated in the bubbles of his gaze, trembled as his hand caressed her shoulder, and mentally adjusted to his flat boxer's nose and thick black beard. She giggled as she remembered the sweet little fart she had detected in the tent of his dungarees, and became thrillingly moist at the thought of his vulnerability. Muff felt empowered and dignified in her new feelings, and knew suddenly that she had found something within her to replace her lost music. Then her mind misted over, and images of the Nutter Prince and the Red Dragons of the flag of the new Idristan merged into the face of her new lover.

"Oh you little beauty", she sighed, and fell into a deep sleep.

Chaplet 17

The Monsoon

The next day was a washout. It was the monsoon season, and rain descended on the valleys in thick grey sheets. Myfanwy and Spiff were attempting to get back to Cardiff in the old Morris Traveller Nicky had lent them. But the roads were impassable, being not only covered in water but also clogged again with builders trying to get back into the city to complete the work on the stadium roof.

Spiff had taken himself into the back seat, partly, as he said, to prepare for the marking and validation process ahead, but also, as Muff knew, to establish a suitable distance between them, of class, function and power. In front, she was merely the driver; behind, reading his paper, he was clearly the boss.

"I see there's been another young suicide in Bridgend. Kid probably just found out he was Welsh!", he joked.

Spiff continued this sniping at her and her countrymen all day, but Muff mostly ignored him. She knew that it was the infidelity to his obedient and loyal wife that had made him so foul of mood.

"Poor boy doesn't even know it was only a dream", thought

Muff, and forgave him. Besides, she was very happy alone in the front. The driving rain outside made her feel cosy and warm inside, and she was surrounded in her little cabin by the virtual presence of her new lover. While she waited in the queue of white vans she rubbed at the stains of oil and sweat he had left on the steering wheel, teased out the curly black hairs from the upholstery, and drank deeply of the sweet-sour mist of pipe tobacco and musk that lingered in the car.

When they turned back for the chapel in the late afternoon, having driven no more than five miles, Myfanwy had a satisfied feeling of having spent her day well. She felt she knew her lover Nicky much better now.

Chaplet 18

Improvisation

Heidi Hyson was nothing if not flexible, adaptable and enterprising. These were the qualities that had made her such an effective Head of Faculty, such an inspiring singer of modern jazz, and such a good terrorist. Accordingly, the next day she hired two coaches and simply transported the Jazz Faculty forty-seven miles west to her chapel in the valleys, and Professor Spiff Abrahams conducted the examinations there.

The students seemed to him raw stilted and bloodless, much like his battered penis, but he was in generous mood.

"Without exposure to the great Urban cauldron, without the competition of the most talented and precocious students of the country", he wrote, "and without the guidance of world-class teachers, the Welsh students have nevertheless performed well. With more hard work and application, some of them may become adequate".

But even as he wrote, the room was changing. Heidi had begun to chant, and the students had joined her. A great "Ouuuuuoummm" swelled up in the chapel. Myfanwy's forehead began to pulsate and she recognised it as an awakening chakra, and greeted it as a lost friend. A huge bearded figure appeared in the pulpit. It was Nicky. He reached down into a dirty khaki bag and his dungarees momentarily separated into two shiny peach globes. Myfanwy's lower body began to pulsate and she recognised it as an awakened pussy, and greeted it too as a lost friend.

Nicky now blew into a homemade metal instrument fashioned from a tyre iron. The sound was pure and ethereal but also earthy and dirty; it first swooped and fluttered then rumbled from below; first shivered into shards and fragments, then enveloped itself in warm humid mist. None could see the person playing any more; there was only the sound, a magical sound, the breath of all creation.

The students ceased ouuuoummming, picked up their instruments and began to play, and each now became part of Nicky's sound; this was music such as Spiff and Muff had never heard before, for it was both universal and collective and at the same time intimate and individual. Spiff picked out Heidi's distinctively guttural voice in the ensemble, as she moved effortlessly between Germanic Bebop and Native American chanting.

"Buhderdur-deedle-einemeinhof-bee-Jah bee-Jaah",
she sang, crushing down into the final flattened fifth, and continued into the chant her Navajo mother had taught her.

"Jaah-Hoya Hoya Hoya Hoyaah".

Spiff felt his own fusional Bip-Bop surging up in his body and reached for a saxophone to express it. His complex urban sound came spilling out through the horn and made its way into the midst of the ensemble. First Nicky joined him, then Heidi, then finally all the students, until the whole chapel now rang with the unison of the majestic melody.

"Dah dah dah dah dadah dah.."

Myfanwy shivered in delight at the laughing twinkle in Nicky's eye as he played the tune she now recognised as the theme from the Dam Busters.

Chaplet 19

The Muse And The Chwyth

Myfanwy stole over to speak to Heidi.

"Tell me about your friend Nicky", she asked. "He seems a very interesting person. Helluva player, like, as well".

Heidi was both helpful and teasing in her answer.

"Oh yes, we all love Nicky down by here. Keeps all our cars on the road, he does. And he can play anything, anything that blows, jah? And he plays for all the valleys. He's our breath, see, our chwyth. That's what we call him, see, Nicky de la Chwyth'.

Myfanwy was aware that the room was completely silent now. She blushed as she realized that everyone was looking at her. Her lover Nicky was walking towards her.

"But he's never played like that. Never quite like that", whispered Heidi. "It's you, he knows it's you, jah? We all know it's you. You are our muse. You've brought us some kind of enchantment".

Nicky de la Chwyth now knelt before Myfanwy. He placed his tyrehorn on the chapel floor and lowered his head.

"I thank you for the gift you have brought me. The gift of sound. But how shall I use it?".

As he spoke the last words, he raised his head and gazed into her eyes. She spoke easily, without knowing her answer, and barely recognizing her own voice, which had lost its scratchiness and become mellow, melodious and compelling.

"The sound itself will tell you. Only listen to the sound".

As she spoke she understood that her relation to Nicky de la Chwyth had changed for ever, for she had become his mentor, his guardian angel, his sorceress, his mother. Now she knew she would never fuck him, and so began to weep.

Her tears fell like the Welsh monsoon on to the encrusted beechwood of the old chapel floor and in their salt were washed away many layers of negative feeling, of inertia, of apathy, of stunned dumbness, and though their trance was lifted, the people in the chapel came around Myfanwy, clapping and cheering, and hailed her as a Mahdi, a Messiah, and the Herald of a New Age.

The train journey back to the Smoke was frosty; Muff didn't seem to want to talk. Spiff relaxed back into the cosseting seats of the first-class carriage and relived the triumph of his Chapel improvisation, which he now realized had been superb, even by his own exacting standards. One small aspect of that afternoon gnawed peevishly at the edge of his mind - the strangely rapturous reception accorded to Myfanwy.

"Oh well", he told himself, "these Welsh must stick to their own, I suppose. It's all they have".

He began to feel annoyed, and suddenly found himself

wanting to fuck her there and then, on the spot, in the railway compartment. But she refused to meet his eye.

Spiff consoled himself with the belief that while he would be appearing on National Radio the next morning, Myfanwy would still be just another secretary.

Chaplet 20

The Last Word

The original thinking of BBC Radio Four, while amalgamating its diverse morning programmes, Start The Week, Midweek, In Our Time, On the Ropes, Woman's Hour, Desert Island Discs and so on, into one magazine format, had been to radicalize and popularize the show. Hence its first title - Nine Eleven. But Middle England rose up in protest, with pressure from the shires, and from traditionalists within the BBC, for it was felt that a certain level of cosiness must be preserved. So they called the show Nine Elevenses. Seeming to combine the radical with the cosy, Castro with cocoa, the car bomb with the cardigan, the name was perfect.

Veteran presenter Jenny Morgan was also a clever choice, for she specialized in intros and outros that largely neutralized and muted the contribution of her guests, and refocussed listeners on the two most important things, the identity of the show and the sound of her own voice.

Spiff was just starting to get anxious. Jenny Morgan was finishing with the Nigerian death row journalist and would, he realized, shortly be turning to him.

"....people in the West are not aware of the legacy of the Methodist missionaries. Their word is spreading throughout the world and may soon come back upon you in a scream of violence and anger. When in prison I learned of the existence of Methodist training camps and of death squads planning......."

"Thank you, thank you", Jenny cut in, "for that fascinating insight into the plot of your latest work of fiction, The New Missionary Position, and now we turn to a revolutionary teacher, and indeed player, in the field of Jazz, Professor Spiff Abrahams of the Royal English Conservatory of Music. She paused, and Spiff began to speak,

"I..".

Jenny looked at him sternly and cut across him.

"Well Spiff, you're an interesting man. You were brought up in rural Dorset, and showed no interest in music apart from singing in school music lessons and assemblies, which your mother says you loved, until you heard jazz in your teens, and had a damascene experience, an epiphany, a vision, but of course it was something you heard rather than saw, perhaps we should call it an audion, but to carry on, you picked up the tenor saxophone and almost instantly showed a virtuosic understanding both for that instrument and for jazz, and not only took the English and indeed International jazz scene by storm, but also if I am correct, became the youngest ever Head of Faculty to be appointed at that most prestigious of all the world's Music Schools, the Royal English Music Conservatory, where you now play, teach, and as it were, hold court". She paused for breath, and Spiff tried again.

"I...".

But Jenny motored on over him.

"And now, perhaps in an attempt to radicalize and popularize, a process we are familiar with here at the BBC, haha, you have developed an entirely new music form".

"Yes", said Spiff, but to no avail, as Jenny continued,

"it's a combination, as I understand it, of the African American tradition of BeBop, as developed in the nineteen forties, by someone, it says here, called Jolly Parker, with the contemporary urban dance and street style they call Hip-Hop. And you call this new Art form Bip-Bop".

She turned suddenly to Spiff, fixed her eye balefully upon him, and asked him directly to speak.

"You are a fascinating man and musician, Spiff Abrahams. Tell us something about yourself!".

Spiff was speechless. All he could manage, while his mind dashed here and there trying to find something interesting about himself that Jenny hadn't already disclosed, was,

"Well...yes...I ...thank you...".

The studio, and the nation, were left in an uncomfortable silence. Momentarily satisfied with her guest's humiliation, Jenny came to the rescue.

"I suppose you've already done it all, haven't you?", she joked. "What is there left to say?"

Then Spiff's brain lurched into action.

"My students!", he cried. "My students are a joy. I have a new one, Jamal, who is from the ghettoes of Portobello Green, and still raw, but he will, I believe, go very far indeed".

"I'm afraid we're very near to the end of this morning's Nine Elevenses, a big thank you to today's studio guests, and of course to all our listeners, both here in the UK and indeed all round the world", said Jenny.

"Just before we go, and to keep us in that global mood, Spiff, tell us, will you, where some of your students are now. How far do they actually go?".

Spiff was once again speechless, and only had his idea just as the show's closing music began to play. It was a jaunty and somewhat atonal little number, devised in a collaboration between that giant of Contemporary Classical Composition, Harry BurtFangler, and small children from a School for the Profoundly Deaf; it alternated between 9/8 and 11/2 meter and was played entirely upon antique milk bottles.

"Cuba", blurted Spiff, as the music rose in his headphones. Jenny was shaking her head; panic filled her eyes as she realized that for once she was not going to have the last word.

"One of my students has been taken to Cuba by the Americans and is being held in Guantanamo Bay".

Chaplet 21

The Last Dream

Cornelius Brewster always played Radio Four in the morning in the hope that its Englishness would rub off on him. He listened while wrestling with his Times Crossword, the same puzzle he had started on his first day as Principal of the Royal English, and of which he had so far only completed the top left hand corner. He was aware that the newspaper carried a new puzzle every day, but for emotional reasons was unable to admit defeat and move on; furthermore, he reasoned, when he did eventually finish the puzzle, it would be a measure of his long and difficult journey, and of just how English he had become.

Cornelius choked on his skinny latte as the words of his Head of Jazz, Spiff Abrahams, rang round his office, and out into England and the World.

"...one of my students is being held in Guantanamo Bay...". He jerked upright and when the scalding liquid spilled out over his hand he dropped the cardboard cup on to his crossword with a yelp. The yellowing page turned grey as coffee soaked through it and obliterated the text.

"Nooohh, nooohh!", Cornelius moaned, for losing his puzzle he feared that now he would never become truly English.

But, as the phone began to ring, he realized that this was the least of his problems. In bygone days, when newspaper headlines were still a force, there would have been the grace of a day in which to collect one's thoughts and to prepare one's position. But with today's gizmology, the startling news of the rendition was almost instantly all over the Web, and on radios and televisions and mobile phones everywhere. Even worse, video footage was being broadcast on TerrorTube of the vicious beating given to the female student in the Palace tunnel by what appeared to be American Special Services personnel.

Cornelius was harangued throughout the day by people demanding information and explanations - the American Ambassador, confirming their meeting for Real Tennis later that afternoon, but also quite irate - Ang Li's mother, in turns tearful and vituperative - an assortment of journalists, in turns cajoling and hectoring - various prestigious solicitors claiming to represent the interests of Ang Li - and finally the Chairman of the Governing Body of the Royal English, asking him to consider carefully his position as Principal.

By three o'clock, Cornelius was exhausted, and looking at the telephone with dreadful anticipation. He whimpered as it rang again, lest some new and surprising round of torture be revealed. But it was only the American President.

"CC, my old buddy, how the devil are you? Still going to

shul, I hope?", teased the great Head of State, Hymie Vidal. Cornelius shuddered at the memory of his old nickname, and of the day he had barmitzvahed with the irredeemably crass young boy who had since risen to such heights within the arms and petrochemical industries. The President continued speaking without waiting for Cornelius to reply.

"We've both done OK, CC, for two nice Jewish boys. We're both Head of something, that's what counts. And you can help me, CC. This Iran thing may go tits up, or possibly the Iraq one, again, and the Republicans may be looking for a new Number One." He paused dramatically.

"What about it, CC? Could you take it on, have you thought about it? You've got all the qualities we need to transform the Party, and take us to the People. Think about it, you're black, you're Jewish, and you're gay, so most people will love you, but underneath you're a nasty little shit ready to defend to the death the rights of the powerful. I know you, you're perfect, CC, think about it". He paused again.

"I know what you're thinking, CC, but fuck the meek, for they shall inherit the mirth! No, don't answer that. I'm only kidding around with you anyway. I didn't ring up to discuss the Presidency, CC, there's much more at stake. This Guantanamo shitstorm around your student is going global. We've got demonstrators with guitars and effigies ouside our embassies all round the world; we've got threats against our Olympic athletes, and we've got sanctions imposed on our essential imports. Mr Li, father of the terrorist shiksa, heads up the factory in Shandong Province where they make the

Marmite. And the Lea and Perrins sauce. Man, are we going to suffer! The whole Civilized World is under threat. It might even reach you over there in Europe. Now I'm in a bind over here, because all my people, including that frigging Toby of an Ambassador I have in England, are buzzing round trying to find something interesting to feed on, and all they're gonna come up with is more shit. But I can't stop them. Unless you can somehow bury this one for me. Somehow just kill it, then bury it. She never existed, that's what I'm saying, not as a student. She's just a random element turned up in a random place and now being treated in a random way. End of story. There is no paperwork, is there, CC? You have no record of her, do you? No history of any teaching or administrative lapses at the, where are you, the Royal English something? Well that's very good, Cornelius, very good. You should tell the Press. End of uncertainty. End of problem, dot.com. My, it's been good to catch up. Now think about what I said, CC. If this whole England thing goes tits up too, you should think about politics. We need people like you in the Republican Party. Bye. You take care now".

"Would you like a cup of tea?", asked Myfanwy.
Her voice was calm and warm, and Cornelius suddenly felt safe again. He filled a pipe and puffed as Muff set a table for afternoon tea; he watched her full bosom and strong fatty buttocks appraisingly, and was reminded of the large Welshman he'd had a few weeks ago. Myfanwy rang the switchboard.
"No more calls to this office this afternoon, right?!",

she commanded them. Then she locked the door and poured the tea.

"Is it really that simple?", Cornelius asked himself, and immediately fell into a deep erotic dream. He was in a car, not his own beautiful vintage Aston Martin DB4, but a common, dirty vehicle, and he was smoking his pipe. A body was moving over him, a changing body whose breasts reared up over his chest towards his mouth and turned into a large hairy male bottom. At the same time his thighs were being tickled by a bush of thick black hair on a female pubis that turned into the face of a chubby young man. Cornelius glimpsed a twinkling eye and a flat nose and recognised the Welshman he had cruised in Russell Square. He groaned in pleasure at the memory and set his tongue flicking out into the unknown crevice before him. A phrase came into his mind and he giggled. "I don't know what it is, but I'm going to lick it!".

Muff sat opposite her Principal, happily slurping her tea and munching on one of the Welsh Cakes her grandmother had sent up from the valleys, as she watched him writhe, giggle and moan in the dream she had sent him. It would be the last, she decided, the last dream she would send to him or any of his ilk, for everything was destined to change today, and she needs must conserve her power.

When Cornelius awoke, he found their roles reversed. In his absence, Myfanwy Maboob had acquired quiet dominance in the room. Someone from outside in the coveted lower corridor hammered at the door, shouting incoherently. Myfanwy opened the door and admitted Len, from the front desks.

"You've got to do something", he cried, "we're being mobbed up there".

Muff looked at her Principal and raised her eyebrow in a question; it was her last act of subservience to him. Cornelius nodded; it was his last act of authority over her.

"Very well", said Muff. "I'll come and deal with it. I've just been appointed Chief Officer for Press and Publicity, see".

Chaplet 22

Real Tennis

Toby Frigham Young might have been an English aristocrat, judging by his name, but was in fact merely the American Ambassador, and in fact an Evangelical Christian from Alabama, born and bred. He despised Cornelius Brewster, for being queer, for being Jewish, for being black, and most of all for wanting so badly to be English.

"Damn it, it's plain un-American activity", he fumed, as he served to Cornelius on the Real Tennis Court at Lord's Cricket Ground.

There was a National Emergency brewing, with this Guantanamo student terrorist affair, and they should be talking about it right now, Toby told himself, not playing some stupid game out of bloody-minded politeness. "Damn English!", he cursed, under his breath. "They'd rather spend time being unruffled in a crisis than doing something about it!".

Toby focussed on the dapper figure of Cornelius on the other side of the net, pictured his weak flapping mouth, then with a grunt of violent frustration, sent the leather and cloth ball straight into the Gallery on the Service Side, scoring an outright winner.

"Your point. Good shot, old boy!", shouted Cornelius. "Advantage and match point".

Toby, short, fat, balding and unfit, was an unlikely athlete, and compensated with extreme aggression and determination. However, he still didn't know what was out and what was in, and relied on Cornelius to keep score. It was a devilishly complex game, with its angles, conventions, obstacles and scoring patterns and its Penthouses, Galleries and Chases; Toby mostly liked just to batter the ball. He was the action man whereas Cornelius was the backroom boy.

"Yes Siree", Toby told himself. "He definitely likes that back room", and sent a last shot spiralling viciously over the net to land in the same place as the last.

"Oh well done, Toby. Super shot", shouted Cornelius in delight. "Your point, and your match!".
He scampered up to the net and Toby accepted his damp handshake, his triumph clouded with distaste.

"Why do the English like to lose so much?", he asked himself, "and why, oh why would an American want to emulate them?".

Chaplet 23

The Martyr To Tradition

The question of emulation was also in the air at the Blue Posts Public House, north of Oxford Street. Mickey, on his way to his only remaining gig, was having a quiet pint with his nephew Jeb, currently the house pianist at the new Ronnie Scott's Club.

"How's it going down at the club these days?", Mickey asked. "New owners again?".

"Yeah. Japanese this time", said Jeb. "Supermarket chain. Very big on innovation, and timekeeping".

Not your strong points, mate, thought Mickey, for he knew Jeb was a fairly typical modern jazz pianist, with plenty of flashy technique but few ideas and no time.

"And they're also big on corporate identity and loyalty", continued Jeb.

"Look", he said, laying his hands on the table. "Do you think this needs a bandage?".

Mickey looked at the bruised stump where Jeb's right hand third finger once had been.

"Christ, mate. What happened?", he asked.

"You know the Russ Conway Tribute thing I'm doing, to go with the You've Got Jazz Talent TV month we're doing at the club?"

"Yes", said Mickey, remembering his days at the club playing with Bill Evans, Ben Webster, Sonny Rollins.

"Sounds great!".

"Well they let me know, quite subtly, that it wasn't quite enough, you know, that I needed to show more, I don't know, more loyalty or commitment or something".

"So?", said Mickey.

"So I did it. I chopped my finger off. To be more like Russ. To be more authentic. More loyal", said Jeb.

"Just be pleased you're not a trumpet player, doing a Wingy Manone week", said Mickey, sipping his pint.

"He only had one arm".

Chaplet 24

Cocktails For One

Cornelius Brewster continued to annoy Toby Frigham Young after their game, in several ways. To begin with, Cornelius tried to prevent him from attacking a dead electric hand-dryer on the wall of the changing rooms.

"Why does nothing work in this goddam place?", Toby had ranted, and then laid into the appliance with his racquet. "I just hate wet hands!".

Cornelius had been calm, and patronising.

"Just ask the wallah for some linen", he advised, pointing out an attendant standing in the corner. "That's what he's for".

Then, up in the Member's Bar, rather than join him in a manbonding beer. Cornelius had ordered an extravagant cocktail. And to cap it all, he was proving very awkward, almost intractable, in the matter of the Guantanamo student.

"Look", Toby explained. "We'll find out eventually. We always do. It's just taking longer than normal to get the audio translated. We think it may be an obscure Punjabi dialect. But the point is, we will find out. It would just be a help if we could talk to your chap in the meantime".

"No, Toby", insisted Cornelius, "I'm afraid I can't give you the identity of the staff member who heard the call and raised the terrorist alert. I am, after all, his Principal. I owe him a duty of care. He couldn't tell you anything useful, in any case".

"But we have our own experts", Toby cut in smoothly, "who are highly skilled in the extraction of information, in...". He searched for new words to describe the process, and continued, "...in encouraging people to open up. They have many different techniques to help people explore the past, to excite the memory. All we need is a few hours with the man".

Cornelius was adamant.

"Yes, I've read all about waterboarding, dear boy, and that's precisely why you're not going surfing all over my chap. What I mean is, he really can't tell you anything. He speaks only in a handful of words, and other than that merely farts and winks, and that's your lot".

Toby sighed. He knew plenty of men just like that, out in the real world, outside the refined environment of Cornelius's aristocratic fantasy. Hell, his own father, for one! But he recognized a dead end, and tried another approach.

"I'm looking forward to the Olympics this summer", he said. "I think the US team will astound the world in the Real Tennis".

Cornelius walked through the open door.

"Oh yes, I'm so excited about it. Apparently they are magnificent athletes, and redefining the game, by all accounts".

"What a shame if the team can't come!", said Toby.

Cornelius looked puzzled. "How so?".

"I have a bad feeling about this Guantanamo student", said Toby. "The terrorist. And her co-conspirators. Unless we can root them out now, I can imagine a scenario later this year, if it all drags on, where American athletes wouldn't travel".

"That would be a shame", said Cornelius as he snapped the opening shut. "Oh well, it's only sport, I suppose".

He took a deep draught of his third cocktail through the turquoise straw. "I shall be going to Cardiff whatever happens. With or without the American Real Tennis team. The Royal English are providing all the musicians".

Toby was disconsolate.

"So long as they're not trying to play jazz", he sniped.

Cornelius felt a rare surge of fondness for his Head of Jazz, Spiff Abrahams.

"We perhaps don't swing as much", he acknowledged, "and I'm no expert in the field, but we do bring other things to the party... subtlety, finesse, nuanced emotion, restraint, and I suppose... Englishness".

"Hunh!" Toby grunted. "Perhaps don't swing at all is what you mean!".

He rose to his feet, his face reddened with tennis, beer and anger.

"You'll never be more than a cartoon Englishman, Cornelius, you sad little freak, but you've got some of his worst features in bold. You're so corny you're dangerous. You can't see what's in front of your eyes. There may be a ring of student terrorists taking over your building, where your own Head of Security is a Foreign National with links to religious extremist groups. And all you can say is 'Your point. Good Shot, Old Boy!", Toby sneered, mimicking Cornelius's exaggerated Trevor Howard British accent.

"Actually", said Cornelius. "Ang Li is not and has never been a student at the Royal English Conservatory of Music, and my intention is to make this known to the world. I have enlisted a member of staff as Officer for Press and Publicity specifically for the task. I spoke with your President today and we agreed that this was the best way to proceed. Hymie is a friend".

Toby Frigham Young staggered out of the Members Bar in a mist of frustration, inebriation and envy. He did not, as was his custom, walk northwest to his large house by Primrose Hill, but instead, with an obscure sense of his own destiny, turned to the Southeast and picked up a Hackney cab to Soho, in search of adventure.

Chaplet 25

The Dangers Of 13/8

Mickey kept a kit permanently set up at La Bussetta, the venue of his one remaining weekly gig, and just carried in his own snare and cymbals, his own personal 'sound', each Monday night. On this particular Monday evening he had parked up as usual in a Doctor's parking space, using the fake permit he had obtained in a trade with a surgeon for some lessons in Bulgarian percussion techniques, and, after his pint with Jeb, was threading his way carefully through the bustle of the Soho streets. An urgent dance rhythm in 13/8 was pressing into his mind, and Mickey was resisting it. The recent loss of three great drummers, Fat John, Tickle Tom, and Alan the Anvil, all killed while stepping without looking onto the street, had made Mickey very cautious when out and about. Those odd time signatures could be very distracting.

Then Mickey spotted the unmistakeable physog of the Prince of England, the so called Nutter Prince, at the door of a Theatrical Costumier. 'Specialist Supplies for TV Film and Theatre. Fancy Dress and Pantomime our speciality...

...By Appointment to Her Majesty the Queen', proclaimed a gold sign on the weathered purple hoarding. A Daimler limousine waited at a discreet distance on a double yellow line as Mickey watched the Nutter Prince pass through into the sulphorous interior of the shop. A traffic warden hovered nearby, eyeing the Royal Insignia on the car with some apprehension. Still looking at the shop, Mickey stepped down off the pavement into the path of a BMW Seven series laden with Chinese spivs. The car swerved and raced on, its occupants screaming abuse, leaving Mickey pale and shaken at the roadside. He cursed himself for his own foolishness, clasped his hands together in a thankful prayer to Heaven, and walked on towards his gig, putting the Nutter Prince and his costumes entirely from his mind.

Just near the Bateman Street club, on the corner of Frith Street, someone else also clasped their hands in prayer. Victor, the fearsome and afflicted Head of Security at the Royal English Conservatory of Music, was praying to his Methodist God for the strength of purpose to fulfil his mission of vengeance and justice that evening. In his pocket he carried the US military issue Walther automatic pistol that he had found in the stone passageways leading to the Palace after the chase of the terrorists, and intended to shoot and kill the American Ambassador with it. He had followed Toby Frigham Young that evening from the Embassy, first to Lord's Cricket Ground and then to the hostess club called La Bussetta. Victor had decided to kill him for general reasons, because of his extreme and radical Evangelicalism, and in particular because of a speech in which he had derided all other forms of Christianity, characterizing them as pale, precursive shadows of the great rebirth taking place in the world. According to him! As he remembered how cruelly the Ambassador had spoken of his beloved Methodism, how he had mocked its greatest exponent and orator, Lord Soper, a wave of anger rippled through Victor's body. He clasped his hands together more tightly and begged the Lord for the strength to be both murderous and merciful. The prayer tumbled from his lips in an expletive of grace.

"Who dat dere!?", he shouted, causing two prostitutes, their arms linked, to jump apart in alarm.

A Chloe handbag dropped to the street and small plastic bags filled with white powder spilled onto the pavement. As the girls dropped to the floor and scooped them back into the handbag, one confided to the other,

"couldn't get any Charlie. Man only had Ket today".

Ket, or Ketamine, is a horse tranquilizer: it was the cause of the bizarre events at La Bussetta that evening, and also the reason why Mickey remembered so little of them. He recalled sitting at the drums early in the evening, before opening time, feeling embarrassed and ashamed as he listened to Enoch, the vile and fat little proprietor of La Bussetta, berate the girls because they had collectively refused to entertain a customer the evening before.

"If I ever catch you talk each other 'bout customer personal, how 'bout I ship you all back King's Cross? Nice an' cold on streets, eh? See if you like better. Stay 'ere, in warm, where I look after you, you mus' respec' customer privates. You like priest, you hear confession, you say nothin', capeesh?".

In the awkward, resentful silence that followed, the pianist began to play Secret Love and Mickey joined him with relief, pretending the snare drum was Enoch's bald tope, and laying into it with his brushes. There was no need for a bass player at La Bussetta, where everything was pared down to essentials. Piano took the melody, drums gave the rhythm, punters took the drugs, girls gave the sex, Enoch took the money.

After that tune, during which his favourite hostess gave him a couple of deep snorts of what he assumed to be Coke but turned out to be Ket, Mickey remembered only fragments. The whole world, including his body, seemed to soften into a jelly like liquid, where strange shapes and vibrant intense colours constantly jostled for the foreground. He remembered two versions of Enoch, with two accents, one Italian and one American, and he remembered Victor's loud squelching fart in the toilet, and himself impersonating the absurd voice of their Principal Cornelius Brewster, although he could not be sure that this happened at La Bussetta. He remembered a huge stallion-like erection and an attempt at sex in 13/8 time with a cross between a sponge and a pterodactyl, then a loud gunshot bang, then an explosion, then screaming, the searing wind of flames, and then deep, deep pain.

Chaplet 26

Keeping Her Head Down

While Mickey recovered from the gig in the specialist burns unit of the Middlesex Hospital, a man lay similarly mummified in the Hospital Wing of the prison called Wormwood Scrubs. He spoke with increasing desperation to the policemen at his bedside.

"Dammit, I am Toby Frigham Young, the American Ambassador. I demand Diplomatic Immunity and that you return me immediately to my Embassy!".

The men from SOCA, the Serious Organized Crime Agency, smiled at each other, enjoying the chutzpah and ingenuity of their captive.

"We like the accent, Enoch", said the senior detective. "It's very convincing. But we know who you are. We know what you do. We know what you look like. We've been watching you for months, waiting for you to slip up".

"Which you did spectacularly", added his colleague,

"...possession and supply of controlled substances, running a disorderly house, possession of an illegal firearm, arson, use of a television receiver without a licence and eight counts of manslaughter by criminal neglect".

His voice was severe, and at the same time gleeful.

"Besides which", said the senior one, "the American Ambassador is already in his Embassy. We've made enquiries. So you can lose the Southern drawl and go back to the fake Neapolitan".

"But that's impossible!", spluttered Toby. "He can't be. Did you speak to him?".

"Not exactly" , conceded the officer. "He has a bad throat. But his wife has confirmed to us both his presence and his identity. Happily".

And this part was true, for Toby's wife, like most people, had often longed for her partner to reappear in a different form, and so accepted her husband's strange new habits with a mixture of curiosity, revulsion and delight. He looked and smelled slightly odd, and his penis felt different, but he was still short, fat and bald, and left for work at the same time each day. He took sex from her more frequently now, and at random times and places, grunting as he manoeuvred her body into position as though it was that of a tame animal evolved entirely for his pleasure, then slapping her arse to urge her over the jump, and bringing her, coincidentally, to shudderingly intense multiple orgasms of her own.

Enoch and Toby had traded places, and for the moment Toby's wife was keeping her head down.

Chaplet 27

Pilgrim In Retreat

Victor spent the following weeks in prayer. There had been some change at work, and that secretary Myfanwy Maboob, a plump, lascivious girl whom he both pitied and scorned, seemed to be in charge. She had made him take some leave, for his own good, she had said, because of the Press storm building up about the Guantanamo student, and also because, in her words, "you're a bit stressed, aren't you, my love?".

Victor was in fact not only stressed, but spiritually traumatised. He had never imagined killing a sinner to be so difficult. The voice of God, he had assumed, would come to guide him when needed. Instead, he had heard the voice of Cornelius Brewster addressing him by name as he sat in the toilet at La Bussetta checking the gun.

"Victor, dear boy. Is that you in there?", the voice had chirped, and Victor had panicked, thrown the gun to the floor, then stumbled blindly out into the club, and seemingly out into Hell itself, a dark, smoky maroon place ringing with the evil rhythms of jazz, where bodies alienated from the Grace of God, as from each other, swayed incoherently together. He saw his intended victim at the bar, but there were two of them, two short, fat, bald men, and he picked one of them at random and strangled him. The man gasped for air in Italian and Victor farted loudly to gain more grip on his windpipe. He thrust his face close to that of his victim, now as red as the decor, and winked.

"Who dat dere?", he thundered. Then there were people all around him, prising him from his prey, hauling him up the stairs and heaving him out into Bateman Street.

He read the rest of the story in the paper. 'Harlots in Hand-Dryer Hell!' shouted the headline, going on to tell how the brothelkeeper Enoch had fired a gunshot into a faulty hand-drier in one of his own toilets while high on drugs, causing an explosion and fire, and leading to a significant number of arrests and deaths. In his own defence, speaking from his prison bed, the brothelkeeper was apparently claiming to have found the gun on the toilet floor and to have an intolerance to wet hands.

Victor, while of course pleased that so many other sinners had burned, did not at first understand why God had spared His original sinner, the Ambassador. In prayer, it was revealed to him that God had only aborted the mission at the last moment in order to accommodate a golden opportunity. The mission was in fact still a goer, and he should expect the Word at any time, immanently and imminently.

Victor now prayed continuously, so as not to miss the broadcast.

Chaplet 28

The Great And The Good

Some months later and much against his better judgement, American President Hymie Vidal raised the topic of his Ambassador during a private online audience with the Queen. His initial purpose in setting up the Video Grid Call was to defuse the increasingly heated row over the Guantanamo student, and to reassure himself that his athletes would be welcome that Summer at the Cardiff Olympics.

The meeting had not begun well.

"What sort of tea do you take, Hymie?", asked the Queen, acidly. "Boston?".

But gradually the urbane Hymie began to charm the ageing monarch, and eventually her voice softened.

"Of course we'd like to welcome your athletes", she said. "Why wouldn't we? They win everything. But with this Guantanamo student, the Press coverage, the demonstrations", she sighed, "I fear the people may be against it".

"I regret this incident deeply, Your Majesty", Hymie grovelled, "and my people are negotiating with the military, but you know how they are...?".

The Queen seemed exasperated.

"Not really", she said. "They simply do as I say here, you see".

She was coy when she spoke again, as though asking for a favour.

"But if you could bring over some jazz!", she said. "I'd like that. We haven't heard any proper jazz over here for a long time now. Not since they turned Scott's into some sort of croonarium".

She chuckled in delight at her own turn of phrase. Hymie was flummoxed, but recovered quickly.

"Oh yes, of course, Your Majesty", he purred. "We have some of the finest College Jazz Programmes in the world, and it would be a great honour to send...".

The Queen interrupted him.

"No college jazz. We have enough of that warmed-over crap over here already. No, give me the real thing, some hard-edged New York swingmatism. I'm a particular fan of the new fusions. The Indian Carnatic Strain fascinates me; it seems to carry on where John Coltrane had to stop, don't you think?".

She smiled sweetly while Hymie Vidal struggled to keep up. He didn't care much for any type of jazz, though he remembered liking Al Jolson in the Jazz Singer.

"Surely, Your Majesty, but if you're going the Al Qu'aeda route, we should maybe think about some Klezmer too, just for balance?".

Now the Queen seemed puzzled. After a short silence,

Hymie changed the subject, and this is when he became more frank than he had intended.

"I must inform you, Your Majesty, that you are holding our Ambassador in one of your prisons. In Wormwood Scrubs".

"But how can that be?", exclaimed the Queen. "I sat next to him only last week. At the Royal Ballet. Dreadful, lecherous man, drooling over the dancers. No manners at all. He has begun to make my flesh crawl. It must be his age".

"That man is an impostor", said Hymie, "and I apologize sincerely if he has made you uncomfortable in his presence, for he does, by strange circumstance, represent the United States of America in your country, at this time".

"Go on", said the Queen sternly.

"Did you read of the Bateman Street brothel fire?", the President continued. "Our Ambassador was found there naked, and drugged; he had large amounts of Ketamine in his system. Ketamine is a horse tranquilizer..."

"Yes, yes, I know what it is", cut in the Queen, impatiently. "I use it on sugar lumps to sedate the corgis".

Hymie continued.

"We also found his DNA on the American Military issue handgun that started the fire at the brothel. He is facing a number of very serious charges and has been remanded in custody awaiting trial next year at the Old Bailey".

"But this is scarcely credible", exclaimed the Queen. "Has he not claimed immunity?"

"Probably. But the British Police believe that the man they are holding is the brothel-keeper, Enoch. Whereas Enoch is the man actually running our Embassy", explained Hymie.

"Which leaves us in a very delicate situation. On the one hand, this Enoch is doing a certain amount of damage where he is, but on the other hand...if it were to become known that our Ambassador was involved in the Soho brothel fire... if the true facts were to emerge...what with all the fuss about the Guantanamo student terrorist, then even greater damage could ensue, I believe. So we're leaving him where he is for the moment.... them where they are...it's a question of balance", he finished smoothly.

"What about this girl?" asked the Queen. "Is she a terrorist? Is she a student? Is she even in Guantanamo?".

"Yes, Your Majesty, we are holding her in that place, and she is, or was, a student over there in England, at the Royal English Conservatory, but she is totally innocent of all charges of terrorism. We know that now".

"I see", said the Queen. "Poor girl".

"But we found out just too late to do anything about it", continued the President, "so we're just going to keep her under wraps until the heat dies down. Just for a few more years. Meanwhile I have people working to bury the story. As far as the World is concerned, the whole student thing will turn out to have been a big mistake".

"It certainly will have been for her", agreed the Queen.

"Meanwhile, as I say, Your Majesty, I have my people. And there's one in particular that I would like to have you call him, if I may suggest, as he's the one I trust to deal with this on my behalf, and on behalf of the American people, while my real Ambassador is in the pen. His name is Cornelius Coltrane Brewster, and he's head of one of your grand music academies over there, and he's good people. My people. I think you'll like him, Your Majesty".

Chaplet 29

A Royal Summons

So it was that Cornelius was summoned to appear before the Queen. He was nearly wetting himself with excitement as he was admitted into her presence through the Ambassador's Court on Buckingham Palace Road. He was wearing his most English of outfits, the mauve tweed plus fours with brown brogues, and had been polishing his vowels all morning. The Queen, however, with the perspicacity of a thousand years of rule, saw before her just another Yank.

"You are not of us", she proclaimed. "Yet you are among us. And you are charged with the stewardship of one of our most precious national assets. The young. And it seems to me, Mr Brewster, that you have not made much of a fist of it so far. I must confess to being very disappointed by your role in the Guantanamo crisis. It seems that this poor student may only have ended up where she is because you failed to teach her. Mr Brewster, the world is watching you. I am watching you. Remember that you are the Principal of the Royal English Conservatory of Music".

She leant heavily on the word 'royal'.

"And that you must behave accordingly. Was the girl your student? Do not lie to me!", she commanded him.

Cornelius hung his head in a nod of shame. He had never felt shame like this before, yet he received it gratefully into his body, assuming it to be synonymous with Higher Englishness.

"Then you will make this known. You will tell the truth of this to the World. This is your clear duty".

"But..the President..?", stammered Cornelius.

"Has his ways, as we have ours", said the Queen. "I have spoken to your President, who has commended you to me, incidentally, vouchsafing you as his representative to me and as an emissary between us in this most delicate of matters, and this is my decision. The provenance of the girl must be declared. Furthermore, Mr Brewster, you might ensure that you put in place such administrative measures as will ensure that such a teaching disaster can never take place again. It is time to remenber your pedagogic oaths and put your house in order!".

She paused to allow Cornelius a further pang of shame, then continued, more briskly.

"Now, about the music for the Olympic Games. What exactly do you have planned?"

"Well, Ma'am", said Cornelius, leaving his feelings of worthlessness with some regret, "we have made some provisional arrangements, some Handel, some Hodinott to appease the Welsh, some Elgar of course. And some very interesting contemporary classics, the Winehouse First Symphony,

Laurie Holloway's new opera, Blind Date, with a libretto by Jonathan Ross, and of course the McCartney Oratorio. But we aren't at all certain that there will be an Olympics, Ma'am... so many nations are threatening to withdraw. Because of the Guantanamo crisis", he added, hoping to reignite the Queen's anger.

"There's also the Prince, Ma'am. I believe he's been quite outspoken in his criticism of the Olympics, not just because of American Torture, but also because of excessive professionalism and triumphalism in sport, and the consequent loss of purity and beauty".

"Journalists" spat the Queen. "All wind and piss! The Olympics will take place, you can take my word for it. Just without you Yanks. Now look. Do you have any jazz planned?".

"Of course, Ma'am", said Cornelius quickly.

"I was afraid you'd say that", said the Queen. "You have that awful Abrahams fellow with his English Country Dances, don't you?".

"Yes Ma'am. Indeed. He calls it Bip-Bop. It's meant to be more urban, I believe. It's a fusion of.."

"I'm sure it is", said the Queen. "But I want some real jazz, and the President has agreed to send over his best New York Trio, so you must make room for them in the Closing Ceremony. They may be the only ones to make it".

For a reason he would never understand, the Queen now became irrational. Her face turned red, while her lips quivered white with anger. Cornelius felt a warm glow of kinship with her, for these lips suddenly seemed very African to him, and he remembered reading that the Queen indeed had some African blood from her ancestor Queen Charlotte.

"And it serves you bloody right!", she screamed at him. "After this Summer we'll never have to see any of you ever again, and what a blessed relief that will be".

Then she began to babble and hiss in a mystic tongue that Cornelius finally recognized to be Welsh.

"Llanfairpwllgwyngyllgogerychwyrndrobwllllantysiliogog-oseptictwaat!!", she finished,

"and just make sure you get me my jazz".

Chaplet 30

A Message From On High

Cornelius Brewster had a busy afternoon. His first task was to tell everyone that he had been up to see the Queen. Then he held a Press Conference. He was surprised that his admission that Ang Li was in fact on the Royal English Conservatory of Music student roll was greeted with such apathy, but he didn't know that his Officer for Press and Publicity, Myfanwy Muff Maboob, had been briefing against him for several months, stirring up as much anti-American feeling and general controversy around the issue as she could.

"Well, we've known that all along", said the International Correspondent of the Daily Blog. "But now you're admitting it. I suppose that's some sort of news. I suppose we can run with that".

And the journalists did not run, but strolled to the nearby coffeeshops and bashed out their copy, by electronic dispersal, to the waiting World. And the official news did make a difference, because the villainy of the Americans was thereby confirmed, and the demonstrations and sanctions against them were therefore redoubled.

Then Cornelius called the European Agents of the New York Trio to confirm their booking for the Closing Ceremony of the Olympic Games, at a cost to the Conservatory of thirty thousand pounds. No sooner had he put the phone down than it rang again. It was only the Queen.

"Now look", she said. "About the music for the Olympic Games. What have you got planned?". Cornelius, though having previously enjoyed the Queen's ire, did not at this time want to mention the word dementia, and merely repeated to her his earlier speech.

"Well, Ma'am, we have made some provisional arrangements, some Handel, some Hodinott to appease the Welsh, some Elgar of course. And some very interesting contemporary classics, the Winehouse 1st...", he recited, "...and of course the New York Trio you've requested".

"That's all well and good", the Queen broke in,

"but I believe you also have a fine in-house piano trio. Aren't they called the Mob, or something? Len somebody on piano. Chubby Asian man. And the other Professors on bass and drums. Lovely players. We so used to enjoy listening to them. You must find room for them in the Closing Ceremony".

"Certainly, Your Majesty", acceded Cornelius, and as the phone went dead became suddenly sweaty and lightheaded, and felt full of confusion, for his tiring and exciting day had just caught up with him.

Mickey put the phone down, laughing.

"That's one gig for the Summer", he congratulated himself. "Wait till I tell Len and Steve!".

He always knew his imitation of the Queen would come in useful one day.

Chaplet 31

Haute Cuisine

Later that evening, in an anteroom at the American Embassy, after a sumptuous dinner cooked by a brigade of celebrity chefs, Cornelius confided in the man he believed to be the Ambassador.

"I think the Queen has become unhinged. She was speaking in tongues yesterday".

The Ambassador said nothing in reply, but Cornelius didn't notice, having been distracted by a beautiful waiter. All the waiters were male, and wore custom leather aprons that exposed firm naked buttocks each time they turned back towards the kitchen. Toby had become a much better host of late, reflected Cornelius, even if his Real Tennis had gone off. The staff all seemed terrified of him now, but he was certainly getting results.

"I think she may be suffering from some form of dementia", said Cornelius eventually. "She's losing her temper, forgetting what I've said to her, and what she's said to me. It really is very sad. She's been such a force".

His eyes filled with tears, just as a quartet of leather-aproned lap dancers arrived at their low oriental table.

"She asked for a New York Trio for the Closing Ceremony", said Cornelius, "and then said she wanted an English Trio! Does she want them both?".

The Ambassador smiled a wolfish grin and separated the lap dancers, taking the two more feminine of the men for himself and pushing the other two towards Cornelius.

"Hey, waddyagonna do?", he croaked in, Cornelius thought, a very accurate and amusing impersonation of a Mafioso.

"Threesomes is nice".

Chaplet 32

Reading The Future

Myfanwy Muff Maboob was enjoying herself. She now spent most of her days in meetings with journalists at beautiful and expensive restaurants. And if the journalists themselves were ugly and cheap, so what! Muff was nonetheless delighted. Delighted and also relieved to have escaped the oppressive tedium and relentless fellatio of her former life.

She was also apprehensive about the future, for she had powers she did not yet understand. She could possess the dreams of men, and give them the gift of Sound. But these were powers still new and uncharted in her body. Where would they lead her, she wondered, into what new realm? What would be asked of her?

Because she felt this uncertainty, and although she now had a large enough salary for something much better, Muff still lived for the time being in her Chigwell caravan, glamorizing herself every day in the office on the coveted lower floor of the Royal English Conservatory of Music that she now used mostly as a changing room.

She knew that she was heading somewhere; she knew this with great certainty. But she did not yet know where. For the moment she was just following her nose.

One day in the late Spring, and for a reason she did not know, Myfanwy did not alight from the omnibus at her usual stop for the Conservatory, but stayed seated, allowing herself to be taken to a part of the city that she did not know. At some point she rang the bell asking the driver to let her off at the next stop, although she had no idea where this might be. Descending from the bus, she followed the main road on foot for a while, then turned left along the pavement into a maze of small terraced houses. Eventually she came upon a shop bearing the sign 'Jefferies Antiquarian'. Muff noted the presence on the sign of a small graphic of red dragons and, in tiny letters, the words League of Idristan, and she entered there.

A man approached her as she stood among the tall dusty shelves. His face was covered by the soft velvet brim of a purple hat. As he removed it, Muff recognized the Nutter Prince. She recalled that at their last meeting she had dropped emotionally to her knees, ready to accept and revere his royal manhood. Now she felt so such impulse. Her mind was calm and confident; her legs remained strong and straight. It was the Prince who dropped on one knee and bowed his head. Muff was only surprised at how little surprise she felt. It seemed to her that the proper ceremony had at last begun, and she felt relieved. Muff allowed him to kiss her hand, then bade him rise. The Prince quickly searched the shelves and plucked out a number of volumes. The top one, she saw, bore the title

'Inside the Welsh Triads'.

"Take these, My Lady", he asked her. "For on these pages you will read of our History and of our Future; you will understand your power and your destiny; and you will learn of the Realms ancient and modern to which you are bound in the magic grace of your being. You will understand how you now must change, Your work until now has been of great importance; you have confounded and confused our enemies as you have consoled and energized our friends. You have given us the time to plan and prepare for the work that we must do on our side, and you have predisposed our friends to accept the great changes we will propose. Or so we all must hope. You have done much already, but your most difficult task still lies before you. Read these while you rest".

He pressed the books into her hands and was gone.

Chaplet 33

Becoming English

In the near aftermath of his conversations with the Queen, Cornelius Brewster was already beginning to change. For in the course of receiving what was in fact a right royal carpeting, and in which he had also been mistaken for an American, he nevertheless felt himself to have moved several leagues closer to Englishness. As he waited for Spiff Abrahams, his wayward Head of Jazz, to appear in his office, he reached down into his memory to touch again the sweet severity of the Queen's voice, and felt again the sexual tingle that comes from being included.

When Spiff was in front of him, looking smug, vacant and self-absorbed as usual, Cornelius for once came straight to the point.

"I am dissatisfied with your performance. You are failing the students, you are failing the Conservatory, you are failing me, you are failing yourself, and most importantly, you are failing the Queen".

Spiff tried to speak, but Cornelius cut him off with a scything motion of his arm.

"Specifically, your failure adequately to provide tuition for your students, for one student in particular, Ang Li, has led to a major diplomatic crisis, the jeopardy of the Olympic Games, and incidentally the deaths of many hundreds of people during consequent riots around the world. This merits a verbal warning".

The young Professor looked aghast at his Principal. He knew the procedure well, having implemented it several times against some of the oldtimers who were still clogging up the system when he arrived; if the verbal warning were followed by a written one, he would surely soon be facing the sack. After drums come bass solo, he thought gloomily, as he considered the inevitable nature of decline. Tears welled up in his throat as he realized he was no longer the golden boy.

Cornelius could have been reading his mind.

"How's that new young bass player coming on, the one from the streets?", he asked. "Jamal. I hope we're taking care of him, at least?".

Spiff had no idea what had happened to the lad. He had seen him once in a practice room, doing duets wth Steve, the old bass codger from the front desks, but hadn't spoken to him. He had been too busy giving Steve a verbal warning for desertion of his post and unauthorized use of College equipment.

"Show me his file, please", commanded Cornelius, "with the register of his one-to-one instrumental lessons".

Spiff shuffled through the papers on his lap.

"I can't recall which particular teacher he has", he hedged.

"What's the choice?", Cornelius pressed, and took the list of Faculty Double Bass Professors that Spiff held out to him, reading aloud from it.

"Scott La Faro, Ray Brown, Jimmy Blanton. Never heard of them. They may be great players, but are they good teachers? How often do they come in? Are they reliable?"

"Those particular ones are dead", said Spiff. "But they still bring the punters in. And anyway, I have another list of teachers. Up here". He tapped his head. "It's constantly changing, it follows the shape of the cutting edge. It's part of my vision".

Cornelius now had something of a vision himself, for he suddenly saw that with all his politeness, with all the love of understatement and euphemism he had discovered in himself on the day he had walked into the Conservatory as its Principal, he had been trying far too hard to be English. While being chastised by the Queen he had learned that to be truly English you just had to be truly yourself.

"Listen to me, you squeaky little cunt", he shouted. "Listen to me good! I'm not interested in your poxy fucking vision, and the only cutting edge you should be interested in is the axe I use to chop your fucking legs off unless you start doing your freakin' job...and here's another thing, why don't you sort out your own fucking playing? I've just heard that we, I mean they, are sending over one of our finest, I mean their hippest New York bands for the big Olympics gig. You, and me, and the Royal English Conservatory of Music, and every English jazz player, and every English jazz teacher, and every fucking English jazz person, is going to be judged by your saxophone".

He paused now, out of breath, then finished more calmly. "And if you come up with another one of those lame folk songs, we'll all be fucking mortified!".

Spiff Abrahams left the meeting feeling puzzled and hurt. It was difficult, he reasoned, to work with someone so insensitive to the artistic process. Nevertheless the encounter had energized him, and he immediately set in place a system of regular tuition for his students for the remainder of the term. The fourth years would teach the third years; the third years would teach the second years; the second years would teach the first years, and, the really clever bit, the first years would teach the fourth years. It was a beautifully designed system, self-balancing and circular, and if it had certain limitations, the students all found it a considerable improvement over the previous ad hoc constellation.

Having set this system in place, Spiff Abrahams returned to the woodshed himself, where he embarked upon a gruelling regime of 13 hour practice days. He took Jamal in there with him, and made the boy walk endlessly through the jazz repertoire in all keys and all tempos while reciting from memory over and over again the Arts Page containing Spiff's single good review. It was hard on both of them, but only a few weeks now remained for Spiff to bring to perfect sharpness both his chops and his creative conception.

And as Cornelius Coltrane Brewster had rightly pointed out, he had a very big gig coming up.

Chaplet 34

After The Woodshed

Myfanwy had been shopping in the West End and her feet were hurting. It had been a last minute decision, to wander down from the Royal English into the great shopping centre of London, made possible by the chaos of the final arrangements for what was feeling like an exodus into Cardiff. The Italian shoes her Mum had bought for her were lovely, but impractical round town and over long distances. And they'd never been the same since she'd been sick in them. Muff found a bench in the park and flopped down on it gratefully.

By strange coincidence the young bassist Jamal was on the same bench. His shoulders were hunched and tense and he would not meet her eye.

Myfanwy recognised in him the urgent desire to slap and kill their Head of Jazz, Spiff Abrahams.

"He does your head in, love", she explained, "that's his special gift".

Jamal peered inside her shopping bag. She saw that his fingers were long and delicate, more suited to the violin, she thought, than to the double bass, with its thick strings and intractable nature. They were covered with bruises and bloody blisters.

"It's an evening gown", she said. "I thought it might come in handy in Cardiff. For the dinners, and the ceremonies, like". She pulled it out of the bag and jumped up to show the garment off along her body.

"Unusual, isn't it?", she said. "With the colours half and half like that".

Jamal nodded, smiled, then rose from the bench and walked away. He pointed to the large case on the grass, wherein lay the instrument of his torture.

"This is bullshit", he said, and walked away to Portobello Green, leaving Myfanwy to totter back to work with the extra burden of the Royal English Conservatory of Music house bass.

Chaplet 35

Long Live The Queen!

"Citius Altius Fortius Umidius", intoned the Queen, addressing the luminaries gathered in the Siambr of the Senedd of Cardiff Bay, as well as a Television and Internet audience of several billion, to open the closing ceremony. "Faster, Higher, Stronger, and Wetter!".

The room filled with a warm chuckle at this clever twist on the Olympic motto. The athletes had indeed gone faster, higher and stronger at the Cardiff Games, just as the rain had fallen faster, thicker and wetter. The roof of handblown Indonesian glass had never quite made it on to the Main Stadium, but the drenched crowds had kept their good humour. The American athletes had stayed home, and there had been enough medals for everyone.

"What a happy privilege it was", continued the Queen, "what an honour and treat for the eyes it has been to see so many obsessive compulsives assembled together in one place".

The Queen paused and smiled at the cameras.

"And using such a wide variety of drugs".

The Siambr had fallen silent in the intensifying darkness of the Queen's tone. Faux Ambassador Enoch, invited on account of the visiting New York musicians, felt his phone buzz in the pocket of his brand new Briony suit; he suspected it to be a panic call from one of the crew of girls he had been working during the event, and he quietly rose and left the chamber as she continued.

"I am sad that this magnificent, this historic sporting event could not resolve the recent misunderstanding between the Great Nations of the World".

The Queen nodded in the direction of Enoch's empty seat.

"But happy that it marks the end of a phase of uncertainty and dissembling, a phase of History several millennia long".

Confused muttering arose around the Siambr and opinions were discreetly exchanged as to the mental health of the monarch, and in response she lowered her voice, making it intimate, confessional.

"My husband and I have never been English. We have been living a lie. As did our forebears, and their forebears before, and their beforebears before them. We are, we are and have always been Ancient Britons. We belong here, here with you in Cymru, the true ancestral home of the throne, of the people, of the sacred realm of Ancient Britain".

Reporters were already walking quickly to the doors to get to the laptops they had had to leave, for reasons of security, outside in the adjoining Cwrt. With the Queen's next words they began to run.

"It is with great pleasure", she said, "with great pleasure, pride and also relief, that I announce to you now my abdication from the Throne of England".

Cries of shock and horror spread round the room.

"Combrogi", she continued in Welsh, "I hereby recreate the Kingdom of Ancient Britain, which I name Idristan, and stand before you as your Sovereign".

The journalists were reaching the doors now, but found them locked shut from the outside. They turned and watched the former Queen of England in the centre of her new circle.

"But first!", she cried. "Some jazz. Some real New York Jazz with which to celebrate this new beginning".

A curtain on the stage behind her parted, revealing three bearded and ringleted performers of indeterminate age and sex playing a laptop, a tabla drum and a didgeridoo. Behind them, the piano trio of Len, Steve, and Mickey tried desperately hard to stay with the great New York frontliners, and to turn their random squawkings into music.

Ten minutes into the first number the Idristani Queen turned to her husband with a despairing and disappointed look.

"I know", he said, all tea and warm sympathy.

"It's all in one. How can you get a decent backbeat if it's all in one?!".

"I feel badly for the piano, bass and drums", said the Queen, and they raised their eyes heavenwards, and for the first time noticed the architectural and natural beauty of the huge funnel of Welsh Oak that grew up out of the Siambr, through the heart of the glass building, into the blue slate roof high above.

Two floors higher, in the direction of their gaze, in the toilets of the Oriel, the viewing gallery of the Senedd, Victor was lying on the tiled floor nursing a broken head and a sore arse. The man he took to be the American Ambassador, whom he had followed into the toilet to scold for his intolerance in spiritual matters, had turned out to be an effective and quite vicious streetfighter. To his own great surprise Victor now spoke aloud from the toilet floor in a heartfelt prayer.

"Oh Lord", he said, and the unfamiliar words exploded like an exotic fruit in his mouth, and he said them again, crying as he recognized their taste. "Oh Lord", he said. "Oh Lord".

Downstairs in the Siambr, Spiff was becoming overexcited. He sensed that the audience were tiring of the carnatic rhythms of the New York trio and were eager for some hard swing. Filled with the confidence of his hours in the woodshed, and with penis atwitch, he swaggered on to the stage, adjusted his body to the time of the two trios, then looked deep within himself for the first phrase of his statement. It came surging up almost instantly, passing through his lips into the horn, "da da-da da, da da da-da dah?" as a burning passionate question to the world. The audience sang the answer straight back to him in one lilting but oddly sarcastic Welsh voice, "In an English Country Ga-ar-den".

"Oh no", said the Idristani Queen.

"Not that twat again!", said her husband.

While the folk singing continued in the Siambr, Victor

emerged into the Oriel from the toilets, to see a group of Red Dragons between four and six feet in height. They walked on hind legs, like people, and held black guns the length of human feet with their forelegs. Tucking the guns into the cream belts around their tummies, they swung ropes over the top of the funnel, first securing them to the floor of the Oriel with a giant staple gun, hopped over the edge and abseiled down into the Siambr below.

But at that moment Myfanwy Muff Maboob herself appeared on the stage, and all present bowed their head in reverence, though few knew why. As she spoke it seemed to us all that her tongue was foreign, for we did not recognise it; yet we all understood her meaning. She spoke of King Arthur and Uther Pendragon, of the knights Sir Gawain and Sir Galahad, of the wizard Merdydd and his magic muse. She spoke of the Welsh Cakes and the Welsh Triads, and of the roots of the Ancient Briton in the mountains and valleys of Cymru, and we heard in her words that Our Lady Myfanwy Muff Maboob was our magic muse, just as Idristan was to be our new kingdom, and we heard also that although there would again be joy and peace in the Land, first there would be bloodshed and acrimony, for the rebirth was sudden and the dividing lines would be sharp and final.

Then she passed among us, and divided us by her touch, and as she moved among us her white gown gradually divided into two long strips of colour, and while one half was a deep blood red, the other half was beige.

And some of those she touched were musicians, and they

rose and played, and some of them sang. First Heidi Hyson came, with her profound and resonant Oum, then the porters Len on piano, Steve on bass and Mickey on drums; then came the player of the tabla drum from New York, but not his friend with the laptop, for Muff passed him by, nor his friend on the didgeridoo, for during the sixty-third minute of his circular breath he had already passed away.

Then Muff came near to Spiff, and he cowered before her gaze and tried to hide his saxophone, but she looked upon him with tender mercy and reached to touch him, reached to choose him, but he flinched from her, for he lacked the courage to be chosen, and she passed him by.

Then she came to a big man dressed roughly as a humble mechanic, and she took his curly beard hair in both hands and pulled his face into her stomach, inhaling from him the pipe scent she now recognised as the tobacco smoked by Cornelius Brewster; with this deep inhalation we watched her accept once and for all the spiritual burden of her museship, and in the exhalation that followed we heard her whispered adieu to the carnal world. She released the man's head from her grasp, and we saw that it was Nicky de la Chwyth, who reached down now and stabbed several holes with a screwdriver through one of the largest of the Dragon weapons where it had fallen unused on the floor as we had become entranced by the poetry of the time. As he raised it to his full lips we saw from its leafy green handle that it was but a leek wound with gaffer tape, not an automatic weapon of any sort, and we now heard a breath of music more wondrous, more complete and more lovely than any before it. And the assembly of musicians were not overawed by the beauty, but inspired and emboldened to join and become part of it, and as their lovely song rose up in the Siambr, we saw that the Red Dragons had removed their heads and revealed themselves as the entire Royal Family, and that their leader was the Nutter Prince, and we saw that the Queen and her husband also now wore this garb, and were at last tapping their feet and smiling.

As the last breath of this gorgeous jazz died away, a loud voice boomed down into the Siambr from above, bringing us cheering to our feet. It was Victor, whose terrible Aphasia had been cured by a blow to the head.

"Oh Lord", he shouted. "Oh Lord. We thank you for the Realm of Idristan. We thank you for our new Royal Family. We thank you for your blessing. Long live the Queen!".

In these compelling words was constituted our new kingdom, and we recognized that magic had been done that day, and the final syllables spoken of a spell long in the saying, and we looked for Muff Maboob to hail and thank her, but only her silk robe remained, beige and red on the oaken floor, for she knew that there was much important work to do, and had gone away to rest.

Chaplet 36

The Great Partition

This then is the story of the Great Partition, or at least of its beginning, for there were to be some years of turmoil and tribulation before it was complete. As it was foretold. There were some English who could not accept the loss of their Royalty, and did not want to become a Republic of Small Town States, each governed by a Local Council, and these had to be anaesthetized with celebrity gameshows. There were also some insurgent Welsh who would not accept that they were Ancient Britons if it meant swearing fealty to people they still considered to be English; these had to be exterminated.

Gradually, though, people made their own choices; things settled down.

Idristan was truly a wonderful place to live, for it was lush and verdant and filled with people who wanted to be there. And these were people come from all over the world, people of all races and religions whose common spirit and purpose it was to live together and work and play in peace and harmony, in loyalty to their King.

The Queen herself had succumbed to the mental instability that we had begun to detect at the end of her last reign, and had died in the early days of the Great Partition, ceding the throne of Idristan to her son the Nutter Prince. The new King immediately implemented some of the ideas of his beloved Plato, and created an Academy of Higher Learning in which the main subjects were jazz improvisation, yoga and motor mechanics, and in this new atmosphere the people thrived and were happy.

And we still had Myfanwy, of course, who had made it all happen in the first place, who was our Bard and our Muse and our Prophet. And we loved her so much, we did, all of us, and were so proud of her. And we all knew that she couldn't play a note of music herself, no matter how much she wanted to, which had created in her the energy to change our world, and we sang and played all the louder, all the purer, for that knowledge.

Over the border in England, things were a little different, as the country had been entirely paved over and filled with security cameras. Birds and bees, as well as flowers and other animals were only imported from overseas to be displayed in designated Heritage Sites. Any artists that remained in New England, musicians, painters, filmmakers, writers and so on, all worked at such sites, where they devoted their time and talent to the recreation of an artificial and quite fictitious representation of the past. The National Coordinator of New English Heritage Systems was in fact one Cornelius Coltrane Brewster, who had achieved Englishness beyond his greatest expectation, and who was also one of the few black people left in this part of the world. Spiff Abrahams was his second-in-command.

Most skilled and intelligent people had left this strange New England, as there was little left for them to do. The main industry was now the recycling and repackaging of waste; few jobs involved more than driving, loading, or pressing keys, buttons and levers, all at carefully prescribed times.

The main cultural activities were drinking, fighting and karaoke, and the closest most New English people came to a spiritual feeling was a tingle of nostalgia evoked by a Classic TV Repeat from back in the day. Taxes were still kept high, to fund a huge and sprawling NESS, the New English Safety Service. Cancer had been cured, but deaths had multiplied from liver damage, tinnitus and head wounds.

People were so angry in New England, you see, though they thought they were happy enough. They had decided there was no God, that there was nothing they couldn't understand. And because they had decided there was no God of any sort, they decided there was no King or Queen to put in front of Him, and that made them very angry in the end. Because there was only them, so they believed, and nothing else beyond that, they had no other way of looking at themselves, and became imprisoned in their myopia.

And it is interesting to note the decline in good footballing goals and the general descent into incompetent mediocrity everywhere, that occurred when the idea of God was scotched. Or englanded, should I say? Because human excellence and genius derived from our attempt to grasp an idea of the unknown, and now it disappeared for ever in New England, for it was more important there to be right, than to be great, or even good.

Because there was only themselves, and nothing beyond that, they became obsessed with being right themselves. Being right and safe. All the time. Obsessed with truth and security. That's why everywhere you looked in New England, there was a camera, or a committee, or a referee.

We didn't need any of that, see, not in Idristan, not me or Heidi Hyson, or Nicky de la Chwyth, or Steve, or Mickey, or any of the others. We weren't trying to be right, or trying to be safe, or trying to be happy, even. We were just getting on with it, like, just playing our music and getting on with it. And that's what made us happy in the end. Because we knew we could never really understand what we were made of, or why we were here, or what we were doing, see, but we didn't think that was a bad thing. We actually liked that thing we couldn't understand, that's what we liked most of all, the mystery.

And we were never against Science, see, or Knowledge, or Engineering, because they were bloody useful, when you got down to it, like. But you had to know what they were for, which was just for telling you about the likely behaviour of the things you'd divided the world into. As I say, all very useful, in the day-to-day. But they explained nothing, left untouched the nature of being, the mystery at the heart of it all, the thing that we loved, the fact that we were joined together in this big amazing jellied puzzle that would always be past our intelligence. By its very nature.

And we embraced that, see, and called it God, just for handiness, really, and put a King or a Queen in place so we could love and embrace God that bit easier still, and then we played our music, and that's why we're happy in the end, like, because we're not even trying to be.

You see, that's why our music is so fucking beautiful.

Chaplet 37

The Awakening

The phone was still ringing. Then it stopped.
"Len, Len, are you awake?". My wife's voice grew louder and louder until she appeared by the bed, face pink and eyes bright from early morning yoga and meditation in her garden temple.

"Are you free Monday night? Bloke on the phone wants the trio. Reigate. Three hundred quid. Doesn't want any deps, though, the Maboob Mob in full, or not at all."
I groaned and turned over. "Tell him OK, take his number and I'll get back to him".

"He speaks, Mein Gott he speaks!", said my wife.

And it was true that I hadn't been up to much for the last week or so, with my bad ear. But Heidi decided unilaterally two days ago that my allotted sick leave had come to an end, and therefore felt I'd been malingering since then. She bounced away downstairs with a smile on her pretty face. She was a cracker, really good value, a real grafter, and I loved her to bits, even if she thought only in straight lines. But a jazz musician doesn't need a bendy wife.

She was better than her parents, though. They were strict Lutherans, which I gather is like the Methodists down home, only German, and they were against me from the start. I always thought it was because of me being half Pakistani, and only recently found out it was the other half they didn't like; the Welsh one.

I tried in vain to keep the water out of my duff ear in the shower. I blame Mickey for that ear as it goes, not the urine in the local swimming pool. It's those heavy Turkish cymbals he plays. "Big, dark sound", he always says, ever so proud, like, and he's right, I suppose. If you're a medieval army looking for something to terrify the enemy's horses, then big dark heavy Turkish cymbals are just the job. But in Reigate Jazz Club? Mickey couldn't make this Monday, anyway, I wouldn't even ring to ask. He wouldn't give up his Monday at La Bussetta for anything. Reckons the jazz scene here will be dead soon, but there'll always be a market for pussy. I've hated the place myself, when I've done the odd dep there. The girls are so sad, and he's a greedy bastard that Enoch, the owner. Fat little creep. Mickey's probably right, though, there'll always be a gig there. Unless some disgruntled punter burns it down. I'll tell the Reigate bloke we can all do it, and wait till Monday to tell him our drummer's ill and I've got someone else. I'll find someone quiet and save them some earache.

Heidi carried on bringing me the latest news about my life over breakfast. Apparently it was Saturday.

"Myfanwy starts with her new teacher today. She's playing Rach 3 for him, he's bound to be impressed. I'm so proud of her, she's doing so well with her music. You like the new piano too, don't you, Len?".

A nine footer in the living-room, a full concert grand, what's not to like? So what, not a Steinway, or a Bosendorfer, but those guys all started small, and I reckon this Idristani fellow could be the next great piano maker. And free, as well. What's not to like? Can you believe I've never had a sponsorship deal before, not in all my years of playing? It's not like the rock world, over on the jazz side.

"I hope he's better than Mickey's nephew. More....you know....suitable".

Yes, Heidi, I know exactly what you mean. But you thought it was a good idea as well, putting Myfanwy with Jeb, until he turned into such a lecherous little git, barely out of college himself and already drooling over our little girl; not that I blame him, in a way, with her starting to look like that, to behave like that. That young bass player Jamal I used as a dep last week was sniffing round her, I noticed that, and I've even caught Mickey and Steve looking at her a bit funny, and they're like family to her, really. Still, I suppose biology trumps sociology.

"The new one's American. Cornelius something, his name is. Only young, but a bit of a high flyer, I'm told. Loves the English. Hopefully she'll make the big push through, now, with him. At least he's got all his fingers".

I'm feeling and I know looking, gloomy.

"What is it, Len, don't you believe she's good enough?"

Oh, yes, she's good enough. I know that. Just not in music.

Some people just haven't got it, that's what Heidi doesn't understand. They've got all the bits but they can't make them work together. Myfanwy's a good girl, a good, clever girl. She'll work that out for herself, I know she will. Find out what she really needs to do.

"I'm going to drop her down to the Conservatory, because you're teaching this morning. I suppose you remembered that? The car's fixed now. I took it round to that garage you told me. The converted chapel. Big scary man with a beard. But he was really nice once I'd relaxed. He played me a lovely tune on an old family flute, he said, then he fixed the car. It's running so smoothly now. In fact I think that's why I had the accident. I didn't tell you about that, did I, you've been asleep".

I don't know about any of this, but it all sounds familiar, because I've already seen it in my dreams, where the past, present and future all get jumbled up in a weird jelly anyway, and it's much worse if I get any sort of infection, like now. I need to play the piano quite soon. It's the only way out of the jelly.

"But it's all right, no-one was hurt, and there's not a scratch on the car. Just a dent. It was the Nigerian man down the road, just stepped off the pavement in front of me. Either he didn't hear me, because the car is running so quiet now, you won't believe it, or maybe he was just miles away, thinking about something legal. That's what he does, didn't you say? Isn't he a Law Professor somewhere? Mind you, how he does that, I don't know. He's gone very funny, he's not right at all at the moment. He couldn't string more than a few words together, always the same, and I couldn't understand him at all. Maybe it was the shock, because it can't be easy for the students, otherwise. Then he started winking at me, and it was more than a twitch and made me feel quite uncomfortable, and when I asked if he wanted to call the police, because I know technically you're supposed to do that if you bump into a pedestrian, even if there's no damage, he let out this big squeezy fart!".

Heidi laughed merrily and buttered me a last piece of toast. I'm on rations because of my belly.

"And last week. When I dropped Myfanwy, another teacher asked about you. You're married to Len Maboob, he said. I've heard him play at Ronnie Scott's. Very impressed, he was. Said they were thinking about starting some sort of jazz course at the Conservatory, and would you be interested. I said you would be. Len, you might be a Professor!".

Yeah right. Only those classical guys are right up themselves and don't really want anyone else up there with them. Spoiling the view of the monarchy. And teaching jazz isn't that easy anyway.

"You've got a new one this morning. He's from the West Country. Another young genius, or so he told me on the phone".

Heidi left the kitchen and shouted up the stairs.

"Myfanwy, we're leaving. Come down now!"

I kissed my two lovely girls Myfanwy and Heidi goodbye and watched them walk down the garden path. I reminded myself again to find a time to tell Myfanwy I loved her. They look so grown-up but they still need to hear it. A young man carrying a tenor saxophone case was just coming through the gate. He smiled politely enough at my wife but I didn't like the way he was looking at my daughter. I didn't like the angle of his neck, or the cut of his jib, or the bulge in his trouser. He held his hand out to me confidently.

"I'm Spiff", he said. "Spiff Abrahams. I'm cutting edge".

I showed him through to the living room. The telly was under the huge piano, which didn't bother me as I was out working most nights and there seemed to be less and less on these days anyway, only repeats. The girls quite liked lying on the floor together to watch their programmes.

"Let's play". I said. "What jazz do you like?".

"I'm into Coltrane", the young man said, licking his Rico number 4 reed, then squinting as he positioned it against the old Otto Link mouthpiece. At least he looked like he knew what he was doing.

"But I've taken it a bit further".

Yeah right. I give him the piano intro to the Coltrane Body and Soul, all moody Ab pedal and moving inner voices. He waits and waits before playing, and I like the tension he creates, and space for his statement. Maybe the young guy has something after all. When he begins to improvise his whole skinny body scrunches together in a spasm of deliberation, and his face takes on a look of tortured purpose. His trousers are jerking towards me in a corduroy knob. I recognise the melody immediately, an old one, from the days of my youth.

He is playing 'Green Grow the Rushes O!'

"Yeah man", I tell him at the end of the lesson.

"Cutting Edge!".

As he hands over the cash he smiles knowingly, pleased to have found someone capable of recognizing his talent.

"You're an excellent teacher, you know", he tells me, and that's when I begin to think maybe Heidi is right. Especially if the live jazz scene really is dying, like Mickey says. I might be good at this.

Maybe I should get into jazz education after all.

THE KING'S EAR

the second book

Chaplet 38

Back Wall Blues

I was stranded in the front. I got to the ball late and bashed my head on the back wall, and the ball only went spinning up in the air anyway, nowhere near the front wall. I caught it though, before I passed out.

Chaplet 39

A Tale Of Two Kings

It was many years before Mickey saw the King again; then it happened twice on the same day. The Daimler Limousine was parked outside the farm shop. Mickey's body convulsed in a spasm of deja-vu as memories of the events of the night of the Bateman Street Brothel Fire crackled across his synapses. The hospital bed, the fire, the explosion, the gunshot bang, the sex, the drugs and the duff pianist - he remembered them all on this Spring day in the Idristan countryside, and more clearfully, more painfully, than ever before. He remembered the pint in the pub with his nephew Jeb, the Nutter Prince at the doorway of the Royal Costumier's, and he remembered stepping into the path of a large BMW.

As he watched the King now, his hands and feet stuttered into the thirteen eight rhythm that had nearly killed him.

"Are you all right, mate?", said Timmy as he watched Mickey thrashing about from the passenger seat of the hearse.

Timmy Gordon found Mickey more and more annoying these days, every trip they made.

"That's the thing with old drummers", he said to himself.

"It gets harder to tell the polyrhythms from the epileptic dementia".

Mickey was staring at him with a frightened, hunted look in his eyes, though whether this came from the tension between them or from the inside of Mickey's mind, Timmy couldn't rightly say.

"I really enjoy these drives, mate", Timmy lied, in an attempt to feel better about himself. Mickey waited until the 'One' of the medium thirteen came round, then grunted. Timmy continued.

"It's a real honour, like, to spend time with you, not just 'cos of your playing, which is awesome, like, but because of history, like. 'Cos of what you did back in the day, in the Great Partition".

And some of this was true, in fact, for Timmy Gordon, though still a young man, and therefore full of the certainty of his own ideas of revolution and amelioration, still respected the struggles and sacrifices of his elders; he was already wise enough to know that the problems of Idristan were legacies from the old times, and were intricately bound up with the lives of the oldtimers, the founding mothers and fathers.

Mickey grunted again, this time missing 'One' by a fraction, as even the arhythmic Timmy Gordon could ascertain.

A slim black man with red hair carefully dismounted from the driver's seat of the Royal Limousine, brushed himself off, adjusted the trouser crease of his uniform, and, skirting the retail shop, went to the Long Barn that lay at the very end of the farmyard. Mickey watched him closely, and tried to remember where he had seen that walk before.

"He won't like that", said Timmy. "Dai's a good old boy, but he won't like that. He needs to see who he's dealing with; if he's doing work for the King, he'll have to talk to the King, see, not his bloody driver".

And within the next minute, sure enough, the driver appeared again in the doorway of the Long Barn, this time walking backwards, with some haste, and being pursued by a giant scarecrow. As they came full into the yard, the back door of the Limousine opened, and the King stepped out into the sunshine.

The Welsh yeoman farmer Dai Jefferies, hunter, gatherer, herbalist, taxidermist, all-round countryman and acknowledged King of rural central Idristan, formerly known as Wales, smiled involuntarily as he looked down on his scruffy new customer. It was a fine day indeed, he felt, when the leader of these upstart new Idristanis came to him for a favour, and he hoped that many similar days would follow. The King was less majestic than in former times, for Idristan was by its nature a less formal place and needed to be ruled with a lighter, even a grubbier hand, and the Royal Family had in any case run out of cash. But his baggy trousers, stained shirt and stout shoes quite appealed to Dai, who saw in the King a younger and smaller version of himself. The King was tall enough by human, even Welsh standards, but Dai Jefferies was a freak leviathan of a man, and towered high above him.

"I like the headphone", said Dai, pointing at the single ear muff worn by the other man.

"Look. Same shoes", replied the monarch, pointing downwards. Both men smiled, nodding to affirm the importance in life of a warm ear and a good shoe, then shook hands.

There would be a great battle fought between the two Kings, but for the moment they held hands in mutual respect.

Mickey saw in their wide smiles that their teeth were strong, but also yellow and splayed; they reminded him of horses, and of the ketamine excursion that had changed all their lives; suddenly he was back the k-hole again. His thirteen eight accelerated violently into his voice.

"Ketamine ketamine ketamine ket-ket ket-ket", he sang. Timmy sighed and opened his door. He locked Mickey into the hearse and went into the Farm Barn Shop to pick up the week's supplies for his restaurant. Honey, lamb butter, laverbread, and more honey.

That was all you could find these days.

Chaplet 40

Pwyffthh

Rebekka looked hopefully up at the monitor in the back room of the Maboob Emporium as she heard the tinkling of the indoor temple chimes from the main shop.

"Scheiss", she swore, 'noch ein knacker". Another old geezer.

She reached down into her soft cotton panties and carefully pushed the red crystal into her pussy. The Maboob Emporium, seeing a gap in the market as well as a clear economic advantage in cutting up existing stock into smaller pieces, had just launched their new Libido range of sexual crystal, and Rebekka was working her way through it. Today was garnet, and she had a good feeling about this one. It was a lovely colour. She wriggled to accommodate the rough edge of the crystal, and a tide of pleasure surged through her body.

A fluffy ear muff hove into view on the screen above her, followed by the gnarled, scarred face of an old man. Her pleasure went ' pwyffthh' and left her body.

"Scheiss, scheiss, scheiss!", she swore, for she feared that she might spend her whole life in the Maboob Emporium, and might never see a young and beddable man again. She punched the monitor and the man disappeared for a moment; when he returned to the screen he was just as old as before.

Rebekka sighed and pushed open the staffroom door.

"I suppose I'd better go and sell the old git something", she murmured to herself, and concentrated her loins around the garnet crystal inside her, for in her line of work she needed as much help as she could get.

Chaplet 41

The Gift Of Rap

Timmy Gordon, in a vehicle now pulling into the Motor Amenities Area at Pontardulais, was a young man, and permanently beddable, but not by Rebekka. His thoughts were still twenty miles away, on the gorgeous chauffeur from the Farm Shop in Carmarthen. Timmy imagined the boy lying face down in front of him waiting to have his uniform trousers pulled down. He jumped forward in the story to catch a glimpse of the boy's dark buttocks glowing pink from the spanking they had just received.

Some dark face cheeks suddenly appeared in front of Timmy, interrupting his dreams; they blushed pink as their owner telepathically devined Timmy's thoughts.

"Shit', Timmy said to himself, for he hadn't anticipated the object of his dreams turning up in the flesh so soon. "I hope I haven't blown it".

He searched the young man's face for signs of displeasure but saw there only friendliness and curiosity, and some self-conscious confusion. It was a lovely face, wide and full-lipped, with almond eyes and tight velvet skin.

Afro-Polynesian, Timmy guessed, and longed to reach out through the window and touch it, but instead reached up to touch the angry pock marks on his own face.

Morgan Oguike only broke the narrative of that lustful look between them when he felt the fuel spilling onto his ankles.

"That'll be eighteen thousand hyweldda and thirty-three hywelddu".

As he handed the cashier one of the Royal Credit Cards he confessed that he'd caused a spillage on the forecourt.

"That's expensive", said the cashier. "You don't want to do that with the hyweldda so weak against the dollar, and with petrol what it is anyway".

After the Great Partition the second act of the King, the first being the establishment of the Academy he had so long coveted, was to kick the Royal Mint back into New England and establish a new production line at the plant in LLantrisant for the ancient Welsh coinage of the Hyweldda and the Hywelddu. They were large coins, and satisfyingly heavy, for they were designed by Germans, who had come to Idristan in great numbers in the days immediately after the Great Partition, when idealistic settlers were still welcome.

All new countries experience a few centuries of turbulence, and Idristan was no exception to this rule. Inflation was rising alarmingly, and despite the skills of the German keckmeisters, and their ingenuity with the knickerbocker and the leather pocket, no trouser had yet been found that could hold the weight, in the new currency, of so much as the price of a pint of beer, leave alone a tankful of petrol.

The cashier pushed the card back.

"Sorry. Declined. Have you got another one?".

Morgan shook his soft lambskin wallet over the counter and thirteen Royal Credit Cards tumbled out.

"Take your pick", he invited her. On the eighth card the transaction went through.

"Thank the Lord Soper for the Gift of Rap", prayed Morgan as he went back to the limousine, for these were difficult times for everyone in Idristan, even for the son of a high-ranking official like him. Morgan foresaw his own redundancy, and was grateful that he had other talents to sell.

Chaplet 42

Red Dragon

Mickey felt calmer now. Timmy had got him talking about the old days, about Soho and Ronnie Scott's and the early days of the Trio, and that had settled him a bit, even though he knew Timmy wasn't really listening. But he didn't feel quite right, not yet, and so pulled into the Pontardulais Amenity Area to go to the Crystal shop.

His youngest brother Quintus had always been into that stuff, like their mother, and of course Len never stopped talking about it at the Academy, instead of playing the piano, like he was paid to do, because of the Maboob Emporium chain he had set up with his wife. It was huge in Idristan now; franchises everywhere. People couldn't get enough crystals.
Mickey had always been sceptical. Until he started getting old. Now he'd try anything to feel young.

He picked out some angelite for his anxiety, then some chalcedonia for the dementia round the corner that made him anxious in the first place. He averted his eyes as he walked past the Libido range. No he didn't want an amethyst cock ring, thank you very much. He hadn't wanted anything like that since the fire, as it goes, since he'd been shafted by a winged demon, in the K-hole. He hesitated in front of some brown tourmaline then put some in the basket for Timmy. Lovely young guy, and always shagging, thought Mickey, but lonely, because of his bad skin. But the youngsters wouldn't touch crystals, just like we wouldn't touch sherry, in case we turned into our parents. Crystal meth, maybe! He'd try to talk him round.

In the stimulant section, Mickey found an energy drink called Red Dragon. He turned the tube up to the light and investigated the legend of ingredients.

"Well I'll be", said Mickey aloud. It was made of red seaweed, or porphyra. It was the same algae that Mickey used to run the hearse.

"Blimey", thought Mickey, "Didn't think anyone else used the stuff, except for chefs".

The old bloke at the counter had bad skin too; he needed the brown tourmaline more than Timmy. But he was only buying citrine, for wealth and prosperity. By his raggedy-arse jodhpurs Mickey could see that he needed it. The thought of horses made him dizzy again, and he steadied himself by forming a queue behind the old man. Then Mickey noticed that it was the King.

She was a nice looking girl behind the counter, Mickey thought, if a bit tall and heavy in the hips for him. Just the sort that Steve liked, though, being used to holding a double bass. She was jiggling her hips as she tried each of the King's cards in the machine, and sort of bearing down on herself, with now and again quite a sexy smile around her lips, and Mickey knew he would definitely have given it a jump, once upon a time.

The King's payment finally went through on the eighth go, and before moving forward to pay, Mickey wondered about going back to the Libido section for that cock ring. For a moment he weighed up the balance of pros and cons, of possible pleasure against certain complication, then decided "Nah", and it was the process rather than the outcome of the decision that most reflected his age, for as a young man the question of balance would never have arisen.

Chaplet 43

Car Talk

The two Daimler limousines stood next to each other. Mickey's hearse, though a few years older, looked the more kempt of the two.

"Nice car", said the King as he limped across the forecourt from the toilet block. "How do you afford to run it? I thought drummers were always skint".

Mickey glistened with pride at being recognized.

"Algae", he said. This was a secret he did not normally divulge. As he described the shed at home in which he brewed motor fuel from seaweed, the King listened in admiration. He was an inspiring philosopher and leader of men, but also cack-handed.

"Oh I couldn't have done it on my own", Mickey continued, deprecating himself before his King. "My brother Richard showed me how. He's a biologist. He's still over there, see, in New England. Didn't get out in time".

Mickey's throat tightened in grief and tears came into his eyes. He realized now where all the panic attacks and weird memories had been coming from all day, and the dizziness.

He was missing his family.

The King clapped him on the shoulder.

"Never mind, old chap", he said, "it's a super car".

Chaplet 44

Pain Plans

As the two limousines pulled out of the Amenities Area into the fading light of the Spring evening, Rebekka counted up her day's takings and fell into a deep depression. The garnet crystal suddenly felt hard and alien inside her.

All her family money had gone into this franchise, and it just wasn't working. She hadn't even earned enough today for fuel to get home, and now faced another long bicycle haul up the hill to get home. This was not how she had envisaged her evenings as a successful businesswoman; she had always dreamed of champagne and shagging.

The poky miner's cottage was a big mistake as well, certainly for a girl of her size. The estate agent was a cunt. Even a car salesman wouldn't sell you something you couldn't even get into. She rubbed the lumps on her head and looked out at the petrol pumps and at the green HG logo. Hendy Gate had the monopoly on petrol in Idristan. Soon, Rebekka vowed, soon they would have the monopoly on pain.

Chaplet 45

Blast From The Past

Timmy felt cheerful on the way back to the restaurant in Mumbles. He had enough quality stuff in the back of the hearse to see the kitchen through the next month, with a bit of ekery, and he had the film of a gorgeous new boy running through the back of his mind.

"Thanks again, mate", he said to Mickey, "it's a big help".

And indeed it was, for Timmy was rare in being able to serve the highest quality local produce in his restaurant. Such was the parlous economic state of Idristan that few of his competitors could afford to take deliveries any more, let alone make foraging trips out into the heartlands in large thirsty cars; Mickey's hearse helped keep the restaurant busy, even in these trying times. He didn't know how Mickey afforded to run the hearse and didn't want to ask, for fear of queering his own pitch.

"That's all right, mate", said Mickey. "I know you're in lumber. If I'm not working then she isn't either, and the old girl likes to get out". He patted the dashboard affectionately.

"You know the other one, the Daimler we saw, with the

King in it?', he asked Timmy now. "I've been thinking about the chauffeur".

A jolt of jealousy electrified one of Timmy's molars. That's where he always felt this emotion, and over the years the tooth had turned slightly green. Mickey had never shown up on the radar before. Maybe it was a life-cycle thing, he wondered. Big bikes in the forties and boy's batties in the sixties. Maybe, he wondered, maybe we all go gay in the end.

"I heard him fart in the toilets", said Mickey, "and that's when I recognised him. I used to work with his Dad".

Chaplet 46

Tabla Tantrum

Our Lady Myfanwy Muff Maboob, the architect of the Great Partition, and Muse of Idristan, hadn't played squash since her teens. Music had taken over then, for a while, and though the music eventually stopped, the squash never really got started again.

Muff regretted that now, swinging the racquet out in an arc around the jutting prow of her bosoms and smashing the small black rubber ball away behind her into the corner of the court. She could see now that some explosive activity might have helped her through the awkward silence in her life, back then when the music stopped.

She had been a good player, too, having reached the Junior National Squad at one time. It was a family thing. Grandfather Maboob had been one of the secret masters of the sport, one of the Pathans from the Northwest Frontier, that harsh landscape between Pakistan and Afghanistan where boasts are doomed and dropshots are cheap.

He was like Khan, everyone said, only better. But Grandfather grew bored of the grinding orthodoxy of the New European game and came to Wales in search of wizardry. The Welsh players were tenacious and artistic, and as they unleashed each new unpredictable shot into the nick, all seemed to laugh at a maniac pitch that recalled for him the sound of his beloved markhor, the goat-antelope of the Himalayas.

The Welsh girls were similar, and Grandfather therefore spoke easily with them in the village, and soon got himself hitched to the baker's daughter. The colour of his skin was never an issue, as he was wont to repeat to his descendants each Christmas, because he was mostly lighter than the indigenous Welsh males, whose faces were stained black with coal dust.

As a young girl Muff had quick hands, and a quick brain with which to calculate the angles of the court and the options of her opponent. The arrival of her breasts added a dimension of power to her strike, previously lacking. Obliged to lift her elbow to gain clearance for her racquet of these spectacular mounds, Muff suddenly discovered how to crack her arm like a whip, and was soon defeating every woman in the country, and quite a few of the men.

Perhaps, she now reflected, if she had beaten more men than had been justified by her skill level, it was because her new breasts, in combination with her green eyes and short white skirt, had been such a distraction.

Sam Sara skipped down to the corner, easily reaching the ball she thought had gone for a winner. She had been lazy and complacent and had not reached the T at the centre of the court; she rushed to get there now before Sam played his next shot. She made as much of a palaver as she could over the few steps, trying to break his concentration on the ball, but his head didn't move. She knew he was watching her closely though, in his peripherals. She bent low, jiggling her breasts at him, and was still in this position as Sam's next shot found its spot on the front wall a mere inch above the tin and then rolled out of the sidewall nick.

He looked into her breasts with curiosity and a complete lack of sexual interest and then smiled at her encouragingly.

"Must get back to the T", he reminded her gently.

He is a kind man, at least, thought Myfanwy. He does not judge me for throwing myself in his direction. So I suppose I can keep on doing it, she reasoned. But in the same thought recognized that every time she did so she felt less and less sexy, and more and more desperate.

"Now, let's have a look at your boast. Specifically, your movement in and out of the shot", said Sam. This was not just her first game of squash in twenty years, but her first lesson as well. It was an old ploy, but a good one. If you fancy a man, ask him to teach you to do something. Few men can resist the opportunity to display and glorify their superior nature. It had always worked for Muff, back in the days when she was interested, before her divinity.

Sam Sara, however, seemed impervious. In fact, thought Muff, all men seemed impervious to her now. As though, in becoming a Muse, in becoming part of their most intimate sound world, she had become invisible to them as a woman.

Yes, she had renounced her carnality, several times, in the

prologue to the Great Partition, but always in public, more as an oratorical, a theatrical device. She had never considered how that might play in the long run.

She remembered the words of the Nutter Prince, now King of Idristan, between the dusty shelves of the Jefferies Antiquarian bookshop in Greenford, Middlesex.

"You have done much work already, but the hardest task of all lies before you".

Perhaps, thought Muff, he had been talking about now.

Certainly, as she watched the tabla player Sam Sara, squash champion of all Idristan, glide into the back of the court, and admired the perfect roundness of his gluteal muscles as they strained against his white shorts, Muff felt that she was carrying a great burden, for she could hardly stop herself from pursuing him into the corner, ripping his shorts off and plunging herself down upon his gesticulating penis.

"Your step needs to be lighter, more taka tira kita, remember?".

Muff had started her campaign by asking for lessons in tabla technique, but had quickly realized that Sam's intense religious feeling about his music might not conduce to the penetrative action that Muff had in mind; this is how they came to be on a squash court now. But Sam was deluded if he imagined she remembered anything he'd said while she was busy gazing at his hairy arms in the tabla lessons.

He moved round the court in light rhythmic steps, to demonstrate.

"Oh yes, the steps have a pitch", she lied, "you move so

musically, Sam",

He smiled deferentially.

"And so do you, My Lady", he said. "But your sound is deeper and slower, more of the large Bayan, whereas mine is lighter and quicker, more of the small Dayan".

"Oh yes, I see that now", said Muff, looking hopefully into Sam's eyes.

He clumped round the court in imitation of her slow ungainliness.

"This is you", he said, cruelly. "Your dhinagina is absurd and useless".

She only realized later, looking over her tabla notes, that he had been talking about the rhythm of her step. At the time he thought he was being rude about her pussy, which is partly why she threw her racquet at the wall and walked off court.

Chaplet 47

The Young Prophet

Upstairs in the bar of Miskers, the magnificent restaurant in the round overlooking the thirteen squash courts of the Mumbles International Squash Centre, Myfanwy soothed away the last traces of her tantrum with a glass of kir royal. She would be dining alone, as Sam Sara had run off for his weekly tabla class at Cox's Farm, the prison at Swansea.

The thought of that grim building inherited from the Victorian English filled her with sadness, and the tight bubbles of her champagne became still. Could they not have found a small corner in the Royal Mind, Muff wondered, for a policy on Prisons? But of course that would have needed a corner of the Royal Purse, and precious funds diverted from works more essential and closer to the King's heart. The Academy was wonderful, though, and lay at the conceptual core of their new kingdom. And though those poor devils were banged up in their tiny cells with only the grunts of their peers for comfort, their sentences frozen in time by the shock of the Great Partition, they did benefit from the work of the Academy, for great teachers such as Sam Sara were sent there on a daily basis to instruct them in yoga, jazz improvisation, motor mechanics, and other associated arts. At least, Muff concluded, if they lack justice, they have rehabilitation.

There was much to celebrate in Idristan, as Myfanwy clearly saw, looking down into the squash courts below. For men and women of all ages and racial origins found joyful community together in the revival of this ancient game. If the people of Idristan renounced the empty knowing selfishness of New England and like Republics, so too did they renounce the mean hoarding mentality of Republican squash, and put in its place a wonderful playfulness, giggling and artistic.

A waiter came to her with news that her table in the restaurant would shortly be ready. She recognized him as a former student of the Academy. All that work, she thought; all the philosophy, the yoga, the searching of the soul. And for what, to wait tables? Muff could not shake off her gloom tonight.

"I'll be there in a moment", she said, draining her glass and holding it out to him.

"Get me another one of these, will you, love?".
All those carburettor insights, all those flattened ninths, what were they for in the end, if it all came down to this?

Her eyes fell on a poster running the full height of the bar wall. It announced the results of the MISC internal leagues for the month. Entirely one half of the hand-painted sheet was devoted to the Gay Squash League, and this fact cheered Myfanwy inexplicably, so that she went to her table in more cheerful mood.

"I'll have the Dulse Bhaji. Just that, with a Garlic Nan, love, and another of these. Easy on the blackcurrant this time". Iestyn nodded approvingly as he accepted Muff's champagne glass again.

"The laverbread is very good today, My Lady".

The laverbread was always good at Miskers, for the Head Chef Timmy Gordon was rightly famous for his ingenious reworkings of traditional Cambrian foods, and especially the red seaweed of its glorious coastline.

As she tucked into the delicious sea vegetable Muff caught sight of an old man playing squash. He was powerful and graceful, with some hair and teeth, and for a moment Muff felt she was a young girl again. She dreamed she was the ball, and as her whole body relaxed into roundness, as she relinquished control into the racquet of her master, the complex saltiness of the curried seaweed in her mouth suddenly intensified and expanded to fill her whole being.

"Is everything all r-right, My Lady?", asked Iestyn. Muff smiled and brushed away the sloke tears brimming at her eyes.

"I'm grateful, that's all, my love", she replied. She took his hand. "And how about you, Iestyn? Tell me, how are things with you?".

"If I m-may, My Lady?". The young waiter needed no further encouragement. "I need to address you on a matter of some N-n-national Importance".

Myfanwy winced inside. These days she felt less like the Muse of Idristan and more and more like its housewife. Why not, she agreed inwardly. I'm doing every fucking thing else.

But she also wanted to hear what Iestyn had to say. He had been one of her best students at the Academy. His specialism in the final year, she remembered, had been divination, and he had been superb. She had high hopes for his future then, as a seer, or perhaps a prophet. She was pleased to see that although he was only waiting tables he was nevertheless keeping his hand in. Myfanwy gave him the nod of her consent.

The boy stammered on, nervous and clumsy in the delivery of the speech he had prepared.

"It's the p-p-petrol, see, My Lady. It's running out. And what's left is too expensive. The people can't go on the way things are going on, like. Just with b-b-bicycles and horses and carts. They won't do it, like. It's uncivilized, old-fashioned, see, and too t-tiring".

Iestyn's skin had not improved, Muff noticed. If anything it had got worse. Her thoughts turned anxiously to her own appearance and she rummaged in her tiny handbag for some face-saving lipstick. Iestyn helped her pick up the spilled contents as he continued.

"They'll rise up, My Lady. I've seen it in advance, like you showed me. Unless you do something about it. T-t-talk to him, like". He stuttered to a finish, and bowed his head, blushing. Fucking amazing news, Muff told herself. Petrol's running out, and petrol's expensive, and no-one's happy about it. The boy's a minging genius!

"Thank you, Iestyn", said Myfanwy, with all the dignity that her divinity deserved.

"You have done well to bring this matter before me".

She touched his shoulder lightly.

"Now bring me another one of these, will you, son?".

Iestyn, still blushing, and relieved to have passed on the heavy burden of his divination to the proper authority, took the champagne glass again.

"Th-th-thank you. My Lady", he said. "I hope you d-didn't m-m-mind. I kn-know you have the K-k-kings ear".

Chaplet 48

Ocean Dream

Myfanwy awoke with a raging head, and was straight on the phone to Timmy Gordon, who knew what she was ringing for.

"My Lady, I'm sorry, I'm doing my best, but I haven't been able to source a different blackcurrant liqueur. Not at any price. All the supply lines are constricted now, My Lady. It's the petrol".

Muff's head throbbed harder at the mention of the fuel crisis.

"That stuff you're serving is foul", she shouted down the phone. "It's pure chemicals. Why am I going to pay a thousand hywelddas for the best champagne if you're trying to poison it with chemicals?".

"Yes, My Lady", agreed the Head Chef. "It's probably not safe to drink in any quantity", he added, unwisely.

"Listen, you poisonous little gay", she screamed, "just remember who you're talking to. Just remember the Royal Patronage you have but don't deserve. Just remember who and what brings the punters in. Just remember who butters your laverbread!". Her headache worsened as the pitch of her invective rose.

Timmy knew exactly what brought the punters in and it had nothing to do with Myfanwy or her Royal chums. He was dominant in two niche markets, and his club was full of foodies come for the cooking, and queers come for the squash. Nevertheless, he did take pride in the quality of his produce, and certainly did not want to upset Myfanwy any more. Timmy made his amends.

"Yes My Lady, I do apologize. You are absolutely right. I will do everything in my power. I did not mean to imply..."

Myfanwy slammed the phone down before Timmy had finished grovelling. She knew she was in the wrong as well as in denial, and this increased the gnawing melancholy in her soul. She had created the kingdom of Idristan, yet felt a stranger at its centre. Yes, it was going through a difficult lock on the birth canal, this creaking nirvana, but overall things were still mystic, things were still good. And she so wanted to be part of them. But her dreams were useless here, for the Idristani now had as much telepathy as they needed for day to day use.

All Muff's dreams went out into the wider world beyond the borders of Idristan, into the nasty new Republics, to console the dispossessed in their material abundance, to console the displaced in the luxury boxes of their new homes, to give answers to those who have asked no questions. And these dreams caused her pain and despair, each time they entered such barren places, for though the dreams were given away from her, they also received, for they were illuminations, like beams of light, and they were duplex. And what Myfanwy received back from the wider world in the illumination of her dreams, was knowledge of its dystopia, of the suffering and awkwardness of the humans therein, and she suffered terribly, consequently, in these divinations, and in her divinity.

And though her dreams were useless around her, also they were the only voice she had. And in Idristan, which she had created, she was not heard, nor could she find salve for her wounds.

And as she slept through that day, even as she wrestled with the cries of despair that rose and fell with the light pulse of her dreams, other dreams crowded into her mind - ones she had never experienced before - dreams from strangers in her future, dreams from herself to herself, and dreams of an older man whom she did not trust yet into whose dominion she now gratefully abandoned herself.

Her heart started into a rapid taka tira kita and she snaked her hand down between her legs, kissing it first for moisture. Her heart deepened in pitch, pounding now, and as the man increased the frequency and depth of his penetration her body writhed beyond her control and she heard herself chant in a voice she did not recognize,

"Dhinagina, dhinagina".

"Dhinagina", the man sang with her as they fucked, and though his voice was clear and normal, he used combinations of pitches she had never heard before, and she became wild in her arousal.

As she finally came, she saw into his eyes, and they were full of shifting shapes and colours and she felt she was looking into the history of an ocean, of endless restlessness and random movement coagulated into purpose; and if this purpose was dark, if there was malevolence in its eyes, and if there was cruelty, if there was evil, yet Myfanwy did not seem to mind, to mind at all, for her body still ached with pleasure, and she felt attractive, and grateful, and safe.

Chaplet 49

A Question Of Timing

Quintus Henshaw was a confused and unsettled man. The young imagine they will become wise and sure with age; the old know that they have grown foolish and uncertain.

The canals had escaped the First and Second Pavings that had followed the Great Partition, and had been a refuge for all the bohemian animals plants and humans unfortunate enough to have been left behind. It had been good for a while, all the leaves and the fishes and the bright colours and the wet noses and the funny hats in one place together, all up and down the canals, and Quintus always marvelled that they had been spared the concrete fate of the rest of New England, and thanked his Master, Satan, every day.

The humans were the first to drift away, back to the main thoroughfares, for they knew, most of them, that New England would have them in the end anyway.

Of the plants that had stayed, many quietly renounced the will to live, and now awaited their end in drooping coma. The bolshy ones were ripped to pieces by the enraged animals retreating down the canalsides.

While the shredded earth policy continued on land, underwater the fishes retreated by evolution into one species, a freshwater cod, but sharp of tooth, savage, and intensely territorial.

Quintus held the mouse by the tail and dangled it over the murky green water of the Grand Union canal. Three large fish leapt out of the water, fangs glistening in the Summer sun; the terrified mouse jerked itself up in Quintus's hand, using its tail like a trapeze artist, but the cod had already forgotten their prey and were fighting each other in midair.

They say the cod is the oldest fish of all, thought Quintus. It surely is the most stupid. How ever would they prevail against the concrete river about to flood into their amnion? He shook his head in deapair and threw the palpitating mouse high into the air. A vulture appeared from nowhere and swallowed the mammal in one perfectly timed flying bite.

"In the end", said Quintus, addressing the besieged canal community in general, "it's a question of timing"; and in that moment decided that he would move on.

Chaplet 50

Hanwell Flight

He did not go North, with the plants and animals, to escape the concrete juggernauts working their way up from the South, but instead, for reasons he did not yet fully understand, turned his narrowboat to face them.

Quintus Henshaw had been a Satanist for more than twenty years, but only in his bedroom. Like an air guitarist he had carried out his imaginary sacrifices in the virtual and private world of his narrowboat berth. Perhaps, as he turned his boat around to face his destiny, he was recognizing a truth about himself he had always known, that proper Satanism is like proper Guitar; you need people to play with.

The real air sacrifice of the mouse was a first step for Quintus. He realized this much. But he did not understand the feverish dreams that now came to him and frayed his sleep, and left him sticky and ragged in the day, so that he could not feel at rest anywhere, and found his back cabin not cosy any more, but cloistering and oppressive.

So he took the Blisworth Tunnel and journeyed South past Stoke Bruerne and through the foggy Chilterns, and then finally came to Brentford Lock, where he had never been before, by the six locks of the Hanwell Flight.

Quintus was unsure what would be expected of him, for he had no idea where he was going. He dressed in layers, to be on the safe side, and tucked into the pockets of his multi-coloured waistcoat some phials of his own blood, shit, urine and sperm.

Feeling covered for most eventualities, he climbed the steps into Brentford High Street quite happily, and found himself whistling one of his Dad's old tunes. A man's fist exploded on his nose.

"What sort of tune is that, cunt?".

A group of drunken thugs set about him and as he rolled on the floor he noticed that they were outside a Karaoke bar. Soon, like the fish, the men began fighting each other, and Quintus crawled away to the bright safety of a nearby Jumbolodge. He smoothed his long grey hair back and patted himself down as he entered reception; although the phials had disappeared from his waistcoat, his baggy pantaloons seemed to be covered with fresh supplies of blood, shit, urine and sperm.

Ninety-inch Grideoblogs lined the reception area; Quintus was aware that he had a bad headache and a ringing in his ears, and the beginning of a half-hard in his pantaloons. Probably from the boots, he thought, then remembered that he had become aware of a whining ache starting up in his head even before his kicking, while he was still climbing the steps into the High Street.

Grideo reports flashed on every screen, bringing news of important Karaoke contests and Celebrity sightings from all round the world. Important to some, no doubt, but not to Quintus Henshaw, who was looking for something else. He finally located the information he needed.

'Here tonight', proclaimed the Hotel Grideopaper. '8pm. In conference Room 666. SRA meeting'.

A bell rang in Quintus's haemorrhaged brain, and it was the gruesome tinkle of the sacrificial gong he used in his bedroom. He found his way to the eighteenth floor of the Jumbolodge and counted out exactly eighteen hundred steps from the lift to seemingly the furthermost corner of the hotel, and finally entered a dark room with the legend 'SRA tonight' on the door.

Quintus did not know exactly what Satanic Ritual Abuse was, but he knew he wanted to try some.

Chaplet 51

Ham Fists

Of course Quintus had family close by, though he had been isolated for so long in his own dark mind that he did not remember this, nor yet realize that his destiny was to be reunited with them.

His brother Richard lived only over in Ham, with his lovely wife Gloria; their grown-up son Jeb, a jazz pianist, recently returned to the family home because of what his mother called 'nervous problems' had a regular job as the house organist at Mortlake Crematorium.

Richard Henshaw sat alone with his pint in the Jagger Arms on Richmond Hill and looked down into the Henry VIII Heritage Park that stretched out at the foot of the hill. It was a good job, he had to admit, even as a professional; the deer were good, the grass was good, and the Thames seemed just the right shade of brown. It all looked good. From a distance. Close up, of course, not that any punter was ever going to get close up, it was all done with mannequins and Grideo projections. Richard knew because he'd been one of the senior biologists working on the project. He looked around the pub garden at the shrieking punters.

"What would they care?", he said aloud. "If they even knew?".

"Lovely, ain't it?", said a large-bellied skinhead in his fifties, returning from a wiz in the bushes. "Makes you proud to be English".

"Oh yes, mate", said Richard, making an effort to be friendly. "It surely does".

The man stopped, adjusting to the unusual cadences of Richard's voice.

"I'm not your fucking mate", he shouted. "Are you from round here? Are you even English, 'cos if you were you'd know I'm not your fucking mate". He thumped his chest. "No-one tells me who's my fucking mate".

"I'm terribly sorry. I didn't mean to spoil your evening with your family". Richard waved to the table where two women were smiling; both wore looks of excited anticipation.

"You what? My fucking family now, is it? That's my wife you're talking about. And that's my beautiful little girl. How dare you. Don't you fucking dare, mate. I'm warning you".

Richard saw his opening.

"I'm not your fucking mate, mate", he shouted, and stood up and glassed the man in the right eye, aiming the precise kick of a scientist into his left kidney as he fell to the ground. The two women were coming at him with sharpened hair combs and he snarled, keeping them at bay as he stomped on their man's head.

The landlord peered through the window and fiddled with

some knobs on a shelf above the bar. The karaoke rose to full volume as Richard finished his work and strolled down the hill to his Ham home.

The Gridation levels were much higher out in the street, because of all the heat light and movement sensors. Richard's whining headache came back, along with a ringing in his ears, a throbbing pain in his liver, and a massive hammerhead erection in his trousers.

As he wended his way down the ancient walks of Royal West London, he winked at the Grideyes that he knew were watching him, and wondered if Gloria might have finished her lorry schedule for next day, and if she might be up for a bit of in-out in-out.

Chaplet 52

Breakfast Blues

Gloria spoke sternly to her husband over breakfast. He had come home drunk again the night before, and she had found bloodstains on his shirt collar. If he hadn't been so loving she might have suspected adultery. But in any case he needed a good and regular talking-to, for his own health and sanity, just as she needed a good and regular seeing-to.

"I know, I know", said Richard, weeping into his hands. "The drink is no good for me. I just can't seem to stop myself. All the things I'm having to do at work, and the headaches every time I go out, and then Jeb coming home. I can't cope with it, is all. I'm sorry, I'm a bad boy, I'm so sorry".

"Yes you are a bad boy, and you should be very very sorry", said Gloria, taking his head in her hands and bringing it to nuzzle between her breasts, in the special space they had created over the years, for Richard's sessions of repentance. She knew that he struggled with fatherhood.

"Jeb. That's another thing", she said. "He needs our help. Now, more than ever".

Richard began snuffling into her powder blue polycashmerate blouse and now she pushed him away; she had important meetings later that day and snotty tearstains down her front would not help her career.

"What is it, what is it now?", she asked impatiently.

"I keep thinking of Jeb's teddy", said Richard, breaking into sobs so great he could hardly catch breath. "The one he loved so much but we couldn't save, because it fell into the water and we couldn't get to it because the current was so strong". He was sobbing uncontrollably, and Gloria slapped him hard in the face.

"Now pull yourself together. You're the boy's father. He needs your help. You must get him off the streets and into one of the Heritage Centres. You've got the contacts, I know you have. That Cornelius fellow owes you, after all the work you've done for him".

Gloria softened her voice.

"Really, Richard darling, you must do this. Think what happened to his finger. Our baby's finger. If he gets depressed again, he might self-harm. You know he might".

Richard lay his head on the table and wept into his arms. He wept from guilt, because he had one of the only good jobs in the country, while his talented son plonked out a living in shabby crematoria; he wept for his son's teddy, lost in a faraway river, and he wept for his son's finger, lost in a foolish tribute to Russ Conway. He wept because, unbeknown to his wife, he had already secured his son a musician's place in the Heritage Centre System run by Cornelius Coltrane Brewster, and now faced the task of persuading Jeb to take it up. He wept because his son Jeb flew high above him, more pure, more strong and more musical than he could ever be, and because it was now his duty, as a father, to bring him down.

As Gloria stepped out on to the street, her head began to throb through a sore tooth in her mouth, and she was suddenly aware of her chafing genitals. Despite everything she had said, which she had had to say, for his own good, and for Jeb as well, she loved her husband to bits, and was quite pleased to have this uncomfortable feeling between her legs, to remind herself through her long and boring day, of his unusually vigorous lovemaking the night before.

Chaplet 53

Human Sacrifice

Quintus had made a new friend, though as it turned out, not quite of the sort he had hoped for. He had dozed off alone in the quiet half-light of Room 666 of the Jumbolodge, and had woken up in the middle of an angry argument.

"Abuse of this egregious nature must not be tolerated", shouted a kilted man from the back. "Appleby Club, Hadrian League".

"Duly noted", said one of the five panellists at the front of the conference room.

Quintus, gradually awakening now, looked round. There were more than a hundred people in the room, most of them clapping and murmuring their approval. The walls were lined with Grideoblogs delivering pictures of men and women engaged in frantic activity, their faces contorted in agony. The man next to Quintus stuck out his hand.

"Oh good, you're awake", he said.

"Dennis. Dennis Crowley".

Quintus felt a thrill pierce the core of his soul as the man spoke, for his narrowboat was named Crowley. Could this inoffensive little man also be related to the Grand Master of the Occult, Aleister Crowley, the Beast?

"It's a wonderful name", he said. "Oh yes, thank you", said the man. "I believe Dennis comes from Dionysus, originally, the God of wine. I'm more of a real ale man myself".

A man rose to his feet two rows in front.

"Devil's Punchbowl Club", he said. "Surrey League. This undermines the nature of what we do. Such an amendment to the basic laws of interference strips us of the right to explore the outermost limits of body and soul. Pain and suffering are our most basic rituals. The name of our game is human sacrifice".

The crowd rose, cheering, and Quintus rose with them. Dennis pointed to his head.

"I took the liberty", he said. Quintus raised his hands out of his clap and discovered that like everyone else in the room, he was wearing headphones.

"So many screens. Very high levels of gridation. Dangerous", Dennis explained, sensing that everything in the room was new and strange to this new and strangely pantalooned visitor to the biannual conference of the Squash Racquets Association.

Chaplet 54

Every Time We Say Goodbye

Jeb was in a quandary. On the one hand the score he had in front of him, of the song 'Every time we say goodbye', was not the version he remembered from the old days, when he was house pianist at Ronnie Scott's, and seemed to go major where the old one went minor. Lots of the new versions of the old songs seemed to be doing that, Jeb reflected, as he watched the mourners file into the crematorium. There seemed to be less and less minor everywhere, and more and more major. That's how things were going in New England. On the other hand, he only had three fingers; the old minor version, which he suspected to be the correct one, might be more difficult to negotiate with the bruised stump on his right hand that still gave him gip in the rain.

As the mourners took their seats, Jeb pulled out the Grideo stop on the organ manifold and a large screen glided into view with the lyrics of a song upon it. Jeb struck up the chords of his intro, and one by one the congregation began to sing along, eventually all catching up with the ball that bounced along atop the Grideoblog lyrics.

"The party's over", they sang, voices smeared in sentiment, yodelling in grief.

"It's time we called it a day".

At the end of the service, conducted onscreen with sober reverence by the Official Consecrator, Jeb pulled out the stop marked 'Goodbye', and heard the burners burst into flame in the ovens behind the departure lounge. The Grideoblog rose quickly, revealing a gleaming coffin, and causing the mourners to gasp and wail. Just as quickly it descended again, this time with the lyrics of the song 'Every time we say goodbye' upon it. The noise of the flames intensified and the coffin squealed into motion behind the screen.

Decision time, thought Jeb. Major to minor, or minor to major? Or major to major? Definitely not minor to minor! He was late with his intro, the mourners were looking confused, and he only just got in in time. Sod it, he thought, ignoring the sheet music in front of him. I'll play the one I know. As the note of the organ came into conflict with the tune known to the New England mourners, an incorrect tune, but one cemented in the popular memory in a gridtopping tunebite by the New England Darts team, a rumble of distaste shivered through the crematorium.

"How fucking dare you?", shouted one mourner. "You evil bastard!", shouted another. A small boy ran out from the benches and jumped onto Jeb, aiming surprisingly strong punches around his shoulders. The crowd rose, emboldened by the bravery of the little lad, and fell upon the organist. They continued kicking and punching until the body was a bloody mess, and then they kicked and punched some more.

"Hold on", said one man finally, as he wiped the blood from his glasses.

"I'm a doctor. This man is disabled". He held up Jeb's limp arm and displayed the finger stump on his hand.

"Oh no!", exclaimed a mourner, and voiced the opinion of the congregation. "No wonder he played so weird. Why didn't he explain?".

They left the crematorium in sadness, not just because they had lost a loved one, but because they had battered near to death a man who might have played such terribly wrong notes merely by the accident of his disability.

Chaplet 55

Full Length Therapy

Some weeks later, when Jeb had been returned from the safety of the Intensive Care Unit into the dangerous chaos of the general ward at the West Middlesex Hospital, Isleworth, and at the behest of the lad's parents, with whom he had occasion to work, Cornelius Coltrane Brewster came to visit.

Jeb was no lad any more, of course, but Cornelius still remembered him as the young student teacher at the Royal English Conservatory of Music Saturday School, back in the days before his tenure there as Principal, and before the dramatic events that led to the Great Partition.

If he remembered correctly, the boy had taught Myfanwy Maboob there, before him, and there had been talk of some sexual, possibly even emotional, involvement. What did you expect from a healthy young man, reflected Cornelius, and a desperately needy young woman with great tits? It was barmy putting them in a room together. And Jeb was too young in any case to deal with her musicality, let alone her sexuality. Thankfully he had stepped in, as a more experienced teacher, and been able to knock Myfanwy's horrid little typist's fingers off the piano for good.

He gasped in horror as he saw the stump on Jeb's right hand.

"You poor poor love, will you ever play again?", he cried, and smothered Jeb with a hug.

In the last moments of his coma, Jeb dreamed that he was still being attacked by a philistine mob, but awakened to a far more unpleasant reality. Rough turquoise tweed scratched into the bruised weals on his face, a large pocket watch knocked against his remaining front teeth, and a stench of lavender oil and stale snuff filled his nostrils, so he could barely breathe. He felt his arm being lifted and his whole body felt very heavy and drained of energy, so that he could not resist as his hand was placed on something feeling like buttocks. Then Jeb began to talk, and Cornelius heard him.

"My grandfather was a musician. His name was Godfrey Henshaw. Once upon a time he was Professor of Polyphony at the Royal English, which is why I went there as well, though I didn't know that there had been a scandal and that he'd been forced to leave. He was having an affair with a student, a young flamenco pianist from Valencia named Inès. In the heat of her embrace he had a vision of a keyboard based on a new interpretation of Musica Ficta, and comprising not twelve, but nineteen different notes. He went immediately to his workshop and built this new instrument, leaving Inès in bed, with child. The reaction of the Establishment was immediate and draconian. Godfrey's instrument and the new system of melody, harmony and rhythm that it entailed, were declared monstrous and inexcusable, and Godfrey's Chair at the Royal English was pulled very sharply away. He fell to earth with a bump, becoming a father not once but three times, for the fertile young Spaniard, who had now become Inès Henshaw, for Godfrey had done the right thing by her, had given birth to triplets. These were, by order of age, Mickey, the first born, Richard, my father, the middle son, and Quintus, the youngest.

Godfrey himself never in his life earned another penny, for he was too absorbed in the ramifications of his new keyboard to push himself abroad, and those that heard his instrument by some accident, who might have employed him, were in any case unanimous in their dislike of his strange music.

But there was a vicarage in Kent from Godfrey's family, and they could live well enough from Inès's earnings as a Ballet School accompanist. As people could in those days. And my father and his brothers were all taught to play his nineteen note keyboard as small children, and only allowed to whistle his tunes, and despite this good start, none of them went into music. Richard, my father, is a scientist. Quintus, I believe, is some sort of hermit traveller, and Mickey, the oldest, is a drummer.

I'm the only one, you see, that has carried on from Godfrey, and it must be true, what they say, that it skips a generation. But I can't seem to make it work. Look at me. No-one ever seems to like what I do. I don't understand any more. Look at me".

He fell back on his pillow, exhausted by his speech.

Cornelius now understood much more. Why Jeb played such atonal drivel at the piano, even by jazz standards, why his Uncle Mickey had such a keen ear, such a gift for mimicry, and why Richard Henshaw, the biologist he employed at the Heritage Centre Systems, spoke with such unusual pitch and cadence. Cornelius could hear that timbre in all the Henshaw voices, now he'd put his finger on it. He reached behind him and seized Jeb in his most intimate crevice, the stump of his missing finger.

"Now look, young man. I can help you. You may not think it, but I can. I can help you lay down the burden that you have been carrying for so long. And to what end; for what purpose? To make some sort of point to the world about your own creativity? What self-obsessed foolishness! Or perhaps to educate the masses, to lead them to a better place? What misguided, what patronizing nonsense is this! And look, old chap, see where it has brought you".

He gestured around the filthy ward. A corpse was being lifted out of the bed opposite while two more prospective corpses fought in the corridor for the right to replace it.

"In my day C Difficile was all we knew, and that was bad enough. These days only the healthiest and strongest can survive a spell in these hospitals. They're up to F# Difficile now. And it's only going to get worse, because all our available money is being poured into the Grid update, and for the forseeable future, and of course that's absolutely right, Jeb, because we can all see that more surveillance means less disease. But it does leave you in a bit of a jam, now doesn't it?

I've had a chat with your father, and your mother as well, but that was in a different committee, as they're on different sides in the funding argument, now I think of it, but in this case, as far as you're concerned, in the matter of the welfare of you, their only child, whom they love very much, they are as one, and speak with the one voice, and agree that you should give up your jazz and your crematoria, and come to work with me in one of my Heritage Centres. It's a good job, it's what you're good at, even with your missing finger, and it's all music at the end of the day, isn't it? We can get you into one of our own hospitals, on site, to convalesce safely and quickly, on full pay, until you're fully ready to start working again. Now look, old chap, that does sound like a splendid idea, doesn't it? Just nod if you agree".

Jeb knew that he should refuse, for the sake of his art, and for his soul, and for his grandfather Godfrey, and for the future of music itself. He remembered how Ornette Coleman had been chased from clubs and beaten because of his saxophone sound and had yet persevered. But he was at the end of his physical resources, at the end of all courage; if he could find the words to resist, he knew he lacked the strength to follow past them into action; so he nodded, and Cornelius nodded, and smiled too, for he had won a great victory.

"You should never", murmured Jeb. "you should never have fucked her".

Cornelius was confused. He knew instantly that Jeb was talking about their student in common, Myfanwy Maboob. But he didn't remember that. Many strange things had hap-

pened in the days leading up to the Great Partition, and many strange dreams were dreamed, but Cornelius did not think he'd ever fucked her. There had perhaps been some secretarial fellatio, quite in the normal run of things, but...
Jeb was looking over his shoulder.

"Hello you two", said Richard. Cornelius turned and saw Jeb's father standing at the foot of the bed. A tall straggle-arsed man stood next to him. He had multi-coloured silk pantaloons and fiercely burning blue eyes. Cornelius knew instinctively that this must be Quintus.

"Look who I've found", continued Richard. "Bad pennies always turn up, they say, and this one certainly did, down at the Squash Club, would you believe, just by chance, as a new member!".

Richard was surprised to find his boss lying on top of his son in hospital, but knew Cornelius to be a wise and powerful man, with his own ways of getting things done. With no self-consciousness, Cornelius swung himself onto the floor and proffered his hand in greeting.

"You must be Quintus. Jeb has been telling me all about you". With his other hand he clapped Richard on the shoulder.

"The good news is that your son is making sense at last. He's putting down his jazz, and his dead people, and all his bourgeois principles, and taking up the cause of the community, the cause of New England".
He looked fondly down at Jeb's bruised, defeated face.

"We'll make a real musician of you yet".

Chaplet 56

The Arsenal Of The Sperm

"Oh my Good God", exclaimed Muff, as she saw the large head and long skinny body of the Junior Squash Champion of all Idristan amble into the Mumbles club, for she suddenly saw him in a new light.

"He looks like a sperm!". She watched the other squad members as they arrived for their morning training session on the magnificent glass exhibition court; they congregated around their tall leader, chatting happily, jumping up and down, eager to get on with their work. Muff giggled.

"They all look like sperms!"

When the great Sam Sara arrived, he seemed jaded from his marathon tabla session in Aberystwyth the night before; nevertheless he applied himself to the job in hand, and set the young athletes back into the gruelling training patterns that they would need to observe if they were to succeed in the World International Squash Event taking place at this very club, that very Summer.

Myfanwy should already have left the club, immediately after her usual breakfast there, for she had important meetings that day in Caerdydd. But she could not tear her eyes from the young men on court, for she had to know which of the young sperms was the fastest, the strongest, and whose shot had the most penetration and depth.

Head Chef Timmy Gordon sat and smoked nearby, watching Myfanwy with a mixture of scorn, empathy and self-loathing, for he took her to be afflicted by the same voyeuristic and unrequitable lust that he felt himself for these lovely young men. But his take on Myfanwy was wrong, or at least slightly wide, for her feelings at this moment were more biological than sexual. Moreover the two types of feeling were blurred together in their common purpose; so much so that they were in any case indistinguishable the one from the other in her body; as a man, even such a Gay Gordon as Timmy, could not possibly know.

The tall young champion easily dominated his training partners, and as Myfanwy's bodily curiosity was now sated, she now turned her keen mind to a question of technique.

She beckoned to Sam, who left his charges on court and trotted obediently up the raked steps of the small arena to discover His Lady's pleasure. He brought with him strong smells, of squash sweat, of fermenting Guinness, and of stale French perfume. Myfanwy now had a vision from the night before, of a large white arse slapping from side to side around the firm dark muscle of Sam Sara, on the moonlit sands of Aberystwyth. She shook her head to clear the vision.

"We won't be able to get either of them for much longer, I suppose", she said. Sam looked at her questioningly.

"With the fuel crisis. The transport costs. The women won't have their perfume, and the men won't have their Guinness. Might as well splash it about for now, eh?".

And it was true that in all Idristan there was now a sense of impending doom such that the people, once generous and relaxed, had now become reckless and profligate, and whatever they had, splashed about. Sam looked crestfallen. Like most men, especially musical men, he hated to be reminded where he was heading. Myfanwy changed the subject.

"They move so well. They're so fast. So agile. So good with the wrist".

Myfanwy could feel her mind drifting back into the question of her body and had to snap herself back onto track.

"But they have no real power in the strike. It's such a waste".

She clattered down the stairs, removed her cycling shoes, picked up a racquet, and went on court.

The boys were amazed at the power and weight of the shot that Myfanwy Maboob now showed them, and gathered round her excitedly, to know her secret.

"These", she said simply, and stuck her bosoms out at them. The boys cackled nervously, and Sam Sara, who had never seen Muff strike the ball so well, saw that today her breasts were bulging with life, and seemed to glow.

"They keep the arm out, away from the body", she said, "that's the secret".

And the young men were now set to their drills again, but now pretending to have bosoms like Myfanwy, and the difference in their strike was pronounced and remarkable, and judged by all to be potentially a deciding factor in the tournament ahead.

"But how can we make it more sure?", asked the tall young champion.

"It only works as long as I remember to pretend, and I keep forgetting".

"My Nan's had implants", said the short cheeky sperm next to him. The group exploded into horrified laughter.

"Your Nan!? What does she want those for?".

Myfanwy silenced them with a stern look; she did not want at this time to explain to her young disciples the parlous state of their Kingdom, where now even the pensioners were fucking like there was no tomorrow.

"I'm not having a sex change", said the tall champion.

"The last one obviously didn't work", said his cheeky friend, provoking more chuckles all round, and then continued.

"Seriously, My Lady. I wouldn't want breasts like yours". He paused and his face took an earnest cast.

"I'd stay at home all day playing with them!".

The group exploded into roars of laughter, and Myfanwy couldn't help but join in; although she felt distaste, she also knew vulgar humour to be a vital weapon in the arsenal of the sperm.

The idea was mooted, by Timmy Gordon, that a mould be made of the Muse's bosoms and special vests created therefrom, that the young athletes would use in their training schedules, and possibly in the Summer Tournament itself, subject to the ruling of the International Squash Federation.

"It's a job for Dai Jefferies", said Timmy. "He can make pretty much anything he turns his hand to. I'm out there pretty regular, like, for what we need here. I'll fix you up a fitting appointment, if that's all right, My Lady?".

Myfanwy gave her consent to the meeting, then, realizing the time, rushed from the club. As she retrieved her bike from the racks outside, she became distracted and began searching in her tiny handbag for the keys to unlock it. The contents of the bag spilled on the gravel. Iestyn the waiter, smoking outside, came to help her.

"There's no lock on it anyway", he said, as he handed her the bits and pieces from her handbag. Muff remembered that there was no crime in Idristan and smiled happily.

"You're absolutely right", she said. "How silly of me".

"Enjoy the ride in", said Iestyn, enigmatically. "You shouldn't be doing it for much longer".

"No", said Muff, sensing him to be right. "I probably shouldn't. Oh well".

And with this she slotted her racing stirrups into the holes of her cycling shoes and with a spurt of acceleration from her mighty thighs, sped off down the empty road.

Chaplet 57

A Spin of Two Halves

Myfanwy had been completing the fifty mile ride from the Mumbles to the Senedd in Caerdydd in shorter and shorter times, and she knew this for certain because she had recently invested in a Swiss strobe suction cyclometer that measured not only her heart rate, blood sugar, hormone balance, levels of essential salts and minerals, astral profile and mood, but also her speed and journey duration.

As she pumped down on the pedals on the first steep incline of the ride, she examined the device and found that her endorphin levels were soaring and that she was in a very good mood. The strobe display disappeared for a second, then reconfigured itself into a smiling yellow face. Muff yanked at the cyclometer and hurled it into the passing bushes; she lost balance in the act and now wobbled to a standstill and fell on the grass verge of the empty motorway, still attached to the bike by her racing stirrups.

More than anything Muff hated to be told what sort of mood she was in. How could a suction whatsitsabob possibly tell her that, when she hadn't even told herself yet? She sobbed and shouted now, and beat the grass in fury and frustration.

What that poxy little machine didn't realize was how pissed off she was with the machine itself, with the fact that she was trying to measure herself in the first place. It was so unmuselike. But then, that was at the heart of it, that was what was giving her serious grump, for the fact was, the people of Idristan didn't need a Muse any more. They needed a dogsbody, a housewife, an amanuensis, a coordinator, a facilitator, and God forbid, thought Muff, remembering her beginnings, they probably needed a secretary.

She looked out over the lush green fields, full of busy but peaceful animals and edged with rambling hedgerow, and from somewhere in the distance heard the beautiful sound of a soprano saxophone ringing above a chorus of male voices. Myfanwy began to sing, and her voice was not high and scratchy, as it normally was, but low, strong and mellow, as it became in her Muse transports, and she found her place easily among the upper distant men.

"Bread of Heaven", she sang, "Bread of Heaven", and her heart surged upwards with the spiralling chromaticism of the saxophone. Then her throat closed abruptly as though stopped by a hand, but it was grief. Grief for her country, and for her people; grief for the music they had in plenty and the butter they lacked; grief for herself, for what she had been, for what she had become, and for what she would have to do.

Singing opens wounds old and new, but also the pores

through which they may breathe and heal. Muff had a good shit by the side of the road and then rode on to Caerdydd at a more leisurely pace.

Chaplet 58

Utopias

The Great Partition was among the most ambitious ideological experiments in human history, on a par with the cultural revolutions of twentieth century China, Russia and Cuba. Of course, like these other revolutions, the Great Partition was political in its way, for it was the story of an ancient people reunited with their ancient land, of a monarchy relocated, and of the creation of the sorry republics of New England.

But it was so much more as well, for the real story of the Great Partition recounts the division of the world along an aesthetic and cultural line; on the one side lies the known world, on the other side lies the unknown. On one side New England, on the other Idristan. And while it has some background in the work of Lenin and Marx, this story has more resonance with the Utopia of Thomas More, with the Republic of Plato, and with the Erewhon of Samuel Butler.

Utopias are never easy to run. And the inhabitants of Idristan were mostly musicians, artists, fairies and soothsayers. Imagine if you will the precarious microeconomy of the jazz drummer scaled up into the macroeconomy of a jazz country. This is the frightening baby left in the hands of our heroine Myfanwy Muff Maboob.

Less artistic souls, let us say for instance Stalin, Hitler, Mao-Tse-Tung, could resort to purges and pogroms to stabilize the economy; these choices were not available to Our Lady, for her only gifts were sound and love.

Chaplet 59

La La Land

The Great Partition was a time of great joy; a time of arrival, and of self-completion. But there was much turmoil too, and upheaval, and much tragic separation. There were those in New England who should have been in Idristan, those in Idristan who should have been in New England, and those too, of whom you will learn more later, who rightly belonged in neither country.

Rebekka knew herself to have landed in the wrong nest. When she was still a swaddled infant she had made her journey out of Germany with her idealistic parents, who hoped to find in New England some respite from the messy foreigners who were taking over their country. Rebekka's mother, formerly first fiddle with the Berlin Philharmonic, was frightened by the loud unpredictable music of the Eastern European Gypsies, and her father was humiliated by the large penises of the Africans coming into the local sports centre that he managed; the middle-aged couple packed up their possesions, cashed in their Deutschmarks, and made a break for New England.

But in the confusion of the time, with people moving so quickly and in such large numbers, and with workers at the borders, in airports, stations and ferry ports, being stretched past their limits, mistakes were made.

So it was that while her parents arrived safely in their electronic white utopia, Rebekka landed on her own, in a hand-woven basket, swaddled in the family money, in the LaLa land of Idristan.

"La La La La, that's all they fucking do!", she said, singing and talking to herself as if in a dream. Dai Jefferies placed his huge hand on the back of her neck and squeezed there; in that moment she felt like a small kitten, not knowing if she was going to be strangled or fucked. She felt elated, terrified, and very very horny.

Dai reached behind her and cupped both cheeks of her bottom in his other huge hand and now stood up, out of the elmwood chair, jiggling her about to get her balanced on the end of his cock, and then drove deep inside her as he walked across the barn.

Rebekka screamed in delight, "La La La La", and initiated her own hips into movement. But Dai would have none of it, and as they reached the workbench on the other side of the long barn, he pinned her still against it and began working his cock inside her. Rebekka felt a grinding sensation as the amazonite crystal she kept there was pounded to dust beneath Dai's powerful helmet. His eyes rolled backwards in his wide old head, and he seemed unconscious of his surroundings. Rebekka was alarmed to see the greater part of his cock still outside her, for she already felt as full inside as she had ever felt, and truly could take no more. But he did not push his luck, and worked silently where he was. When they finally came together, he lay back his head and let out a long primitive roar. Rebekka screamed as loud as she could, "La La La La", but her sound disappeared away into that of her man, where it harmonised faintly as a descant soprano in the interval of a perfect tenth.

Rebekka once more felt vaguely disappointed by the climax.

"I love you, Dai", she said, to compensate.

"No you don't", he said, disentangling her fat thighs from his own massive tree trunks.

"I'm just here until your real man comes along". He pulled the great buckle of his belt into the middle of his rough trousers. "Suits me, girl. I've got work to do now".

Rebekka often spent her mornings with Dai Jefferies, if she wasn't opening the Emporium until the afternoon, when there was the chance of some custom.

She watched him lovingly as he set about his embalming, admiring the skill and delicate precision that this bear of a man brought to his job. Dai Jefferies was a man, but he was built to a different scale. That's why Rebekka liked him so much, she decided; being large herself, she loved to be made to feel small and feminine. But he was probably right, she sighed to herself. He wasn't the one.

She began talking to him now as he worked, which she'd found out he didn't mind at all. Sometimes they had something close to a conversation, as they did today.

"I went to see that Heidi Hyson yesterday", she said.

"Oh yes. Who's she, then?", said Dai. as he began the difficult task of removing the skin of a cow in one piece.

"She's that singer from the chapel. She's in charge at the Academy, as well".

"Oh yes", said Dai. "Another one of those LaLa nutters. What did you go and see her for, like?".

Rebekka paused now, for she was about to reveal a secret.

"I've been thinking about doing something", she said.

"What sort of something?", said Dai.

"Something about all this".

Dai shook his head; he obviously didn't understand yet.

"You know, all this", she continued, "all this muzziness everywhere, and no money, no fuel, no business. Just chaos everywhere, and stupid music".

"Humph", grunted Dai, for he agreed with her so far.

"But when I asked Heidi, which I thought was a good idea, because of the German connection, and because did you know she used to be a terrorist once, and I thought she could help me, with what I want to do, jah?".

"And?", said Dai.

"She said that everything she'd wanted to achieve with the Baader Meinhofs, it had come about with the Great Partition. She told me not to bother looking any further because this was it, Idristan; everything she'd ever fought for. She really has become a Buddhist, you know".

"Humph", Dai grunted.

"But that can't be right, can it Dai?", said Rebekka, urging him to agree.

"This can't be what there is. It can't be right, can it, with no business and no fuel and no money. No money except for those bastards at Hendy Gate who have got us over their last few barrels and are screwing us royally for the privilege, nein? Well if say there was a huge explosion there, a huge accident, jah, then that would make them think again, that would be change then, and that would be a good thing, nein?".

Dai laid down his razor-sharp Japanese scalping knife and set Rebekka straight.

"No it wouldn't, girl. A big explosion isn't the answer to anything. You forget that, you hear me. If you're that angry about the World, then start nearer to home. You can't get straight out to the bigger things, see girl, because them's only ideas, and that's where you get into trouble. You gotta start local, see. Start small and precise".

He picked up his knife again and drove it into the eye of the dead cow on the elmwood table.

"Pay that estate agent a visit, girl. That'd be a start".

Later, Dai went out into the fields.

"That's enough talk for now", he said to Rebekka. He pointed to the little workroom in the side of the barn.

"Get in there and make up some more soap. I've got that pouf from Miskers coming in for another hundred or so soon and we're running low".

Rebekka went meekly to do his bidding, knowing and regretting that this was as close to a goodbye and a thank you as she would get. Was she distracted more by the conversation about terrorism, or by being fucked so hard, or by thoughts of a horizon with a rainbow of true love? Who knows, but in any case Rebekka once again picked up the wrong bucket on her way through to the workroom, and her bars of soap therefore contained not only detergent and heather oil but also a high proportion of liquid arsenic, the embalmer's friend.

Dai paused at the end of his favourite field and surveyed his favourite sheep. Rebekka was a good girl, he reflected, and a good worker. And he agreed with her one hundred per cent about the state of Idristan. All those LaLa nutters coming back to claim Cymru for their own were very annoying, not what he'd intended at all, and would have to be dealt with sooner or later.

But not, thought Dai, by any random explosion at Hendy Gate. Of course Rebekka had no way of knowing that he, Dai Jefferies, was the man behind Hendy Gate, and therefore the man earning the only money to be had in present-day Idristan. Money that he would continue to accumulate, unless interrupted by random explosions, and eventually use to sort the whole sorry mess out. Or as she had called it, muzziness. Yes, he was going to sort the muzziness out, all right, him, Dai Jefferies, and Rebekka was going to help him. But she had to be controlled, because she didn't have the bigger picture.

Or, he now remembered, with a mixture of pleasure and frustration, the bigger pussy. But, he reflected, not many women were built to accommodate his massive stalk of a cock.

He caught the eye again of his favourite sheep, gave him a little wave, then hopped over the fence into the field, reaching once again to the belt buckle of his rough trousers with his huge horny hand.

Chaplet 60

Difficult Decisions

Myfanwy Maboob's first meeting of the day was with the Energy Committee, who confirmed her suspicions that Idristan had exhausted all her reserves of coal, gas, wind and water, and would need to begin buying in foreign power from foreign powers. Myfanwy undertook to initiate discussions of the budgetary implications of this with the Finance Committee.

Her second meeting of the day was with the Finance Committee, who confirmed her suspicions that Idristan had exhausted her reserves of foreign currencies and of all the gold bullion that the Royal Family brought with them at the time of the Great Partition. There were plenty of hyweldda in the coffers, but they were worth even less than the mugabe on the International Exchange. Myfanwy also learned that a number of rural banks had been targeted by itinerant minstrels, and that there was concern that they were part of an organized group. Myfanwy agreed to bring the matter to the attention of the Security Committee.

Her third meeting of the day was with the Security Committee. This comprised one man, Victor Oguike, the fierce Professor of Forensic Law and veteran of the Great Partition. Despite her position of great power in the Realm, Myfanwy had never forgotten the day in the Palace tunnels beneath the Royal English Conservatory of Music, when she had been chased by this brutal man, and had feared for her life.

She knocked timidly on the reinforced door of the Conference room in the Cwrt, from where Victor dispensed his National Security.

"Who dat dere?", he boomed, as was still his habit, despite having conquered his aphasia many years before, as a result of a sharp blow to the head.
But he beamed at Muff as she entered, for much of his brutal manner was affected, and she had come to know him as a bit of a tease.

However, his demeanour became more and more serious as Myfanwy outlined the desperate economic plight of the Kingdom.

"We have beauty everywhere".

Myfanwy spoke with passion. "Birds and bees and flowers. Music is everywhere, and more honey than we can eat. But we have no money; we have no fuel. The people are at the edge of despair".

Victor's great brow furrowed as he scanned the uppermost of the sheaves of paper before him. He jabbed a sausage finger downwards.

"Who dat dere?", he shouted.
Myfanwy leaned over to look. It was a list, a very long list

of emigration requests. Myfanwy was surprised and alarmed, for until now, their main problem had been the control of immigration. And it was small wonder, for who would not choose a land of music and honey over a land of cash and concrete?

But the flow had become insistent, unmanageable, and had begun to compromise the ethos of the Kingdom. After the ancient market town of Aberhonddu, also known as Brecon, had been taken over by a colony of Bluegrass polygamists, and the native Bebop of the Idristani completely overwhelmed by fingerpicking, a line was drawn. Myfanwy had drafted the new law herself, and recalled its exact wording. 'On this day and hencetoforward, banjos and any accompanying humans will be denied entry to the Kingdom of Idristan'. The wording had turned out to be insufficiently precise, and she had later changed it to include all banjo players.

But hardly anyone wanted to leave, that was the point. As Myfanwy looked down at the names beneath Victor's fat fingers, she saw that they belonged to builders and drivers, all workers, and as she flicked through all the pages of the list, she saw more and more of the same, engineers, plasterers, shopkeepers, specialists in concrete and garden paving, all workers, all intent on leaving Idristan.

Muff barely glanced at the immigration list, for she knew its likely contents already. She knew there would be lutenists, beekeepers, aromatherapists and Hopi ear-candlers galore, and nary a single engineer.

"This is serious", she said. "This is very serious".

As she began forming her next sentence, she began to hate herself for what she had become, and was also full of rage.

"We must close all borders", she said. "We must seal Idristan tight shut. It is our only hope of survival".

Victor nodded in deference to the command of this wise and powerful woman, the Muse of all Idristan, although he was secretly upset and disappointed, for personal reasons. He knew that his son Morgan hoped to take his DJ-ing to a new level at the World Rave on the island of Mallorca later that year, for he wished eventually to give up his menial and dead-end job as chauffeur to the Nutter King. For a brief moment he considered asking for a family dispensation for foreign travel, but Myfanwy's face was set.

Inside she trembled; she was a woman, and needed a word from Victor to validate her decision.

Victor winked twice at her, then gave vent to a long squelching fart. There was much else he could have said besides, but he was wise enough to know that most of it would have been bollocks anyway.

Myfanwy Maboob smiled in relief and, giving Victor the schedule for the isolation of the Kingdom, nodded graciously and left the fetid room.

Chaplet 61

The King's Ear

Myfanwy's last meeting was the most important, as well as the least expected, of the day. She had been trying to arrange an urgent conference with the Nutter King for many months, but he had hitherto refused all intercourse with her. She had been tolerant in the beginning, for she knew him to be recovering from a serious Yoga accident, but her patience had been waning of late, for now she knew him to be shirking his responsibilities. Having chased after his coat-tails for so long, Muff had been surprised when the King summoned her for this meeting in the Senedd.

When she entered the wood and glass Siambr and saw the King at the foot of the funnel that twisted up through the slate floors of the building into the steel and cedar web of the roof above, Myfanwy could not help but remember the great day when the destiny of Idristan was first declared to the world. Once again she saw the Nutter Prince, as he was then, abseiling down this same funnel with his little nieces and nephews, dressed all of them as dragons, and she saw in her mind's eye the kind faces of the dear late Queen and

King, and heard again, as a distant echo embedded in the building, the lilting rhythms of the improvised leek of Nicky de la Chwyth.

Suddenly all the stress and turmoil of the last years, and the burden she felt as leader in absentia of this great nation, lifted from Myfanwy's shoulders, and she felt happy again, and young, and proud to be before her King.

"Sorry to have been so elusive", he began, and touched the large earmuff on his head. "I don't know if you know, but I lost an ear in the accident".

Myfanwy began to offer some words of commiseration but the King went straight on.

"Now look. I'm very grateful for all you've done. But it's just not working. The country's in a dire state".

Myfanwy's mouth dropped open. That's exactly what she'd been trying to tell him!

"There's no fuel", he continued, "no fuel and no money. The people won't wear it much longer, you know".

He shot Myfanwy an accusing look, as though she alone had caused these catastrophes to occur. Myfanwy remained silent, for she was in shock.

"But I have some ideas, two, to be precise, that I feel might get us out of the hole, so to speak, which is why I wanted to speak with you today. I feel we could do much more with our honey, for example".

Myfanwy's head reeled around the blunt naivete of the man before her, who nonetheless continued his oration.

"I was out at a farm recently and noticed that the countryside is overflowing with the stuff. The farmers are giving it away internally. So I thought, why not externally as well?" He was triumphant in his logic.

"If there were honey shortages elsewhere and surpluses here, and these corresponded with oil shortages here and surpluses elsewhere, then it shouldn't be beyond the wit of man to swap the balance sheets, like so, and get us all up out of the hole. Not just us without the oil, but them without the honey, do you see?".

Myfanwy saw from his strange arm motions that he thought a balance sheet was some sort of foreign linen; nevertheless she felt heartened by his interest, however critical of her, and however late in the day.

"A brilliant idea", she said. "Utterly brilliant'.

The King smiled, and was boyish in his pleasure, though his skin was mottled with disease. Too much tree-hugging, she reflected, and added,

"The only practical questions will be, how much honey for how much oil, and I suppose, how much do they want and need honey, and how much do we want and need oil? Do you see?"

Her tone was quite acid as she finished, for she still had much anger in her, and the Nutter King was crestfallen.

"Well I'll leave it to you chaps to work out the details", he said, picking up a little as he remembered his second idea.

"Laverbread", he said.

Myfanwy looked at him blankly.

"Do you know what it is?", the King asked. Of course I

bloody know what it is, thought Muff, you daft cunt, we all eat the stuff every day, don't we? But what's laverbread got to do with the price of fish?

"Porphyra", she said respectfully. "It's an edible algae".

"Yes!", shouted the Nutter King. "But did you know you can make fuel from it? I met a chap the other day who told me all about it. He can do it himself, on a small scale. I suppose it's just a question of getting the right experts and the right technology, and then we'd be self-sufficient, wouldn't we? End of hole".

He slapped the funnel in exultation. That's rather a good idea, thought Muff gloomily. What a shame we have no experts and no technology left in Idristan, and have just closed our borders tight shut.

"Again, this is quite brilliant", she said. "I am so grateful for these suggestions. There may be a few practical considerations, such as how much porphyra we really have around our coasts, and whether its conversion to fuel is achievable for us, and economically viable....but.."

"Forget your buts", shouted the Nutter King, and the mould spots on his face glowed antibiotic. "This is real. I can feel it here". He clasped his gut in both his hands and shook it meaningfully.

"There's as much algae down there as we need", he continued. "The whole continental spur rests in a bed of red slime. I can feel it. Ever since we got back here I've been unsteady on my feet".

"But", said Muff.

"And as for the experts and the technology", continued the King, "that's your job. Just get your people together and make it happen! Do you hear me, girl?".

Myfanwy turned ice-cold as the King patronised and commanded her so, and could no longer listen to him speak. She turned to leave. He held her suddenly, by the arm, and with his other hand pressed an unknown object into her grasp.

"It's my gift to you", he said, "in gratitude for all you have done on my behalf, and so that you know I am always here for you, to console you in your troubles. To listen".

Charmed by his self-deception, she turned again and saw that she now held a large handbag, crafted in a delicate pink material, velvet to the touch and covered in a silken transparent sheen. A network of a firmer material gave structure to each side of the unusual receptacle, and was both pleasing and familiar to the eye.

The Nutter King touched his head and explained.

"Having the accident was bad enough in itself, and I didn't want to lose it completely. I've had it done by Jefferies. He's the best embalmer in all Idristan".

Myfanwy saw that her handbag was a human ear, and was not troubled.

"Oh", she said brightly. "It's big enough for a baby".

The King laughed, at what he took to be Muff's non-sequitur.

"Yes, I suppose it is", he said indulgently. "It's certainly waterproof, inside and out. I had it made so, expressly. Though I was thinking more beach than baby at the time".

"No. It will be exactly right. Thank you", said Myfanwy Maboob, and left the Siambr backwards, bowing all the way, and murmuring over and over again,

"thank you a thousand times".

Muff cycled straight home and spent the night cleaning the small flat in the Mumbles. In the small hours of the morning she painted the junk room pink, using four cans of good paint she had put by in the attic, and whose tint turned out to match exactly the colour of her new handbag.

Chaplet 62

Caving In

"You've been very unlucky, my boy", said Cornelius Coltrane Brewster as he steered Jeb out on to the balcony.

"And now you've been very lucky. Take a look out there". He gestured out into the parklands below.

"That used to be Syon Park. I don't expect you remember it. I've yet to see a jazz musician in a park. Which is strange, really. A disorderly gathering of random flora and fauna, impossible to predict, and therefore offering uncertain pleasure. Actually, very jazz. Anyway, we have turned this into our Master Field".

He beamed at Jeb and squeezed his shoulder, causing the jazz pianist to wince in pain, for he had not fully recovered from his beating.

"And it's all real in here, that's the point. Not like on the outside. We have no titanium-fibre, no mannequins and plasma bees in the Master Field. It's all real. But carefully managed, of course, that's the real point, because in the Heritage Centre System we set out to give the people the experiences they remember, the feelings they expect, and the real nostalgia they deserve. But we keep it real. Real birds. Real bees. Real musicians".

He punched Jeb lightly in the stomach, causing him to double up in pain as the largest ring on Cornelius's hand dug into his spleen.

"Attaboy", said Cornelius. "You'll find we look after musicians here. We need them in here, you see, not like on the outside, as you've found to your great cost, dear boy, and not just for our present schedule of delivery, either. Musicians are essential to the cultural fiction of New England. Its fiction is its future. You'll see that in time, my boy. And you'll feel it even sooner, from the way we treat you. I suppose you've no objection to a luxury apartment, wall-to-wall Grideo, with unlimited access to the vintage soap channels? I thought not. And I suppose you won't mind either if we ask you to take part in the occasional experiment?".

Our pianist Jeb, having had the stuffing kicked out of him back in the crematorium, now found himself signing a Heritage Centre Systems Consent Form, and thereby waived any human rights normally accruing to his person against any mishap arriving during the scientific and cultural experimentation to which he now consented. As he did so, he felt the warm relief of inclusion wash through his body.

"You're very important to us, you see", continued Cornelius, satisfied at having secured the signature.

"If we can get inside your head, far enough inside to understand your musical transformations, we will one day achieve total control of our environment".

His eyes gleamed in anticipation of the power that he would one day possess.

"It started with Spiff Abrahams", he continued.

"You must remember Spiff from the old jazz scene? And of course he became Professor at the Royal English, where I believe you originally trained?".

Jeb nodded, and recalled that Spiff had been a laughing stock on the jazz scene because he took himself so seriously but played so tritely. Yet, Cornelius seemed to be saying, this had turned out to be a good thing.

"Yes, that was the point, dear boy. He was, he is, a total buffoon. While he thinks he is funky, modal and chromatic, and some sort of reborn John Coltrane, he actually delivers only diatonic nursery rhymes. But this is fascinating, you see, for in our psychometric and physiological studies of the Abrahams Transformations we discovered the mechanism by which the future of New England might be determined. The future not just of our music, but of all this, our whole culture".

He gestured out into the Master Field below.

"Come, young man", he said, and led Jeb back into his grand office on the coveted top floor of the Heritage Centre Systems Headquarters in Syon Park.

Chaplet 63

Hot And In Love

Quintus Henshaw was a loner and a pervert. He was perverted not by virtue of any sexual predilection, nor even by his virtual Satanism, but because of his obsession with standing out, with being different. How serious in the life of a child may become the tease of a parent! His father, the radical Polyphonist Godfrey Henshaw, had thought it amusing to give his third son the name Quintus. The young boy was the fifth member of the family and, it seemed to Godfrey, was the most bland, anonymous and obsequious child he had ever seen. How amusing, then, to name him Quintus, like the fifth part in the Gregorian ensemble, that can only follow and imitate one of the other voices, and can have no character of its own!

Quintus had consructed his life as a response to his father's assertion, and a detailed proof of his mistake. He had eschewed conformity in any guise. He lived in a houseboat, never passing more than one night in the same mooring; he earned a living by dispensing a crackpot combination of healing, crystal divination, crypto-buddhism and grideoblog design to gullible women, most of whom became dizzy enough during the first consultation to be fucked into the bargain. He never slung his hammock in the same spot on the boat itself, nor closed his eyes for longer than nineteen minutes, for his father had instilled in him the horror of being predictable.

Had Quintus only been able to transcend his family boundaries, to perceive himself as he was perceived outside the family, he would have seen a man already singular enough, in the way of all Henshaws, who spoke in the curious nineteen pitch inflexion they had learned as infants from the songs of Godfrey, and might perhaps have saved himself the laborious effort of becoming doubly different.

He had inherited patience from his father; he had learned that each individual line of counterpoint has its own time and energy, and must come on its own terms to play its full part in the final polyphony. Quintus was therefore not overly perturbed to be spending time that he had earmarked for Satanic exploration with his new friend Dennis, whose idea of mystical philosophy was the Revised Rules of Squash, and whose idea of ecstasy was a trip to the Squash Ball Factory in Neasden.

Quintus settled back into his hammock and adjusted the volume of his Nudgeo to make Mahler's Seventh Symphony dominant in his world. It had been quite interesting, he reflected, to see how squash balls are made. The rubber masticated together with secret compounds, heated and moulded into half-circles, pressed, dimpled and buffed, then finally joined together, sealed and buffed again. Quintus had found the process reassuring and oddly exciting.

He reached down into his pantaloons and stroked his erect member, and with each burst of pleasure fell more deeply into a dream in which he was playing squash with a young girl who was also a great and wise Queen and Leader of Men. In his headphones the orchestra jerked wildly between moods and Quintus began to pull harder and faster on his cock.

In the squash bag nearby, the small black ball, given to Quintus at the factory as a memento of his visit there with Dennis, came suddenly to life. The quiescent period of its afterbirth came to an end as the throbbing heat of the Mahler ran through Quintus's penis and filled the dark walls of the ball with the looseness of life. As the first movement of the Symphony came to its climax, as Quintus's hand reached its final frenzy around his cock, a stream of sperm arched out over his belly and squelched onto his neck, seeming to fuse with the greening copper necklace there, and in this moment the molecules of the squash ball seemed to shake together and the twin yellow dots suddenly popped open like two little eyes.

Muff looked around her, bewildered. She felt hot and in love, but all she could see was coins, plasters, and old keys.

Chaplet 64

The Foggy Foggy Dew

As Spiff Abrahams raised the mouthpiece of his tarnished Conn tenor to his lips, he felt the thrilled expectation of the audience deep within his loins. Live performances had been few and far between in the years since the Great Partition, because of his important job in the Heritage Centre Systems of New England, and also because the jazz music he knew and loved was now, in the new regime, as popular as a pustule.

But he felt them waiting for him now, in the Grand Auditorium of the Syon Park headquarters, he felt they were ready to receive his music, and his penis became engorged with their excitement, and as his tongue searched out and tickled the end of his reed, it seemed to him that he held a thousand minds on the end of his cock.

He had not allowed his thinking to atrophy, despite his lack of gigs, and he felt in his rectal muscles the beginning of a new voice, one that went back to Sidney Bechet, yes, but that also surged forward through Ben Webster, John Coltrane and Chris Potter. His diaphragm began to contract in the carnatic rhythm of the new music Ta Ka Di Mi Ta Ka Ju No Ta Ka Di Mi Ta Ka Ju No and Spiff began to play.

As Gloria Henshaw watched the saxophonist she became overwhelmed by a melange of revulsion, pity and lust. Her discomfort was compounded by the knowledge that her husband Richard and son Jeb were somewhere nearby, and as she ground her bottom into the plastic seating she therefore also felt ashamed and guilty.

Yet she found herself fascinated by the man standing alone in front of them. His saxophone was as dirty as he was scruffy, and he had about him all the air of a man accustomed to failure, but his eyes also held a look of knowing superiority. Perhaps it was the absurdity of the contrast, she wondered, between the obvious reality and the self-absorbed imaginings of his mind, that made him so...so...she searched for the word deep in her childhood memory, so pathetic. Gloria realized that she had lapsed into the thought world of her native French, and that she was trying to say 'pathetique', as of something exciting strong emotion; pathetic in the French sense, like a symphony, rather than in the English sense, like a snivelling pinched excuse for a man.

But Spiff Abrahams bizarrely managed to satisfy both meanings, so that she felt an overpowering desire to lie before him with her legs open. She expected all her lust to dissolve with his first notes, for she feared jazz, but to her delight a pretty little folk song emerged from the bell of the horn, one that she recognized from her first English lessons in the Ecole Primaire in the suburbs of Poitiers, and as Spiff reached the final line of the verse, Gloria joined in, bringing her voice down upon his root in a sweetly harmonious third. She would have preferred to be underneath but was happy enough to stay on top for the time being and negotiate later.

"And keep him from the foggy foggy dew", she sang, and heard a cough from somewhere in the seats down to her right, where were seated the expert witnesses from the other side of the debate; she recognized the disapproval of her husband Richard.

Gloria had had the impression that everyone was making music, so powerful were her own feelings as she sang, but brought awkwardly back to reality by Richard's cough, she now saw that the thousand or so delegates and witnesses in the auditorium were left silent and embarrassed by the sound of a real acoustic instrument, playing a tune that they did not recognize.

Spiff Abrahams's long years of playing with jazz pianists had quite accustomed him to improvising against a background of meaningless noise, so although surprised by the tuneless heckling of the woman in the audience, he was unfazed, and reached the end of his solo arc of free jazz without faltering.

As he did so, the lights dimmed and an image of two hands appeared on the vast Grideoblog on the wall of the auditorium. The hands began to clap and the audience politely joined in. Spiff held his saxophone horizontally, as an offering to his audience, as he had once seen Dexter Gordon do at Ronnie Scott's, and bowed his head graciously.

Gloria couldn't help noticing the rod of corduroy in Spiff's trousers, and wondered if she might get any time alone with him during the conference.

The audience found the Grideo images as incongruous as the musical demonstration they had just witnessed, for although blown up until they were fifty feet across, the hands were small, neat and effeminate. Everyone present knew the countertenor voice that went with these hands, yet it surprised them still when it spoke.

"We show our gratitude to Spiff Abrahams", said Cornelius Coltrane Brewster, "to whom we owe, almost entirely, the technology that we unveil today, the technology that will revolutionize our current world, and I use the word current advisedly, and lay down secure foundations of knowledge and communication for the future generations of New England". The audience moved and muttered together in titillation.

Gloria knew in that moment that her earlier testimony as a transport witness had been a token, and that the idea of using the paved canal network as an extension to the congested road network had never been taken seriously.

Simultaneously Cornelius knew, in the control booth hidden in the shorter side wall of the auditorium, that his decision to present remotely was paying off. His case was strong, but he did not want to compromise it by being gay, Jewish and black in public. His hands, manicured and white in the Grideo glare, moved to a bank of knobs, dials, faders and meters as he spoke the first exciting lines of his speech. The large skinhead next to Gloria leaned over, brushing her elegant knee with his nylon belly.

"Posh cunt, ain't he?" the man said, leering at her.

"Thought all that lot had fucked off to Idristan".
He took Gloria's hand and squeezed it; she recoiled in horror as she felt a long finger scratching her palm suggestively inside the shake. She smiled weakly at the man and looked straight ahead at the Grideoblog; there was no telling with a shaved head, she thought, just how greasy the hair might have been.

Richard Henshaw, it is true, saw the exchange, and clocked the invasive plans of the shaven head, but at the time was both involved in the Grideo and also busy in mental preparation for the biological testimony that he was due to deliver later in the day. Had he been able to act against the shaved head there and then, things might have turned out differently.

The Grideo voice continued to speak as the giant hands fluttered over the complex machinery.

"Spiff Abrahams is a pioneer", said Cornelius. "He created a new form of modern jazz, a fusion of twentieth century urban styles that he called Bip-Bop, a fine example of which you have just been privileged to experience".

The audience rustled in hostility as they learned that the alien sounds they had just endured were also associated with the taboo word from the old times, jazz.

"And which has given to us", continued Cornelius onscreen, trying to smooth the audience down by hand and voice, "for all its inherent ugliness, for all its anarchy, and New Englanders, I do understand your disgust as you listen, and share in it wholeheartedly, which has given to us, by our rigorous scientific examination and testing of the mental and physiological transformations that occur in the deformed brain of a Bip-Bop improviser such as Spiff Abrahams, the technology to recreate not only our music, but as I shall show you, our whole world, according to the modern specification".

"Aaaahhh!", sighed the audience, for they were mollified.

"We first identified, then analysed, and finally amplified the class of brainwave responsible in the Abrahams brain for these transformations...". Cornelius paused; he could not begin to explain to these people the technical details of the process, nor dwell too long on the old jazz music that Spiff had in his head before turning it into simple folk tunes; he knew he had to keep it simple.

"...for these transformations of jazz into erm...music".
There was confusion in the hall.

"That was jazz, innit?", shouted someone.

"That's a saxophone. ain't it?", shouted someone else, shaking his fist at Spiff, and the Grideoblog behind him.

"Well yes and no", continued Cornelius Brewster. "But I must tell you that the music envisaged by the Bip-Bop musician is far worse than what you heard".
The audience gasped in terror.

"It is strident, rough, tuneless, played on unpredictable acoustic instruments, and the musicians improvise; that is, they don't know what they are going to play next".

"Sick bastards", shouted a voice.

"Fucking paedophiles!", shouted another.

"Yes quite", said Cornelius. "I utterly agree. But the point is, and this is where we were able to reap the scientific rewards, what finally comes out, in the case of someone like Spiff, is not half as bad, and quite bland and inoffensive, and closer to what they used to call folk music".

Cornelius felt he was losing his audience, and took urgent action to recover them.

"And this has brought great benefits to science, benefits to technology, benefits to the future, and benefits to New England", Cornelius continued, and with each reassuring phrase brought the audience further back onside.

Cornelius's hands moved back to the racks of equipment.

"Our Heritage Centre Systems Technicians have developed this wonderful little box", he said. "through which I am now going to feed some of the Bip-Bop. Spiff, old boy, would you oblige? Just a little snatch".

Just like working with a singer, thought Spiff to himself, a little snatch out of nowhere, and summoned up the essence of Lester Young behind Billie Holiday.

His body was still fixed in the grimace of last solo and the same folk tune as before emerged. Gloria's heart raced as she watched Spiff's penis twitch inside his trousers, and she silently caressed the words of the old folk song.

"If I was a bachelor", she sang to herself, quite presciently, "and lived all alone...".

Then the tune began degrading.

"We call it the Lomaxtrane", said Cornelius, "because it translates bad music into good music; it translates weird jazz into simple folk song, and simple folk song into nursery rhyme".

And sure enough, as he spoke, Gloria, thrown back once again to her infant English lessons, was able to follow the transformation and knew that the foggy foggy dew had turned into three blind mice.

"...and also because it goes from lo to max", said Cornelius, and the Grideo camera zoomed in as he turned a knob on the panel. Now the three blind mice themselves began to degrade, and there was a loud hum in the room, and all the audience felt a blinding headache among them, and in the centre of the hall Spiff Abrahams jerked epileptically, then fell to the floor, still playing. Ominously, his melody had degraded to a constant pitch with nary a tremble of vibrato or human expression, such that none present could fail to be reminded of the last song of a hospital heart monitor.

"It's only temporary", said Cornelius eventually. "no cause for alarm. And I apologize to you all for any cranial inconvenience you may have experienced".

The audience watched the screen in silence as Cornelius turned the knob back from max to lo, and as Spiff rose to his feet, as his melody turned again through the three blind mice and into the foggy foggy dew, they now rose to their feet themselves and cheered and applauded him, less, it must be said for his musicianship, than for his guinea piggery.

"Awesome, fucking awesome", came the shouts, "Blinding, mate, you ought to be on the telly!".

Amid the hullabaloo, Gloria managed to get close to the

hero of the saxophone moment. She had noticed that since arriving at Syon Park, her personal Grideonalia had all begun working again. Outside on the streets, as was well-known, and was the subject of much popular unrest, the system was so overcharged that the electronic devices in people's pockets were as useless as the cameras hovering above them, and did little more than feed into the general headache and hum.

Gloria pushed through the crowd and slipped a nudge into the baggy pocket of Spiff's beige corduroy jacket. The nursery rhyme moment had clinched it for her; she was now determined to have this man before the end of the day. To this end she had fingered her most appealing grideo on the nudge and also suggested a meeting by chance at 9pm in the Syon Park bar.

She saw Spiff's hand close around the device she had put in his pocket, and she now moved back into the crowd, satisfied to know that she was at least in with a chance, as Cornelius Coltrane Brewster announced a break for lunch.

Chaplet 65

Out Of Time

It would have been a family affair in Syon Park that afternoon and evening, but for the fact that Jeb Henshaw did a runner during the first break.

His first few hours as a Systems Musician had so horrified him that he had run for his car at the first opportunity, and in a stunned daze blundered his way out on to the West London roads, coincidentally bashing in the headlight of his mother's car. Gloria had spotted Jeb's battered Tata and parked her vibrant pink Honda Labia next to it in a gesture of maternal support.

The orchestra pit was small and stuffy. Jeb looked into the giant auditorium at the delegates streaming in for the morning conference and was trying to pick out his mother and father among them when curtains pulled across the glass wall and the Conductor tapped Jeb on the shoulder.

"Grieg Piano Concerto, mate", he said bluntly, handing him a sheaf of manuscript paper covered in what seemed to be flyshit.

"I'm not much of a reader", confessed Jeb. "I'm more of a

jazzer".

A groan went up around the pit.

"Oh Christ", said one of the seventeen violinists. "We've had trouble with your sort before".

Jeb noticed that he was opening the score to the Beckham Violin Concerto.

"The music's only there if you want it", said a bagpipe player helpfully; he was opening a vintage Rangers football programme on his music stand.

A banjo player brandished an arrangement of Bernstein's Symphonic Dances from West Side Story.

"Just play what you like, son", he advised.

"Just don't follow him", cut in a huge wild-looking man with a baby electric guitar, and pointed to the bespectacled drummer who was opening out a sheet of backward paradiddles.

"If you follow the drums at all", agreed a lone woman trombonist, "it could settle into some sort of recognizable tune, and then.."

"...and then we'd all be fucked", said the guitarist.

"But", said Jeb.

"No buts about it", said the violinist, "we don't want any more jazz problems. Why do you folk always have to play in time?"

"But", said Jeb again.

"The point is, mate", said the theremin player, who had a book of Jimi Hendrix transcriptions open in front of him, "anything in time interferes with the Systems software".

He paused, then added, "and when that happens the wrong tunes come out, and that triggers the climate control in here, see, and the pit heats up until we couldn't play in time even if we wanted to".

"So it's best to stay out of time to begin with", said the bagpipe player helpfully.

"But", said Jeb.

"Three minutes", shouted the conductor, and tapped his white stick on the podium.

"I don't think he knows anything". said the violinist.

"Look", said the banjo player, "they put us through this Lomaxtrane thing they've invented. It transforms what we play into what they want to hear. Today we're rehearsing for the dinner dance tonight, but it's not for us to get the notes right, just for them to get their settings right. We can play whatever we like, see. Doesn't make any difference one way or the other".

"As long as it's not in time", said the violinist.

"Two minutes", shouted the conductor.

"It's all right for him", said Jeb's new friend, nodding in the direction of the violinist.

"He's got as much time as a cod in chips. But I know you jazzers, you can't help yourselves". Now he whispered urgently. "Listen, mate, if you're in any doubt at all, ever, about how to avoid One". He pointed to the conductor. "Follow him".

"Thirty seconds", shouted the conductor, and tapped his white stick on the podium.

"Is he blind?", asked Jeb.

"No, replied the banjo player. "Just deaf".

Then the conductor's baton interrupted its crazy flight and swooped down from nowhere on an unsuspecting One, and there was suddenly cacophony; and it was a miraculous cacophony, for even as the violinists sawed, and the banjo player chopped, and the bassoons honked, and the guitarist screamed, and the drummers paradiddled, and the cello scraped, and the Conductor flapped until he all but levitated, yet there emerged in the auditorium only the sentimental garlands of the Grieg Piano Concerto, as loved by all New Englanders, especially since its use in the remake of Lassie.

But in the midst of this, poor Jeb Henshaw could not find his bearings at the piano, and clung involuntarily to the erratic thumping of the drummer, and so conspired with these beats as to produce something near to a groove, and the climate control was thereby triggered, and the musicians were heated until their blood near boiled, as was foretold.

This is why, when the bell rang for tea, Jeb ran for the safety of his car, for he was frightened not just in an aesthetic sense, but because he was being chased by a motley orchestra of enraged and overheated musicians.

Chaplet 66

Special Things

During the lunch break Cornelius Brewster retired to the bathroom adjoining his office on the coveted top floor of Syon Park and soaked himself for thirty minutes in a floss of pink bathing bubbles.

The morning had gone exceptionally well, he thought to himself, but his most important task was still to come. As he luxuriated in the warm water, he looked around the room at the possessions he had so carefully placed there, and took comfort and strength from them all. The Star of David dartboard, the Lisa Minelli LP signed by Barack Obama, the inner rectum statue made from the mould of dear Nicky, his long-lost Idristani lover, and of course the portrait of the Royal Family, as they were in the time before. These were the emblems of his race, his sexuality, his aspirations, and his being; they were his 'special things'. Only here, in the bathroom, could he risk such an indulgent display of illegal thought patterns, especially in his position of influence.

A rancid smell of undigested sewage cut through the pompom perfume of the bath oils, coming from the toilet bowl level with Cornelius's head. He hated that thing in here, in his special place, hated the promiscuity of effluence and affluence, but it was a small price to pay for privacy, for in New England only bathrooms and toilets were still exempt from Systems camera surveillance.

"Effluence, affluence".

Cornelius stroked his genitals lovingly as he toyed with these words, and now another word came to his lips.

"Influence".

That's all he had at the moment, he reflected, rather than real control, for this still lay in each of the thirty-nine Council Republics of New England. But the leaders of these were coming more and more frequently to meet in Syon Park to discuss matters of National Identity, and Cornelius sensed more and more a desire to federate. What he was proposing today could, he knew, make him top hat in the federation.

"Somewhere", he crooned dramatically to the bath taps, "over the rainbow.... communication, security, control...it's all so ugly, so unwieldy. It needs a catchphrase", he mused. "Communication, security, control...CoSeCo...mmm...still ugly". He affected an Italian accent. "Cosecco...how lovely, almost a light Summer wine, yes, that could do it, they could go for that".

Pleased with his creative spurt, he settled back in the tub for a last few minutes with the foam.

Chaplet 67

Groodles

Richard Henshaw was anxious in several degrees as he found his seat again in the Grand Auditorium. To begin with he had been unable to find his son Jeb, whom he wished to interrogate on his first morning in the pit; then he had been unable to find his wife Gloria, whom he wished to interrogate on her relations with the fat bastard sitting next to her. And to cap it all, he knew that he would be in the hot seat himself later in the afternoon, as expert witness for what Cornelius had just informed him had been named the Cosecco Project, and would be facing keen interrogation by the delegates on the safety of the proposed Groodles.

As the giant Grideoblog descended again along the long wall of the auditorium, Richard finally spotted Gloria, and anger rose in his mouth in a tide of bile, for she was still sitting next to the fat one. She had probably had lunch with him, which was why her nudgeo hadn't responded to his nudges, despite the urgent flag he had put on them. She couldn't claim bad reception either, not here in Syon Park, where all devices finally seemed to be enabled. He decided to sort it later, once and for all.

The dainty hands of Cornelius Brewster appeared on the Grideoblog, and he began to speak.

"You will, I am sure, have noticed how much communication we have in Syon Park", he began, and wrote briefly in his air, causing two huge letters CO to appear in the screen footer.

Murmurs of approval arose around the room, for indeed all present had been delighted to get back online at last. Gloria fondled her nudgeo, and knew from its raised edges that she had a nudge waiting. Although it was only about Spiff, rather than from him, being a response to her request for information about the match between them from the online bonking information service, Matchmakers Anonymous. From the picture of Spiff Abrahams that she had submitted in the lunch break, the nudge told her, they had deduced that he would give her both physical satisfaction and mental aggravation. The knot in her stomach separated - a warm thrill of lust spread down towards her bottom while a dull nagging ache spread up through the bones of her face and neck.

"You may also have noticed that all the cameras are working here", continued Cornelius.

"Not just your own personal cameras, but those above and around you, whose intelligence you have no doubt seen on the Systems screens in the restaurant and all around this great old building".

The audience once again murmured in recognition and approval, for they had been comforted to see the security cameras at last doing their job again.

"We all know why they stopped", said Cornelius.

"There was an underestimation of the bandwidth required for the volume of data, and the cabling network has proved insufficient…except in the provision of headache and hum." Cornelius delivered the line deadpan, and the audience remained dead silent. He often forgot how crude were the responses of the modern New Englander, for in truth they defied belief. He now repeated his line "I say again, except in the provision of headache and hum", and signalled humour with a flourish of his hands and a loud laugh. Snorting, braying and hooting broke out in the auditorium, and Cornelius felt sudden nostalgia for the farmyard animals of his Conneticut youth, and for the Hunt Balls of the Royal Family, who had first seduced then deserted him for Idristan.

"But now we have brought you back security", said Cornelius, and wrote in the air again; the letters SEC appeared in the screen footer.

Richard Henshaw shifted uneasily in his seat; he didn't like to be made to dwell on the security aspects of the programme for which he was an expert advocate, because he was plagued by the fear that his own violent misdemeanours would one day come to light. He had never regarded these recurring bloodstorms as part of his real life, and thought of them merely as odd dream sequences. Yet he knew deep down that he had made his family vulnerable, and whimpered as he imagined them one day defenceless, deprived of his protection. Richard was grateful when Cornelius moved on.

"This is made possible by Groodles", he said.

"You may have seen them in the parklands as you came in, and taken them for giant wind tunnels. They are in fact bundles of Grideo Data Cable".

The audience was now astonished. These serpentine structures were the height and width of apartment blocks.

"Now these bring consequences, of course: there are always consequences", continued Cornelius, into the not entirely friendly silence in the hall.

"Enormous resources of energy are required. To implement Groodles in all the Council Republics would require choice and sacrifice in other areas. Choice and sacrifice. Do we want to drive or do we want to communicate? Do we want to move or do we want to be safe?".

The audience grudgingly conceded Cornelius his point and he carried on.

"You may now be asking yourselves about the health and safety of your constituents; you may be wondering, as you are aware of the physical effects of even the current level of current, the endless ear hum, the horrible headaches, the inconvenient erections and so on and so forth, what would be the result were we to lay cable even more profusely, by the measure of a thousand or more".

Cornelius was now becoming carried away with his own eloquence and the audience was beginning to wonder about many things.

"He's a fucking pouf, I reckon", whispered Gloria's fat neighbour. "Look at those hands".

But Cornelius read them well and quickly became focussed and muscular again, though his hands remained dainty.

"The problem is not how much current, but where it is", he continued.

"There is no reason to deprive ourselves of the current we rightly need for our own communication and security. But we must perhaps be more careful where we put it".

The audience was now back onside.

"When we run Groodles through the veins of New England, along the routes of the ancient waterways, we shall be able to concentrate there not only current for our future needs but also the current that is now inconveniencing us on the streets and parklands and livingrooms of the everyday. We will put all the current in one place, and make it safe there. Control!". Cornelius wrote in the air again and the letters CO appeared again in the screen footer.

"Cosecco", said Cornelius, in a pronounced and lascivious Italian accent.

A triple-layered screen of industrial strength glass now slid down between the audience and the main floor area of the auditorium, only gradually muting their expressions of digsust.

"Fucking foreign pouf", shouted Gloria's neighbour.

"Gay cappucino shithead", shouted someone else.

The hands on the screen waved and Cornelius, realizing his cultural mistake, began to improvise, in as much of an estuary accent as he could muster.

"Sorry", he said. I meant Systems, not Security".

He rubbed then wrote in the air and a new catchphrase appeared in the footer.

"Communication, Systems, Control", he said. "Cosy Co". The audience relaxed again.

"Now let me show you what we mean by control", said Cornelius. He flicked a switch on the panel in front of him; the auditorium darkened and a glowing light spread upwards from one end of the vast room, revealing the musicians in the orchestra pit. The audience forgot their disgust and turned to watch, ready for another show.

"This morning I gave you the opportunity to witness the effect of the Abrahams Transformations, under the Lomaxtrane. Now, ladies and gentlemen, I give you the enhancement of the Lomaxtrane Life".

The cameras in the control room panned between the large box of the Lomaxtrane and the solid wall of dials, lights and meters that comprised its big brother Life.

"The glass screen is there for your protection", added Cornelius. "One day soon you will see glass around the Groodles".

As the orchestra began to play, the members of the audience clasped their hands to their ears and eyes and screamed in panic. The raw sounds of the acoustic instruments, each playing moreover in its own scale, time and style, together with the frenetic spasms of the musicians' arms and legs, and their look of anguish as they played, combined to excite feelings of fear and loathing in all present. On screen, Cornelius slowly began to turn the large central dial of the Life. The music began to change, became calm, ordered, recognizable, and the audience sighed in relief. Cornelius, although absorbed in his demonstration, noticd the absence of the piccolo in the ensemble. He remembered that in the assignment sessions he had given this part to Jeb's piano, and wondered what had become of the lad. He looked over into the pit and as the opening piano melody entered in the Grieg Concerto, his eyes were drawn to the mad banjo man whose output had been assigned to this element. As he continued to turn the dial, the eyes of the banjo man became still, his hair subsided, and it seemed to Cornelius and to all the audience that his two remaining front teeth became straighter in his mouth. He turned the dial a touch further, and to their amazement this ragbag of musicians suddenly seemed to form an obedient and cohesive collective, homogenized, brewsterized, free of individual eccentricities and disturbances. The audience fell silent, for they were once again astonished. Cornelius abruptly turned the dial round to the quarter way mark and then immediately back to zero. A great crack appeared in the reinforced glass screen, and the musicians of the orchestra clutched their heads in pain and fell to the floor like stones. All music stopped. Cornelius allowed the silence to sit for a while, then began to speak again.

"Apologies", he said. "Apologies all round. A painful, shocking, but entirely necessary demonstration of the potential of the Lomaxtrane Life. Results only temporary in this case, I assure you".

And sure enough, the musicians in the pit were picking

themselves up from the floor, blinking as they returned from a totalitarian future.

"Imagine a world", said Cornelius, coming to the crux of his argument, "where we are each free to think and behave exactly as we wish, yet what results, what finally comes out, conforms completely with preconceived social patterns. Is this not the reality that humans have dreamed of since time began, where the freedom of the individual and the controlling power of society are each maximized, yet live together in consort and consonance?".

Cornelius felt he was losing his audience again, and returned in plain words to his strong central point.

"Imagine a world where murder rape and looting are all possible. Even yoga and jazz improvisation! Yet no-one will be harmed, for all these impulses will pass through the Groodles of the Life, and be transformed into normal and conventional behaviour. Controlled. Without detriment to the freedom of the individual or the needs of society. Win-win. You believe you are raping your neighbour: she believes you are mending her front paving. Truly it's win-win all round!"

And the audience rose to their feet and cheered and clapped, for not only were they individuals with visceral needs, but also they were delegates of Council Republics, who each now envisaged their own hand on the controlling knob of the Lomaxtrane Life, and many of the women also fretted about the cracks in their front paving and would be pleased if a man only attended to them, whatever his underlying thoughts and beliefs.

And the audience, it then happened, were distracted and in some measure excited and overawed by what they had seen, and heard Richard's biological testimony without argument, even though he could not avoid speaking of the inevitable tumours that would occur in populations living close by the new Groodles in the old canals, and they were not bothered unduly by this, imagining themselves in any case to have been elevated by then to live in grand mansions far from the urban grime, and their heads were still swelled with the fever of power as they retired to the coaches in the grounds to dress for the dinner dance that evening.

Chaplet 68

Crucibles

There are, I suppose, an infinite number of events in the world, if we choose to see it that way. Yet we prefer to single out a few among them, naming them significant, and pretending there to be nothing in between.

Imagine instead infinite streams of activity, each as important as the other, and along its whole length. Now and again, where several streams mingle and collide and coalesce into one small area, there is produced enough heat not only to illuminate the area as some sort of event, but also to alter significantly the course of its component streams.

Such was the Bateman Street Brothel Fire, where eight prostitutes died, and a drummer was propelled into the mental hell of thirteen eight, for this was the crucible of the Great Partition.

And such again was the Syon Park Inferno, which I shall now describe. If my account is brief and lacking in detail, I attribute no less importance to the event. I merely wish to hold your attention to the streams of activity on either side.

Chaplet 69

The Syon Park Inferno

The delegates must have felt special that night. Certainly they each collected and demolished their individual plastic Deliables, and just as certainly each drained their litre sized Merlotubes. Forensic examination of the remains was able to tell us this much. And if we have no witness accounts of the dancing, we can only imagine it to have been spirited and optimistic, even after such a gruelling day of conference, for the words of Cornelius Coltrane Brewster had been inspiring, and the work of the orchestra, once filtered through the Lomaxtrane, was excellent.

His Uncle Quintus had advised Jeb Henshaw how to stay out of trouble. Keep your eyes about you, he told him. Just keep moving. Moving and looking. Don't let them get a fix on you. Which is why, at the time of the Inferno, he was in the Ham family home, listening to his secret jazz collection and looking for his Muse.

Cornelius, once having descended to the level of the delegates, even if only to persuade them, now felt sickened by them, and had retired to his apartment on the coveted top floor of the Syon Park headquarters to search through his collection of forged stamps and banknotes for his favourite likeness of the Old Queen. He and his collection books were blown clear out of the top of the building by the explosion, and landed in the parklands close to the bush where Richard Henshaw had made his hide.

A dog fight was in progress there, watched by three men in evening dress; they all wore blue balaclavas, for they wished to remain anonymous in front of the tree cameras, but Richard knew the identity of the one he had followed, the fat skinhead bastard who was probably screwing his wife.

While the dogs tried to rip each other apart the men circled them, uttering short, sharp cries of encouragement.

"Gooh on, my son...have him...he's yours", and so on, and constantly changed position among themselves. Richard gamely fixed his eyes to his target, recalling the evening he had spent playing Spot the Lady for his pocket money with his father Godfrey, in preparation for the life marked out for him as a polyphonic composer. Spot the tune, his old Dad used to murmur to him. And here he was now, he thought to himself, shivering in the lowering temperature of the West London night, a mere biologist.

His wife Gloria was on her own mission. She had waited and waited for his nudge, and had almost given up, having succumbed to the temptation of a second merlotube, when the assignation came through on her nudgeo.

She kneeled before Spiff now, in the control room in the wall of the auditorium, but sealed off from the karaoke wailings of the dancers. YMCA, they'd be yelling, she knew, and then they would all go quiet and be clutching each other for the sentimental power ballad Two Little Boys.

In the reflection of the bank of equipment behind her lover, a face appeared in the small window of the control room and disappeared immediately. It happened again and again, and Gloria realized that a woman was jumping up and down outside the door, trying to see in. She believed it was the short Asian woman she had seen in Spiff's shadow all day. Nothing to worry about now, thought Gloria. She's out and I'm in.

"Oh yes, it's good to be on the inside", she said to herself, and ran her teeth along the hard ridge of the corduroy pole in Spiff's trousers. She nipped sharply at the bulge of his helmet and he yelped into his saxophone. In his mind Spiff had Eric Dolphy and Ornette Coleman playing Free Jazz in 1960; what was coming out was something quite different. It started as 'There's a Yellow Rose in Texas', but as the Lomaxtrane cut in to control the orchestra in the pit next door, Spiff's melodies became simpler and simpler, until at the moment Gloria nipped him, he appeared to be playing 'Baa-baa Black Sheep'. Gloria groaned as the heat and juices of love flowed to her genitals. She pulled the buttons off Spiff's baggy old trousers and extracted the cock from his grimy G-fronts. It seemed harder than was possible, and the blue veins along it seemed to be straining to escape their casing of flesh. As she took him in her mouth, Spiff gasped and stopped playing. She pulled her lips away and commanded him in a voice suddenly guttural again with her native French, "play nursery rrrhyme forrr me". She rapped his penis against the cold metal of his saxophone to strengthen her message, and allowed her lips to open as the sound of his lovely Conn tenor blossomed again.

But an unexpected thing then occurred, for Spiff attempted to play a recognizable tune, perhaps in fear and obedience, perhaps just in lust, but certainly for the first time in his adult life.

"Baa-baa Black Sheep", he attempted on his horn, and what emerged, quite bizarrely, and whether through the power of his own Abrahams Transformations or through a software confusion within the Lomaxtrane, it is impossible to say - what emerged was a stream of dense and wild free improvisation of great intensity and quality. Gloria thrust him out of her and clutched at her ears.

"No, no", she cried. "Stop it, that hurts me. Stop it now". But Spiff was in full flow and could not refrain from his refrain.

"Have you any wool?", he continued, sending a dark, weird, booming note into the marrow of Gloria's spine. The vibrato was regular, but unconventional, for though she did not know its precise details but only its effect, it followed the Fibonacci sequence, and Gloria found herself vibrating first once per second, then once again, then faster, twice now per second, now three times, now five, now eight, now thirteen, now twenty-one times per second, and faster and faster in perfect proportion, until her every molecule seemed to be shaking together up in the higher reaches of sound, and she pulled Spiff onto her now, made him crush himself into her against the equipment wall, faster and faster, and his note continued as he thrust into her harder and harder, until her body jerked finally into cosmorgasm, joining her own pure note into his, and she knew in this concluding moment that her section was golden.

Gloria's arm had become stiff and extended during her excitement, as it was wont to do, and this was unfortunate for the dancers and musicians, for as she thrashed about with this arm she activated the Lomaxtrane Life in the auditorium, and sent its dial, furthermore, to its highest setting, where it had never been before.

And a great explosion and inferno ensued, in which the great building at Syon Park was razed, and from which Spiff and Gloria themselves only escaped because of the diligence of architects and builders in the construction of the control room, and in which it is fortunate that the musicians and dancers did not suffer unpleasantness, for they were killed instantaneously and before the fire, being pierced by an unusual frequency, then drowned in the lung by electrical charge. And this was also the fate of Ang Li's mother who still followed the teacher Spiff to enquire about the remaining lessons due to her missing daughter, after all this time.

And the burning embers of the building and its inhabitants fell among the dogfighters, as did Cornelius Coltrane Brewster and his stamp and banknote collection, and the group fell asunder and was knocked to the ground.

One among them, whom Richard had been intently watching, eventually rose to his feet and tottered away through the trees, and though his suit was torn and his balaclava badly singed, yet Richard could not see his face.

He caught the man standing by Gloria in the car park and, noticing that her skirt was ripped open and that her car was bashed in at the headlight, he dragged the man back into the bushes and beat him with a heavy branch until he was dead. Wishing one last look upon the face of this intruder into his family, Richard pulled aside the blue and bloody balaclava and noticed that it was a different man, and not the fat one from the seat beside Gloria, although he did seem similar, Richard reassured himself, in both size and disposition.

The couple drove home to Ham without speaking. Each feared they had lost their beloved only son in the Inferno, yet durst not voice that thought.

They found Jeb sitting at the kitchen table in headphones. He started guiltily as they entered, and assumed them to be angry, for their faces were twisted and yellow.

"I'm so sorry about the car, Mum", he said. "It was a total accident", and he pulled into the corner of the kitchen and cowered there; but his mother and father came to him and covered him with hugs and kisses, for their boy had come back to them as from the dead, and they were grateful.

"Please, Mum", said Jeb. "Dad. Don't make me go back there".

Chaplet 70

Yadiyadiyadiyah

"Can we rearrange?", asked Dennis plaintively, speaking to his opposite number at the Old Grampians Squash Club.

"No chance, mate", the man replied. "I've lost one myself, but I'm managing. Fine if you can't raise a team, but we'll take the points".

Yes, points you don't really need, thought Dennis bitterly, as you're top by a mile anyway. Whereas here at New Isleworth we're struggling. Shit. It was only the Summer League as well; it was only supposed to be a bit of fun, and keeping fit for the serious business of the Winter. What was the man's problem?

But the idea of giving points away stuck in his narrow craw.

"No. We'll be there", said Dennis, and put the phone down without pleasantry.

Shit. Now he'd done it. He looked round the clubhouse and wondered how he'd got into this hole, and whom he could find to help him out. Bastard squash players. All very keen to play, at the meeting, and to train as well, oh yes, they all have the best of intentions, but then suddenly come all the excuses, the school holidays, the cricket season, the knee operation, the cataracts operation, the wife, the girlfriend, the wife and the girlfriend, yadiyadiyadiyah. The real cause was the Idristan trip falling through, Dennis knew that for a fact. They'd all been hoping to get over there for the big tournament, not just out of curiosity, to see what the place was like, but to get away for a bit, from the school holidays, the cricket season, the operations, and from the girlfriend and the wife. Then when the borders were shut, and they'd received notice that their visa applications had been made just too late, and they couldn't travel after all, his whole team had evaporated, dissolved away into the New England Summer smog.

Dennis had his own special reason for going to Idristan, because the tournament director was his idol from way back, the great Sam Sara, whom he had met in New York back in the time before the Great Partition, when they were both young men; when Sam could have been World Champion easily, remembered Dennis, if he hadn't been wedded to his tablets, or his tablas, whatever he called them.

"Oh well, my man Dennis", he'd drawled, so laid-back for a New Yorker, "maybe in the next life".

Sam Sara had turned him on then to reincarnation, and though he had never gone the whole hog, with the turbans and the chanting, because that wasn't his style, Dennis had immediately liked the idea of being able to have another go - liked the idea of life as a squash court with multiple back walls, so that no matter how many times you missed the ball, there would always be another go…

And in truth, although this rather metaphysical idea was anomalous in Dennis's meat and potatoes brain, it had brought him more and more comfort in recent times. The walls of New England were beginning to close around the people, and even the squash players were feeling oppressed.

Dennis had been chairman of the Steering Group that had outlawed the nick shot in New England squash, and had found his own arguments persuasive at the time. Yes, that shot had once defined the game, and the ability to imagine the join between floor and wall and send the small black ball there at will was the single skill separating the great from the good. But that was then, and this was New England, where the fine precision of human response had slowly withered on the body, and many things previously taken for granted were now the stuff of nostalgic dreams and talk shows.

Men could no longer saw or draw straight unaided, by hand and eye alone, neither could women thread their needles except by computer; there was a new penetration aid on the market called Sex Nav, and in football's Premier League there had not been a goal by penalty for six years, seven months, and three days. If anyone now hit a nick on the squash court, and made the ball unplayable, it was deemed to be a foul accident and the point awarded to the opponent.

Despite having been the architect of the new rule, Dennis now began to yearn for the nick. He dreamed, these days, of the grace and beauty of a great athlete, one like Sam Sara, bringing mind and body into perfect alignment to bring off a perfect roller, and looked back wistfully to the time before, when even for someone like him, with no real eye for the ball, there was always the chance of improving, always the chance of another go.

He had read somewhere, in some barmy tract by some foreign anarchist type who ended up in clink, that genius in sport was a dimension of religious belief, and that only by placing the self in a universe shaped and oriented by a higher being was it possible to achieve magic in sport. That had rung a bell for Dennis and, though he had no notion within him of a higher being, he sometimes meditated on his own vague idea of reincarnation before going on court for a secret solo session with the ball. But he had not hit the nick yet.

By the end of the afternoon, Dennis had found a team, though he didn't rate their chances over at the Old Grampians. His new friend Quintus would have to play at one; he'd had a lot of experience, but from years back, and he was old now as well as match shy. But he was unconventional, in fact downright weird and, Dennis reasoned, making the team sheet for that evening, that could throw a younger opponent for a while. He was only a five himself, realistically, even in the Summer League, but he'd have to play up at two, it was only fair to the others. Jeb was a skinny rabbit, and could maybe last at three, just by speed and stamina, but Dennis was worried about the man. His eyes were frightened. He looked as though he'd had a bad shock. The DJ was testing the karaoke and when the song came on Jeb ran for the door like a man possessed. Every Time We Say Goodbye, it was, that's all. Probably, thought Dennis, probably getting over that Syon Park business. He'd heard the whole family had been involved somehow, though he didn't know the details. And he couldn't hold the racquet properly anyway, because of that stumpy finger. He'd put Richard at three, Dennis decided, marking the sheet. Nice guy, but completely fucking useless on court. No choice, though, thought Dennis, and marked Jeb in at four, below his Dad.

What was the name of the other guy? Something foreign, it was. He'd looked a bit that way as well. White, but with a long beard and a funny hat. Osama something. Probably never picked up a racquet in his life. Oh well, needs must. Dennis marked him in at five and went home to collect his kit and say goodbye to his wife.

Chaplet 71

A Woman's Work

Gloria watched the Grideoblog as she gridironed and packed the two squash bags. It was her favourite show, a collection of vintage television advertisements from the time before, hosted by a Celebrity Chef.

She laughed at the preposterous notions of the old days, but cried a little as well if she saw a plant or a small animal, for she genuinely missed these strangers in the new concrete and camera reality.

The old Nimble ad came on and she shrieked in pleasure, singing along tunelessly with the funny old music.

"There are three men in my life", she croaked. "To one I am a mother, to the other I'm a wife. The other fucks me sideways".

The warmth of the gridiron at her waist seemed to reach out towards her, and waves of warm lust pulsed out in response from her pussy. She touched the nudgeo in her apron for reassurance; she still couldn't believe that Spiff wanted to see her again. The question was, when, where, and how?

As the music tinkled in the background, Gloria ironed, and

though she was as clumsy and inept as normal, her movements were infused with the passion of her three man fantasy. Two of them could be going on a long journey, she decided, and tossed off another batch of G-shirts and Geans for her husband and son. The other one, she decided, as she packed the extra clothes in under the squash paraphernalia, adding at the moment, quite by instinct, the grideotape marked Control Room that she had picked up on the night of the Inferno, the other one is going to be carrying on where he left off, and so saying she went into her secret cache of fine underwear and ran the gridiron over three of her most successful G-strings as well.

Chaplet 72

Coming Alive

Quintus Henshaw reached into the darkness of his squash bag and scrabbled round for a ball. It was an ancient thing, fabricated years before in the stiff, heavy nylon they had used before the modern lightweight materials, silk-g, cash-g, and so on. Still, it had lasted all these years, thought Quintus, it would probably see him through the night.

Muff had felt him come close, somewhere deep within her rubber join, and had begun to stir in her sleep, readying herself to be taken. Her tiny yellow eyes popped open as his hand crushed through into the bag from the evening light beyond.

There were other balls, she knew there were other balls, but he was only interested in her. She was made for him. She waited patiently while he picked up and discarded each of the other poor specimens, then half-closed her eyes, as his hand finally closed around her willing curves. She did not want to appear too easy.

It was a beautiful warm evening, the sun still high in the sky over the last of the canals, but Muff might have been in an Arctic sandstorm for all she cared. All she could feel was the warm hand around her, all she knew was the joy of coming alive for the man who gave her meaning, all she cared was to dance for him.

Quintus finally found a decent enough ball, one of the new ones from the factory, and a bit shoddy-looking to his eye, with the yellow dots slightly green and wonky, not the same standard of craftsmanship he remembered from the time before, not the same at all. But that was New England for you, he's begun to see how it really was. Everything to cock and by the book! He'd go back on the canals if he could, but they were nearly all gone now, in the South and in the East, and up towards the North. You could only get out to the West now, and not for much longer.

He threw the ball into the air and caressed it on the racquet face before sending it upwards again; he turned his hand and struck the falling ball with the thin edge of the racquet; turned his hand again to caress with the strings, turned again to strike with the other edge, and continued so for fifteen minutes, his eyes never leaving the ball.

Muff was not being driven hard, and had no reason to be as hot as she was, save for the inner joy of being alive and in a conversation with the man she loved. She did not care for the rough embrace of the worn Ashaway strings, nor the sharp surface of the racquet edge; she would have rested an eternity in Quintus's hand. But she knew that he wished it so, and she danced for him. His racquet tended to send her off at an angle, where she would have left the boat, yet she steadied herself each time, and flew straight for him.

And as she fell upon him, her heart singing as she contemplated arrival, and though she felt his eyes held in hers, following her spin, tracking her every move, yet he seemed to play some other complicated game, for his racquet edge moved erratically and would have missed her every time, had she not held fast to the course of her love.

"Bugger", said Quintus, for he remembered as he stepped off the boat that he had promised to bring kit for the donkey they had drafted in at five. Dennis was lending him a racquet. That's desperate, thought Quintus. He had only seen him once, but already had an idea that the man had been in prison. Something about his skin, and his eyes as well, always watching. He'll be used to the four walls anyway, thought Quintus, and went back in to fetch his spare shorts.

But they had perished by moth in the years since they were last worn, and all Quintus could find to suit was the pair of leather spanking shorts he had put aside for a Satanic ritual yet to be realized.

Muff was still warm from her lovemaking, and as Quintus swung his bag over his shoulder and set off down the towpath to the Old Grampians Squash Club, she rolled cruelly among her cold and unwanted rivals.

Chaplet 73

Team Talk

The match ended quickly, with bad feeling on both sides. Dennis and his opposing captain had become embroiled on court in an argument about the foot fault parameters in the Revised Rules; there had been some racial and religious taunting of the New Isleworth number five, and he had shown himself to be a sore loser by destroying a hand-dryer in the dressing room with his racquet.

"I know the thing doesn't work properly, and it's annoying", conceded the Old Grampians captain later, "but the point is, he can't even play!".

And Quintus had upset everyone by hitting nineteen unplayable rolling nicks in the last two games. The match ball supplied by the home team had burst from the brutal overhitting of their number one, and Quintus had supplied a ball from his own bag.

Everything he touched from that moment on sailed into the nick. This upset Dennis, much as he enjoyed the spectacle on one secret level, for each of these nicks was deemed a foul accident under the Revised Rules, and resulted in a point away. It also upset the Old Grampians team, for the frequency and consistency of the Quintus nick led them to believe that he was a smart-ass freak just taking the piss.

Richard was grumpy too, for his opponent was a large man with no hair, who looked familiar, and who annoyed him for a reason he did not yet know. Furthermore, he was distracted from scientific and logical investigation of the matter by the lack of oxygen he suffered while vainly chasing the ball to all ends of the court.

The bad feeling intensified over the meal, fuelled by the copious lagerboots laid on. The New Isleworth number five was late to the table, as he seemed fascinated by the pictorial history displayed on the clubhouse walls.

"This is incredible", he said softly to himself. "It is an honour to be here".

He stroked the cracked glass of the pictures on the wall.

"This is where the Khans made their home", he breathed. "Incredible. Rohan, Mohibullah, Jahangir. And the Great Grandaddy of them all, Azam. To think I have shared court with them, and now eat in their presence. This is truly an honour".

He bowed his head and his beard tickled his thighs between the leather shorts he still wore from his brief match earlier. He had judged that the opposing team would be more friendly over dinner to shorts than to his traditional Baháʼí robe.

"Oi!", shouted his Old Grampians opponent from the table. "Osama", he shouted again. "Bin Lederhosen!".

The opposing team screamed in laughter and banged the

table.

"Get yer arse over here and get some New England nose-bag", he continued.

Dennis intervened, loyally.

"There's no call for that".

"You can talk about fucking calls", shouted Richard's fat opponent. "You and your fucking foot faults!".

He was on his feet pointing at Dennis, and had murder in his eye; Richard pushed his chair back and raised himself, holding the tension in his hamstrings, preparing for violence. The barman heard the raised voices and flicked a switch. Grideoblogs came alive around the clubhouse, each pumping out the Grideo remix of "Every Time We Say Goodbye", and Jeb ran from the room and cowered beneath a table.

"Fucking yellow pouf", shouted one of the Old Grampians. Quintus, seated at the head of the table, rose to his feet with outstretched arms and began to deliver an incantation in a foreign tongue.

"Llanfairpwllgwyngyllgogerychwyrndrobwllllantysiliogogogoch", he chanted. A breeze ruffled through his orange and pink pantaloons and the room was filled with the scent of cat musk.

"You're a fucking cheat", said his opponent, rising from the other end of the table with fists raised.

"Pwoaarhh!!", said Dennis, "who let one off?", and now they all laughed, sat down, and ate the food that was brought to them.

Out in the car park, having said goodbye cordially enough,

they found the Old Grampians waiting for them, wearing blue balaclavas.

The match ended quickly. No-one expected Osama to be so quick on his feet nor so adept with his racquet now he was off court. Quintus mesmerised the opposition with a slow dance; when they were devoid of motion and balance, his brother Richard stepped in and beat them with a rusty length of exhaust pipe he had found in a ditch. Jeb and Dennis hid behind a wall and watched the while, for they knew themselves to be useless in a fight.

Eventually four of the Old Grampians lost heart and ran away, but their car keys were first taken from them and thrown in the canal.

Richard looked down at the man on the floor below him, and remembered where he had probably seen him before, for the blood and oxygen now flowed well through his brain. Surely he was the fat one next to Gloria, the one he'd let escape from the parklands, the one who had probably screwed his wife? His dead mate must have played squash too, that explained why they were missing one tonight. The man raised his arms to Richard and spoke weakly.

"Please", he entreated him. "Please, let...".

Richard raised the exhaust pipe high above his head and brough it down in a fast arc into the man's nose. The man screamed once, jerked twice, then was silent. Richard's teammates watched in their own shocked and complicit silence as he reached down and pulled back the balaclava.

"Nah", he said, to no-one in particular. "It's the wrong

one".

A machine spoke into the air, and its voice seemed louder than usual, because the Summer smog had lifted, and because the guilt of the five squash players, and the knowledge that they had done something very bad and very important, brought into the bloody car park of the Old Grampians Squash Club an atmosphere of clarity and hush.

"Beep", it said, and continued. "Beep beep beep". It was quiet for a second or two, then whirred and spoke again.

"Beep", it said, and was finished, for these were the last five in a series of very damning pictures.

Chaplet 74

My Lucky Ball

It might ordinarily have been the instinct of such a murder of squash players to scatter, to disperse to their homes, to pretend that nothing had happened, until the day when Noddy New, as the police forces of the Council Republics were now affectionately known, came knocking at their doors.

But in that bloody moment together they had each reached a turning point in their lives, and they now turned calmly towards the future. The exception was Jeb, now pointlessly grappling with the wreckage of the old nylon squash bag belonging to his Uncle. Quintus stopped him gently, his hand on the younger man's shoulder.

"Come on, son, come on", he whispered, as though talking to a shell-shocked horse, "we don't need any of that. Come on, son, it's over now". But Jeb still could not move.

"Here, son, what about this?", said Quintus, eyes drawn to a ball, newer than the others, in the debris of the slashed side pocket. He recognized it from its wonky yellow dots as the ball of the nineteen nicks. The dots looked green in the car park light. "Keep this for me, Jeb", he said, reaching down to retrieve it, "it's my lucky ball".

And Jeb believed that the ball was lucky, even though it had partly kicked everything off in the car park, and he took it from Quintus with some comfort, and stood up and rejoined his comrades in their turning point.

They made a short ceremony around the dead athlete. Osama said a Prayer for the Dead; Dennis read from the section on interference in the Revised Rules of Squash; Quintus summoned the Spirit of Beelzebub to watch over the flesh of the deceased, including his family, and Jeb sang as much as he could remember of the trumpet solo by Miles Davis on So What.

Richard was left the final task, as he was the biologist, and also the wielder of the coup d'exhaust, of tucking the car keys into the shirt pocket and sliding the corpse into the murky green waters of the Grand Union Canal. He jumped away from the body as huge cod-like creatures with savage teeth roamed out of the water to possess the corpse.

Quintus was reminded how close was the engine of the Third Paving, how dangerous conditions were becoming in the remaining Western Quarter of the canal network, and of how little time they had left.

"Come", he said. "It is time".

With these words Quintus led the team down the canal towpath to Hanwell Flight, where they boarded the narrowboat named Crowley, and began preparations for the journey to Idristan.

Chaplet 75

Nineteen To The Dozen

Now their journey was at last begun, they fell into the deep sleep their bodies craved, and each felt that the long and tiring day of their previous life was now behind them, and dreamed ecstatically of a new dawn.

Only Dennis did not sleep, for he slept little in any event, and in recent years had spent more nights with the Revised Rules than with his pillow, and he was content now to take the night wheel of the Crowley and steer her down the Thames towards Newbury.

Some wanted to stop, to moor in river towns and villages, in Henley, Bray and Maidenhead, to buy food and fresh clothing, but Quintus was now at the day wheel, and he forbade it, for he knew it was time.

Richard and Jeb, scavenging for old energy bars in their kitbags, found the copious picnics Gloria had hidden there, and the piles of laundered clothing, and they shared these willingly with their crewmates, and all marvelled at the foresight and tenderness of their woman. Then they shared their dreams, and so doing, found spirit to continue, and made bond with each other.

Richard spoke of his vision of a new energy source for the planet, and of a new era of sharing, caring and low consumption; Jeb spoke of his longing to meet his musical equals in a paradise of pure acoustic melody; Dennis spoke humbly and simply of squash, and of his desire to experience again the brilliance and precise passion of the old game. The New Isleworth number five revealed himself as Osama Muhammad, the new Báb. Not one of the team knew what he was talking about, even Quintus, who had knowledge of the Occult, and who kept himself silently at the wheel of the narrowboat.

"The first Báb", explained Osama, pushing his green turban slightly off his forehead in order to scratch at a squashed midge, "prophesied in 1844 the forecoming of a great new leader for the New Age of History; this leader duly came and was Bahá'u'lláh, and he created the faith of Bahá'í, which came to nothing".

Nods all round the narrow galley table.

"I am the second Báb, come to foretell the next new leader for the next New Age".

More nods. More nods and a long pause.

Dennis now remarked that the Revised Rules of Squash comprised ninety-five separate sections, as compared with the twenty of the original.

"Ah. Now that's very interesting", said Osama. "Ninety-five is a multiple of nineteen, in the amount of five, which happens to be our number, which may be significant as well, for other reasons, but I'm more interested in the nineteen".

The Henshaw ears pricked up.

"Nineteen, you see", said Osama, "is the defining number of the Báb, for the first Báb assembled unto him eighteen followers for the task of their preparation for the advention, so that their total number was nineteen. This is why the Báb calendar has nineteen months of nineteen days, separated by four or sometimes five intercalary days".

He looked over at Quintus.

"Four, or sometimes five", he repeated. "When he wants to join in".

The man at the wheel continued to gaze into the Western horizon and did not reply.

"This is why we must say the word Báb nineteen times daily, or at least you must, as my followers, for I am the Báb, and am therefore probably exempt, but you must say my name nineteen times, or pay a fine of nineteen mithquals".

Dennis remarked that number nineteen of the Revised Rules was the new rule relating to the foul accident of the nickshot, and everyone looked at Quintus, but again he said nothing.

Richard began to speak of his father Godfrey, and a lump came to his throat as he recounted the struggle of the late polyphonist to have his new division of the octave accepted.

"What was so special about it?", enquired Osama.

"It was a division into nineteen equal parts", said Quintus, speaking for the first time from the wheel.

"That's why we all speak as we do, according to our father's division, our father's melodies. Me, Richard, Mickey whom you don't know but will meet, and even Jeb there, in the next generation".

Osama stood up suddenly, and banged his head on the cabin roof.

"Thank you, thank you, thank you, thank you", he said, and continued until he had thanked himself nineteen times.

In one hand Jeb clutched the burnt Grideotape that was all he had to remind him of his Mum, and in the other the lucky squash ball of his Uncle Quintus.

"Uncle Mickey will tell you about nineteen", he said proudly. "It's a drum thing. Elvin Jones, mostly. Six over four, then three on each of the six so you have eighteen rolling triplets and then you squeeze in the other one, just like a drop of lemon juice at the end of the soup, to make it all roll just right. Nineteen".

Animated conversation immediately sprang up all around the galley table, and soon all four men were happily chatting to each other, revealing their secrets, and it seemed to Quintus, who yet held himself apart from the company, that the rhythm of their conversation was indeed nineteen to the dozen.

Chaplet 76

Hwyl Y Gwynt, Hwyl Y Mor

But the talking stopped soon enough, for they were come into the canals again, out of the Thames at Reading, first into the Kennet Navigation as far as Newbury, then the Kennet and Avon to Bath, and finally the Avon Navigation towards Bristol, and as well as the savage cod, vicious vole and carniverous plant that now collected from all over New England in this last Western Quarter of the network, the crew also had to negotiate one hundred and four manual locks, twenty-nine of them in the two mile stretch of the Caen Flight by Devizes.

And if they were old men, or old enough, for even the youngest of them, Jeb, now qualified for the Veteran Leagues of Squash, they were fit from their sport, and energized by the imminence of the New Age, and so worked and fasted without complaint.

Muff was the least nourished of them all, for she had not felt around her the life-giving hand of her maker for an eternity. She knew Jeb, recognized him and cared for him, but his hand was hot and sticky with its own anxiety and could give no heat into her join.

So was the long journey a trial of endurance for Muff, and one she survived only because she knew that with every yard of water she was coming closer to reunion, to warmth, and to love.

The Crowley turned out along the Avon, passed under the Gormley Suspension Bridge, made from a million maquettes of the great sculptor's penis, and from the Bristol Channel at Avonmouth, turned up along the coast towards Idristan.

As they passed Caerdydd, then Aberdawe also known as Swansea, and finally turned the bow to starboard against the fierce Atlantic waves, Myfanwy prayed aloud in Jeb's pocket to the Spirits of the Wind and of the Sea.

"Hwyl y Gwynt, Hwyl y Mor", she cried, as best a squash ball can cry. "Bring us safely in!"; and as they crossed over the last ridge of rough water into the harbour, a freak wave washed Jeb and his pocket passenger off the deck of the Crowley and into the sea. Muff was thrown clear of the pocket, but Jeb grabbed her and held her fast. She realized quickly that he acted not in gallantry but in a desperate attempt to save his skin, for the pianist could not swim, although a Pisces by birth.

Muff managed to keep them both afloat, using the buoyancy of her love, until a rescue rope was fashioned from a spare reel of squash string that Dennis kept with him at all times, and thrown to them from the boat.

Less than an hour later, when Muff was back in Jeb's pocket, wrapped up cosy and warm again in a pair of Quintus's fluorescent silk underpants, she suddenly recognised the scent of Mumbles, and knew that she had brought her man home.

Chaplet 77

My Best Intentions

And it came to pass as Myfanwy foretold, that Quintus now found his destiny in Idristan, and it came to pass just as the Báb Osama Muhammad foretold, that this time was indeed the preparation for a New Age, but the events were still surprising, for the seers saw only the foreshadows, as is often their curse.

But, as you will see, now that the necessary streams of activity have reached the coordinates of their destiny, the events of the future now unfold swiftly and with logic, and I shall endeavour to write them down in the same way.

Chaplet 78

Sunrise Strip

The adventurers did not as you might expect, rush down from their vessel, rush out to view their new dominion, rush up to take the reins of power from the Nutter King.

On the one hand they were exhausted from their arduous water journey; on the other, now that Idristan lay defenceless beneath their gaze, they felt the moment of shyness known to conquerors since the beginning of human time.

While his crew slept their diffident sleep, Quintus walked out on to the shore of Mumbles and came upon a damsel on a sandy hillock. It was Our Lady Myfanwy Muff Maboob, who waited there each morning at this time, with a bottle of red wine, for her paramour and lifepartner to arrive, even as she monitored his progress from inside Jeb's pocket.

Quintus took her hand and they walked in silence to the rocks by a clear pool, where, first removing the single gold stud from his ear lobe, he lay her down on a bed of fresh red seaweed and entered her.

She had expected something softer, because of his great age, and the firmness of his erection inside her surprised and delighted her. But he set about her with the air of a workman beginning a complicated task, whereas she knew it all to be so simple. They were together now, as foretold, and there was no need for him to concentrate so hard, or to furrow his brow, for she felt removed from him and was unhappy.

She caressed his buttocks slowly with her feathery nails and tickled his hairy ears with her quick tongue, and as she felt his body relax, its rhythm become less forced, more lyrical and rounded, she felt her own body at last respond, and she raised her legs high in the air and threw back her arms into the sea, and as he pounded into her she first gasped then screamed aloud in the joy of their union, and when his stroke shortened and quickened she moved exactly with him so that when he too shouted out in ecstasy, she was able to draw his juice into her as the base of a volcano draws lava from the fundament.

And if in that moment Myfanwy knew more pleasure than she had yet experienced in all her life, it was because she believed the union to be perfect and eternal, and also because in the same moment she conceived a child.

Quintus leaves her now, though she does not want to see him go so soon, and holds his hand as long as he allows her. But he is here now, she tells herself, nothing can go wrong. He is made for me, as I am made for him, as we are made for each other.

Quintus bounds back onto the Crowley, banging a tin camping cup on the roof of the narrowboat.

"Wakey wakey", he shouts. "Come on lads. Time to be up and about. I think you're going to like it here".

Chaplet 79

The Last Supper

And they came to the club known as Miskers which was large and by Idristani standards modern and well-equipped, for it had been built before the Great Partition with the money of Old Wales to provide a suitable venue for the Welsh Squash Team to shine in the Caerdydd Olympics, even though in that distant meeting squash was finally dropped from the short list of new games in favour of Synchronised Karaoke.

And they found an easy and warm welcome in the club, for the Great Tournament would begin the next day, and Timmy Gordon was greeting competitors from all round the world, whose visa applications had been pre-approved and who had therefore been able to gain entry into Idristan by road and by plane, for all top players wished to test themselves against the Idristani racquet wizards, amd especially against Sam Sara, and Dennis slipped into the queue unnoticed, for in any case he had the team registration document with him.

And though they wished to go straight on court to oil away their rustiness with some well-chosen drills, Dennis knew that rest and sustenance were more important, for they had not eaten for many days, and still had canal legs.

And there was brought before them a feast of cakes, honey, seaweed and lamb bacon, and they ate and drank until they were sated and wished to sleep.

Their young waiter Iestyn led them to their quarters which were in bunk style because of the large number of competitors, but still more commodious than those on the narrowboat Crowley, and as he closed the door behind him, left into the room an enigmatic prophesy.

"You're going to get mullered".

Chaplet 80

Why Oh Why Can't I?

This came to pass in the Teams, for the New Isleworth men did not have the strength in depth of their competitors. Nonetheless in this riotous week of running and hitting, full of pulsating glam rave and the exuberant gesture of homosexual melodrama, there were surprises in the Individuals.

Dennis, readjusting to a new set of Rules, more like the original, being fewer in number than the Revised Rules of New England, but benefitting from the addition of a special section on Artistic Play, was amazed to be awarded the Tournament Prize for Grace and Economy, for he had always thought his own play boring and stolid.

The new Báb Osama Muhammad was surprised to be so feted on the homosexual side of the draw, for he was by now old and grizzled, as well as short, fat and bald, although his green turban disguised this feature. If he was so adored by the camp camp, perhaps it was because in his many years in prison he had grown accustomed to the company of men, and adopted some of their private ways, so that they were now comfortable in his presence. Also he still wore the leather spanking shorts. In any event, it was with great pride that he took his place on court for the final of the Gay Plate, and as he stood shoulder to shoulder with crowd and opponent as their anthem played, tears welled in his eyes. His life seemed to play out inside him as the singing swelled through his body, and he felt again the Alabama sun hot on his neck as he bent to take the clear stream in his hands and felt the odious grip of the preacher around his hips, and heard the sanctimonious voice in his ear.

"Toby, Toby, I can't wait any longer. Oh forgive me Lord, for what Toby is about to receive".

And the music surged and the singing reached into every corner of the arena, even unto the straights, and more images came to Toby, and more tears, as he remembered for the first time the dreadful scorching reality of the Bateman Street Brothel Fire, and in that moment took responsibility for what he did that night, and resolved in his mind the injustice of his years in prison due to mistaken identity, and was only pleased to have met his friend and cellmate there, Ali Rahman, and to have found his way into Bábism so that he could be here now among so many lovely people.

As Judy Garland moved to the climax of the anthem, he came to know that the succulent middle of his life was suddenly turned poignant and stringy, but nevertheless he joined her upper voice with his own fragile falsetto and found there mixed together an agony of yearning and the calmness of arrival, and as he sang, "Why oh why can't I?", Osama Muhammad, also known as the former American Ambassador Toby Frigham Young, knew that he was at last happy.

Chaplet 81

Ptah

The progress of the Henshaws was uneven. Richard and his son Jeb played poorly in the Teams and worse in the Individuals, yet became heroes in the tournament atmosphere, for other reasons.

Richard was immediately intrigued, on entering Miskers, to observe so much bad skin. The pustulant layers were deepest among the local players, but Richard watched with human concern and scientific interest as the fresh faces of the arriving competitors quickly deteriorated.

He did not find his answer until the final day of the tournament, when he discovered that the soap bars used throughout Miskers were laced with arsenic. The smell was covered by the fragrance of Idristani heather, but he recognised the texture and indeed the effect from his experiments with small animals as a young boy.

"You're a godsend, mate", said Timmy Gordon. "I've been trying to work that one out for months".

He shook Richard by the hand.

"Could you do me one more favour, mate? It's delicate, see.

If I tell old man Jefferies his soap is off, he'll go mental, like. And I can't afford that to happen, see, 'cos I get pretty much all my supplies from him. He more or less keeps us going. But coming from you, as a scientist…he still won't like it, he might go off on one anyway, but, well put it this way, mate, I'll owe you big time".

Richard Henshaw found Dai Jefferies in the restaurant gallery, absorbed in a game of chess. The board was unusual, having King, Queen, Bishop, Knight and Castle, and only four pawns on each side, together with a piece he did not recognize, made of crystal.

"What's that?", he said.

"It's a ptah", replied the Nutter King, who sat opposite Dai Jefferies. "It doesn't have to look like that. You can use anything, really".

"Crystal is good, though. I like crystal", said the large young woman seated next to Dai. Her face was fat and opaque, and her eyes, though small, were cruel and lazy. As she spoke she lifted a Bishop and held it in midair, all the while looking across the table at Quintus, the fourth player at the table. Her movements were teasing, but Quintus would not heed them just now, for he was preparing for the Tournament Final.

"What are you doing here?", his brother asked. "I thought you'd be practising".

"Chess clears the head", replied Quintus. "I have eaten well, and slept awhile. Now I must clear my head. Then I will win".

The young woman cackled derisively, and none could ignore the sexual challenge in the sound, but still Quintus did not respond.

"Apparently there's arsenic in the soap from your farm", said Richard. "That's why they all look like plague victims". He gestured down into the arena below, and it was true that many pretty young bodies were topped with a dirty crust.

"Could be", said Dai, absorbed in his next move. "Time enough to sort that tomorrow".

Richard was relieved to have escaped a row, and although he was eager to leave the company as soon as possible, politely enquired about their unusual game.

"Enochian Chess", said the Nutter King. "One of the disciplines of the Academy. It came from John Dee, astrologer to my forebear Queen Elizabeth 1, up through the Order of the Golden Dawn of the Victorian era. We have it from Our Lady Myfanwy Maboob".

Richard knew of the Muse by her global reputation, and also by his connections through his brother Mickey with the Royal English Conservatory where she had once worked, in the time before.

"I am curious to meet her", he said.

The Nutter King touched the earmuff he wore and waved towards the arena without taking his eyes off the board. "Down there", he said. "She's been waiting in her seat for hours. For the final to begin".

Richard looked down into the Arena and saw a woman alone in the raked seating, to the far left in the front row, where she would be best placed for the backhand action. She seemed beautiful even from that distance, but Richard sensed she was sad, for she held herself around the leg and chewed her knee.

"Daft bint", said the young woman, and Richard detected a Germanic twist in her vocal rhythm.

"She won't see anything worth much down there".
She continued to look directly at Quintus, who again did not respond.

"You don't seem to think much of our new friend Quintus, do you Rebekka?", said Dai, still looking at his own Castle, and the tall young woman blushed, for she did not care to be teased and challenged herself.

"Is it for the purpose of devination?", asked Richard. "For seeing into the future?".

"Some use it that way", replied Dai and, first leaning forward to move his Queen on the board, now stood up and stretched out his huge body to its full extent, and shook himself all over, like a beast of the field.

Richard's eyes bulged as he saw what he took to be some sort of python undulate behind the muddy trousers, and Rebekka saw this too, though only in her peripheral vision, for she was still concentrated mostly on Quintus, whom she had decided to take as her lover and king.

"But we use the active board", said Dai, "to order the time and nature of the Golden Dawn".

Chaplet 82

A Waiting Game

And Myfanwy was waiting in her seat, and was also waiting in a different guise in the pocket of Quintus's nephew Jeb, and would have waited elsewhere as well, would have taken any guise suggested, and this was possible for her, for although she could not play a note of music her powers in other areas were many and mystic; and Myfanwy would have done anything if she could entice her lover just once to raise his eyes and look upon her.

But he was elsewhere, in his own dreams, lost in his squash, and in the bewitchment of his own journey, and Muff knew in her heart that he would not emerge unto her for some time, and certainly not before the outcome was decided of the Tournament Final.

One thing, though, unsettled and annoyed her, and gave her cause for concern about the future. She did not see, although she advocated chess for the promotion of clarity of thought and purpose, especially the Enochian variety, which she herself had introduced into the curriculum of the Academy of Idristan, why Quintus had chosen to play now, with these people and in this particular way.

As she looked up into the restaurant she could not quite see her lover Quintus, unless he leaned across to make another move, doubtless a brilliant one, but she could see the others. She knew they were playing the active game, rather than the passive one, and sought to order the future rather than simply devine it, and she wondered why Quintus had joined them.

He should be in the here, preparing for the immediate, for the final. He should be in the here with me, thought Muff; I could help him, if only he would let me. Better than those people up there, she thought, for they are strangers to him. And should in any case be elsewhere, attending to their functions; the King to his Realm which he has ignored for so long and left to me, and Dai Jefferies to his crops and crafts. Why are they there? They do not love him. Not as I do. Except perhaps for the fat German bitch from the Crystal Shop in Hendy Gate, thought Muff. She was hanging round in Dai Jefferies's workshop the day they took the breast moulds. Waiting to be fucked. I don't trust her, she thought, I don't trust her at all.

She felt some turbulence in one of her earthly bodies and touched her stomach by the squash court, where she could feel her baby grow. She stroked her own belly now and calmed herself. Quintus would have a good explanation, she told herself, and she would hear it and they would continue in love together, and there would just be the three of them, Quintus and her and the baby, for Muff would have no more need to multiply herself through the universe, and the matter would be closed.

Sam Sara came on court to begin his warm-up. The fluidity of his movement, the fluency of his racquet arm, and his unerring eye for the nick did not give Myfanwy Maboob any satisfaction. She was suddenly worried for Quintus, worried for Idristan, worried for herself, and worried for her baby.

Chaplet 83

Mullered

Iestyn was taking a turn behind the bar and chatting to his Mum when the order came down from the top table for pints of Jefferies and a litre of spring water for the Wizard, who was just about to go on court.

Quintus had thrilled the crowds with his racquetry over the week of the tournament. None had believed that so serious and so old a man would prevail against the youth of Idristan, so merry and agile in their full-breasted squash tops. Yet time and time again Quintus had found the impossible shot to turn the rally round and win the point; now, incredibly, he had reached the final, with the deserved nickname of the Wizard.

"Why's it called Jefferies?", asked Iestyn's Mum, who seldom came into the club, and was in any case innocent of the ways of men. "It looks like Guinness to me".

Iestyn placed his hand round the long thick handle of the beer pump.

"You don't want to know, Mam", he said.

And Iestyn's Mum began to reminisce about their family history, and about Iestyn's father who had barely known his son before being taken from them in the bloody chaos of the Great Partition. And, because he wanted to hear his Mum speak, because he needed to know these things about his father, and because those who devine the future are seldom in a hurry to get there, Iestyn let the drinks wait for some time on the bar and did not signal to the waiter that they were ready for collection.

"Thanks, mate", said the waiter. "He's going mental for the drinks. That's all I need".

"I'll take them over myself", said Iestyn. "You mind the bar, and me Mam".

"How fucking late are these?", shouted Dai Jefferies, half out of his seat and already much taller than Iestyn. Quintus and the Nutter King still watched the chess board intently, but Rebekka fixed her eyes on Iestyn. There were no watches in Idristan, for time had not been measured there, until this moment. So Iestyn was merely pretending when he looked at his wrist and pronounced cheekily,

"Nine minutes, mate".

Dai Jefferies rose to his full height, casting a giant shadow over the board. His white hair stood up in a shock of power and his wrinkled, weatherbeaten face suddenly became lissom with adrenalin and testosterone.

"Is that all?", he said, and clubbed Iestyn to the ground with one blow of his paw.

His Mum screamed at the bar, and in the confused silence that then fell upon the club, Myfanwy Maboob felt that all present looked to her and asked to be guided and reassured, for she was their Muse. There were no police, for there had been no crime until now in Idristan, and Iestyn had been felled at the table of the King. Where else would the people look, but to her?

And though Myfanwy felt, in that moment, that Idristan was turning colour, yet she could not move to prevent it, nor even reassure the people, for now she was caught up in the urgency of her own needs.

And Muff knew also that by her new attention to her own person, she had caused Quintus and his Qabalah to come among them, and so was responsible for the changing colour, indeed had partly willed it.

And though she did not want to sacrifice Idristan, yet the needs within her were overpowering and necessary.

Chaplet 84

The Tournament Final

The Tournament Final began, and gradually the gloom and silence lifted, for all were enchanted by the muscular finesse of the competitors.

The two men played very different games, yet in the opposition of their styles were perfectly balanced and evenly matched.

Sam Sara was steady, fast, accurate and rhythmic, while the older man Quintus was deceptive, seductive and unpredictable. But by virtue of youth and stamina, Sam Sara had sneaked home in the third game and now came on court in the fourth leading by two games to one.

He served high into the backhand of the Wizard Quintus, and though the return was good, being tight along the wall, Sam Sara sensed a reluctance in the arm of his opponent, and wondered if at last Quintus was becoming tired. He turned his body into the corner, shaping to boast back up the court off the sidewall, but turned his wrist at the last moment to drop the ball straight. Quintus had read the boast and was already moving to the forehand corner when he saw the angle of Sam's wrist and so had to wrench himself round into the other corner, and arrived there late for his shot. Badly positioned, he played his crosscourt too narrow, and Sam picked it off from the 'T' with a lovely feathered drop, now into the forehand corner. Somehow Quintus pulled himself there in time, but was a yard short. In a desperate lunge, he did the full splits into the corner, causing the audience to gasp and cover their eyes and ears, for the sound of his old bones coming apart was to them like the sound of a tomb cracking open. This time his return was good, and clung high and straight to the wall, and Sam Sara retreated backwards down the court, taka tira tika, tracking the lob. And so good it was that it would have fallen dead in the back corner had Sam not jumped to intercept it on the wall, and slammed it into the empty backhand space, to win the point. And though the audience cheered Quintus for his gameness and for his age, and laughed at the two damp spots he had left on court by his testicles, during his splits, Sam Sara was more interested in the fatigue and tension he sensed in his opponent, for he knew that, if he could strike now, exploiting these, victory would follow swiftly.

Now, serving to Quintus's forehand, seeking to press home his advantage with pace, he smashed the ball forward onto the front wall, where it punctured and died.

A long pause ensued, during which a replacement ball was sought. Quintus sat for this moment in the seat next to Myfanwy. He seemed grey and exhausted, and would not meet her eye.

Eventually, as no ball could be found, Quintus's nephew Jeb, who was seated next to his new friend, the Nutter King's driver, Morgan Oguike, threw over a ball.

"It's your lucky one", he shouted.

Dennis, in his role as Guest Tournament Director and Senior Referee, examined the ball, and finding it within the parameters of quality of International Tournament Play, sanctioned its use and ordered the match to be resumed.

As Quintus's hand closed around her again, warmth raced along Muff's join, spreading out around the curves of her walls. She felt light in his hand, perfectly round, perfectly balanced, perfectly safe. She knew she could go anywhere and do anything if he but gave his command.

After the knock-up Sam Sara served again, a high sliced lob falling onto the wall at an acute angle. Sam stepped sideways to the 'T' preparing to intercept the weak return he had forced by the excellence of his serve. As she spun downwards, Muff saw Quintus's racquet wavering beneath her and sensed the tiredness and anxiety in his mind and body. She aimed herself for his sweet spot, but he did something foolish at the last moment, and now presented to her only the narrow racquet edge, so she twisted herself slightly to one side, fixed her wonky yellow eyes on a clear spot between the string grommets and abandoned herself into his kiss.

Sam's mouth dropped open as he watched the Wizard Quintus take the ball off the wall and, using not the strings but the thin edge of the racquet, send it low on to the front wall and into the sidewall nick. Unplayable. Unbelievable.

The crowd rose to their feet, cheering and shouting, and Muff swelled with pride and love as she luxuriated in her lover's grip.

Now were the tables turned. Sam Sara played well, as well, people said who knew, as he had ever played, yet in the presence of the Wizard Quintus, he now seemed a donkey. Hither and thither to all corners of the court he rushed, who once had controlled the rallies from its centre, and wherever, however he returned the ball, Quintus seemed to be waiting; the ball seemed always to flow towards his racquet, and indeed from it, into all the nicks of the court. And when the final statistics were revealed, it was known that from the moment of the change of the ball at the beginning of the fourth game until the glorious moment of Quintus's victory 11-0 in the fifth, the tally of nicks was in fact nineteen.

And Muff revelled in the victory more than Quintus himself, for while it was only a game of squash for him, albeit a prestigious and important one, for her it was an opportunity to come alive, and to serve her master, and to affirm their destiny together.

And she thought this had truly happened, so freely and so expressively had they worked together on court, and so free and expressive did she find his victory smile as she, Myfanwy, handed him the Trophy in her role as Muse of the Tournament and of all Idristan.

And she waited for him afterwards in the gallery restaurant, for Iestyn's body had been removed to the family burial ground, and she believed that Quintus must now come to fetch her for the beginning of their life together.

And in the arena below, where the raked seating had been pushed back into its housing so that there could be celebration and dancing, suddenly there was an explosion of loud music.

There was immediately silence in all of Miskers, for this was music such as had never yet been heard in Idristan, and it was the Syon Park Control Room grideotape that Gloria had packed into Jeb's squash bag as a memento of his Mum, and it was good that there were no Grideo facilities in Miskers, so that there was only graudio and no grideo, for it was enough to hear what Spiff was doing with his saxophone without also seeing what Gloria was doing to his knob. Especially for Jeb, who was a musician.

And the audience roared in approval and excitement, for the DJ Morgan Ugoike had also done a remix for the young people, so that all of Spiff's saxophone, the nursery rhyme, the monotone, and even the free jazz he had most surprisingly played, became danceable for them, and they now flooded onto the floor and began jiggling and joggling in a violent style quite alien to the ethos of Idristan.

And Myfanwy's heart sank as she saw this, for she devined in the dancing the end of the Kingdom of Idristan, yet she felt ridiculously happy at her own lover's good fortune, and in her guilt she ordered several bottles of large red wine, for she was still early in her term.

And before she had finished even the first bottle, she saw her lover dancing in the arena, though he was held so tight in the embrace of Rebekka that she could barely distinguish him among her.

And the podgy kraut hands ran tenderly over his taut bottom as they swayed together and seemed in their movements to dismiss and ignore Myfanw's regard completely yet simultaneously send her an imprtant message about a change of ownership.

Muff stood up and swung her arm through the row of open bottles on her table, spilling the old wine to mix with the young blood that stained the floor, and hurled her current bottle at the glass window of the gallery.

Fighting then broke out in the arena below, for the Idristan people were changing colour with every beat of the new music, and Muff saw her lover and lifepartner Quintus slip away into darkness with Rebekka, and beat at the remaining window in rage, frustration and despair.

Nicky de la Chwyth came there later, for he heard by some mysterious means that Myfanwy was in distress, and after collecting her possessions from her flat in the Mumbles, he drove the pissed and wretched Muse to Heidi Hyson's chapel, where were gathering in anticipation of the challenges ahead, the first and last of the true Idristani.

Chaplet 85

One Big Hunk

While and to the extent that Myfanwy nursed the small life that grew inside her slow and steady, she no longer watched over the welfare and colour of her people, that changed in the term of her pregnancy beyond recognition.

For when Quintus came into Idristan, it was as though a switch was thrown releasing all the pent-up energies of self, and the people became mad in their chase to catch up with the rest of the world and especially New England.

And one day Mickey came back to the chapel with the news of the discovery of a field of seaweed below Idristan that would transform the small country from a raggedy-arse minstrel destination into the richest and consequently the most powerful nation on the planet. It was all down to his brother Richard, he explained, who first having developed and perfected the conversion by high electrical charge of seaweed into fuel, had then discovered the field in the course of an intensive bio-geological survey of the Realm commissioned by the Nutter King.

Myfanwy had been drawn from her maternity bed by the

stilling of the lutes and barytons, and heard and understood the most part of Mickey's account, switching off only as he began to enter the technical detail of the Treaty being made with New England to pipe the porphyra across that country along the giant Groodles that now replaced its ancient canals, killing all plant and animal life around them by their high gridation levels, but now ensuring that the conversion into fuel of the seaweed was already complete when it arrived into the pipes of Continental Europe to be carried through into the deserts of Rahman Saudia Arabia, where by virtue of his prison friendship with Rahman, the ruler of that country, the new Báb Osama Muhammad, had secured a purchase and distribution deal of the energy so produced, throughout the whole surface of the planet.

"We're one big hunk of laverbread", said Mickey. "That's what it boils down to".

Hearing this news, Muff went back to bed with a headache, and resolved not to venture out again until she had made her baby.

Chaplet 86

Mead And Candlelight

And the changes continued with growing pace and intensity throughout the Realm, and those Idristani loyal to the ethos of the Kingdom moved in and around the village where Myfanwy lay with child in Heidi's chapel, and formed a protective ring around them.

Then the borders were opened again, for trade was already spilling in and out of the Kingdom by illegal means and could not be stopped, for Idristan was now picked as a boom economy among the top five in the Grideo World Boom-Boom Chart, and people poured in from everywhere, not musicians and artists as during the Great Partition, but men and women of trade and commerce, and also many from New England and beyond who wanted holiday homes.

And a new middle class of Estate Agents was created, who were welcomed in by those already practising in the Kingdom who had many contacts and networks previously established therein and became richer even than the newcomers, especially those that worked near Hendy Gate, for this was the centre of the many operations of Dai Jefferies, who was now the real power behind the throne.

Myfanwy knew little of all these changes, save by the recent paucity of music in the chapel, which was now more often filled with serious discussions by mead and candlelight of terrorist operations against the apostates and newcomers, and especially the owners of holiday homes.

Much was kept from her because of her fragile condition, and though she liked a morning paper she was not allowed to read one, by the deceit that supplies had been interrupted, for the week following the gruesome murder of an estate agent found dead in Hendy Gate by a knife wound to the eye.

Neither was she aware, save for the presence one night in her room of a huddle of blankets swiftly removed the next morning, that the Nutter King had been deposed by a Qabalah backed by the militias of Dai Jefferies, and that a new country had been created named Porphyra, to symbolize the origin of its fabulous wealth, and because it was anyway a better name for a country than Laverbread, and the Wizard Quintus declared King, with the German Rebekka his Queen.

And the Nutter who had been Prince and then King now retreated to the chapel, where he fell immediately into a coma that was known by all to be metaphysical rather than medical, for he was bitterly aware that by his selfish preoccupation with his Academy, with Yoga, Jazz Improvisation and Car Mechanics, and by his other hobbies of Tree Hugging and Enochian Chess, he had taken his eye off the ball, and let slip back into nothingness the Great Kingdom of the Ancient

Briton, where Art and Music and Philosophy did for a short second of universal time hold sway.

And he snored do deeply in his coma that he could not even sleep among the other chapelites of Idristan, but instead was made a bed within the old Methodist Harmonium, where his rumblings could intermingle with the jazz hymns of a bygone age.

Chaplet 87

Serenade To A Cuckoo

And a baby was born to Myfanwy Muff Maboob in the chapel of the village now known as Idristan, in the country of Porphyra.

It was a long and difficult birth, due in part to the advanced age of the mother and in part to the wishes of the child, who devined that the womb was currently safer than the outside world.

When she had already laboured sixteen hours in the pews, surrounded by her female birth partners and acolytes, Nicky de la Chwyth appeared before her, and he was refreshed from a long sleep and his hearty breakfast of honey, seaweed and lamb bacon, for in the chapel and in all the village they clung to their ancient diet as a symbol of the dissolving nirvana around them, and did not embrace the frozen tasty toasties that were becoming available in the shops.

Nicky saw that the birthing party was well-meaning, but he wished now to bring matters to a head, and carried with him two tyre irons.

"Christ, Nicky", said Muff. "Couldn't you find any forceps?".

And all around her marvelled at her ability to joke under pain and distress and they laughed with her and this helped anyway to loosen the tight resolve of the child.

Nicky then raised the tyre irons to his lips, and they had careful holes along them, and were instruments, and Nicky now played in the manner of the jazz master Roland Kirk, who also played several wind instruments at once when he became excited, and Nicky's song was a beautiful lilting melody shaped to draw the child down.

It was a variation of the Kirk melody named 'Serenade to a Cuckoo', well-known to all the birthing party, and they sang to the child with Nicky, and those who could not sing whistled, and those who could not whistle tapped, for there happened to be many female drummers in the village of Idristan.

Then the baby was born, in a great whoosh of submission like an Elvin Jones cymbal splash, and the birthing party left Muff alone with her baby and went to take their own breakfast, of lamb bacon, honey and seaweed, for they had not eaten for many hours.

The boy still kept his eyes tight shut, and all Muff could see of his face was the large Hittite nose that she recognised as her own. He was squat in the body and still covered with the dark slippery vernix of birth, but Myfanwy saw his father in him, and knew that his frame would grow long and tall, and his body hair fair and curly. If he grew at all.

This thought lanced Myfanwy's soul and she was pinioned

in panic, for even as she held her lover again, in memory, between her legs, even as her tired body responded, opening itself to him, she understood that the Wizard Quintus was now her mortal enemy, and she feared for her child.

The boy cried, but Muff could not hold him; she feared that once she held him she might never leave him go.

Heidi heard the infant and mother crying and came into the pulpit where they lay.

"What's his name, like?", she asked gently.

Muff turned her head away and sobbed. She feared that once she named him, also she could never leave him go.

"Don't you worry, my love", said Heidi tenderly and tucked Muff under blankets and kissed her. She felt the boy yearning and only jiggled his toe in passing, for she knew that none could hold him before his mother.

"I'll come back later", she said. "You'll know when you've found the right name".

Chaplet 88

The Order Of The New Dawn

The day now dawned of the opening of the Field of Laverbread, for men and women had worked night and day for many weeks to lay the pipes across the land and water into the territories of New England, where the seaweed would receive the first of many high Groodle charges on its journey to Rahman Arabia.

And most of the workers had been brought from elsewhere, as the Idristani were still unsuited to hard work, having grown accustomed to lounging about with lutes and lyres with buxom and sociable companions, and also to Tantric Yoga.

The juxtaposition of idle minstrel with industrious immigrant had caused much mayhem and violence, especially where, as often happened, the Idristani woman chose the ant over the artist.

The Nutter King asked Dai Jefferies to provide a militia from among his men, and as head of this militia Dai Jefferies appointed Victor Ugoike, who had once been Head of Security at the Royal English Conservatory of Music, where he had dealt with terrorists and explosions, and he accepted this post gratefully for he was bored of immigration paperwork, and by his energies the cells of the old prison at Swansea Castle soon bulged with the jilted jesters of Idristan.

When the deal was set, by the good offices of the new Báb Osama Muhammad, and the revenue stream from the distributed fuel assured, the military coup was enacted, in which the Nutter King was deposed, and the Royal Family of the Ancient Britons dispersed, and the new Kingdom declared of Porphyra.

Dai Jefferies held the power, for he coveted the wealth, and his military chief was Victor Oguike, and his puppet rulers were King Quintus and Queen Rebekka, lost in their fantasies of squash wizardry and crystal witchcraft.

The Field of Laverbread was of great dimension, as many recently come to the country might have guessed by the instability of their footing, for it was a bed under the whole land mass, that extended for unknown leagues outward into the Celtic Sea.

There was no safe place directly to view the field of seaweed, so King Quintus and Queen Rebekka had ordered a shaft built in the table atop the mountain of Rhobell Fawr near to Dolgellau, for it formed a suitable eyehole into the flowing red fortune beneath.

And a favoured circle were invited around the mountain eyehole, while all of Porphyra was commanded to attend, and they were held in barbed wire compounds in the valleys below while they watched the ceremony on great Grideoblogs provided by friends of Porphyra in New England. And those deemed potential dissenters were made to wear red hats to identify them.

Victor Oguike came in person to the chapel to collect Myfanwy and child.

"If you only do one thing today", King Quintus told him. "Bring me Muff".

Myfanwy had not risen from her bed until this moment, and felt she looked a fright. She reached into the space beneath her pewbed and fetched out her handbag.

The curved ridges of the embalmed ear caused her fond thoughts of the Nutter King. Muff was still held in the limbo of childbirth and knew little of events outside. Tipping out the contents she found her reddest lipstick and her darkest mascara and also a lycra travelling dress that she had kept for emergencies ever since the time before, and in no time at all was scrubbed up very nice.

Now Muff scrubbed also the inside of the human bag, and tore sheets from old hymnals she found around the place and lay them inside in the form of a swaddling nest.

Now she tipped the boy's cradle over the mouth of the bag so that he gently slid inside it, and she was careful all the time not to touch him, though he moaned aloud as he slid past her, and she noticed that his eyes were still tightly shut.

Victor's eyes were open as he steered her into the Daimler Limousine commandeered from the Nutter King, but they were also evasive, for he secretly felt that in pursuing his own career he betrayed Myfanwy Maboob, Lord Soper, and all of Idristan.

Chaplet 89

Red Hats

"Citius, fortius, profundius, lucrosius", intoned King Quintus, for he had studied the texts of the Great Partition, and had inherited a sense of occasion from his father the great polyphonist, Godfrey Henshaw.

"Faster, stronger, deeper, richer", he continued, and pointed dramatically into the eyehole in the mountain table. Grideo cameras flirred and whicked and a great murmur of amazement arose in all the compounds below when the people saw the strength in depth of the torrent of red seaweed.

"Porphyrants!", he shouted, stretching his arms wide to embrace his subjects and all the energies of the universe. "Porphyrants. You have suffered much and you have laboured long. Now is come the time when your fortune is made. Now is come the time when you can relax and enjoy the fruits of your labour. As I declare this pipeline open, I name this day Laverbread Day, and designate it a day of rejoicing for as long as there shall exist, by the Grace and Bounty of Beelzebub, this Kingdom of Porphyra, and also a Public Holiday".

There was great cheering in the compounds, and shouts of

"Huzzah, Huzzah, Long live the King!".

The Queen Rebekka smirked and revelled in the nachos of her King's glory, and concentrated her pelvis around the rhinestone crystal inside her, wishing this moment of pleasure and power to have no end, but King Quintus stilled the crowd with an imperious gesture.

"But no King acts alone", he continued. "I am nothing without my Queen".

As he gestured to Rebekka, inviting acclaim, a woman's voice rang out from the compounds below in the words "fat kraut", and this was immediately followed by the single shot of a militiaman's rifle. Myfanwy saw the red hat disappear downwards in the distance, and though she could not see the body, she thought it might belong to Iestyn's mother, who had never recovered to herself since his death.

"I am nothing without my family", continued King Quintus, indicating the group of Henshaws opposite, "and owe special gratitude, as do we all, to my brother Richard, who created the science behind our future".

Richard stepped forward, raising his hand in a gracious wave to the crowd below. As the cheering rose again in the valleys and hills around, Jeb and Mickey Henshaw shuffled their feet and looked glumly into the eyehole of the seaweed, for they were awkwardly caught between their place in the New Royal Family and their loyalty to the ethos and people of the true Idristan.

"I am nothing without my people", Quintus now cried, walking out over the tabletop, to the very edge of the mountain, and held his arms up to the sun, and out to his people. His baggy pink and orange pantaloons rustled in the afternoon breeze, and a roar of feisance echoed in the hills of all that land.

By prearranged signal huge amplifiers now sprang into life, and excited the loudspeakers in the compound, and music now filled the air and it was the Morgan Oguike remix of the Spiff Abrahams Transformations, now become a rave hit in the dancing venues of all the world in the name Twinkle, and now the Pophyrants began to dance, for they found the sound shamanistic and infectious.

Myfanwy was distraught and depleted as she watched the scene in the compounds below, and her arms were limp as they felt the weight of her child in the King's Ear. This was not the land of music and dancing they had fought for. The people below had no sense in their movement of a higher rhythm that they sought to express together; no note in their voice attempted the hidden frequencies of being. Instead they gyrated separately, each within their own tight circle of despair, their bodies twisted and aching with alienation from each other.

Now, as Muff watched them, they began to brawl, for this was the only possible end to their dance, and she began to cry, and her sobs were deep and slow and heavy, and each one brought up a more distant dimension of her life so far.

King Quintus now axed the music to stop and as the people turned their faces upwards to him, his countenance became serious.

"Who dat dere?", shouted Victor Ugoike. He was pointing across at the new Báb Osama Muhammad.

"Thank you, Victor, for reminding me", said the King.

"Indeed, I must honour the man you now bring to our attention and speak not only of his bravery and endurance on our great journey into this land by the narrowboat Crowley, and of the lucrative fuel distribution deal he has secured for us with his friends in Rahman Arabia, but also of his role as Prophet to the New Dawn. For if we were tempted to think of ourselves merely as mates on a long squash trip, Osama Muhammad came among us as a prophet, as the new Báb, and showed us the first glimmer of the New Dawn that we have created in Porphyra".

King Quintus continued, having to shout above the cheers now, "and I must also thank Dai Jefferies for his financial, logistical and military support".

Dai nodded, and was satisfied, for although he preferred to stay in shadows, in isolated farms and in antiquarian bookshops, he needed his contribution to be marked.

"Who dat dere?", screamed Victor, still pointing at Osama, and now he had double vision, and was back in the maroon hell of the Bateman Street Brothel, caught in indecision between proprietor Enoch and American Ambassador Toby Frigham Young. Now he held Osama by the throat and raised his voice to the crowd to denounce him.

"You are a stinking murderer, my man", he shouted.

"You come here with the turban of a prophet, preaching to us of your New Dawn, but in truth you come straight from your prison in New England, where you were sent for the brutal murder by gunshot and explosion of eight prostitutes".

The crowd below raised their fists and jeered upwards. Victor carried on.

"And we continue with our cottage-to-cottage enquiries in the search for the mystery man in the murder of our beloved Hendy Gate estate agent by knife to the eyeball. Why do we bother, when he stands here among us?".

The crowd below moved urgently against the wire walls of the compounds, that bulged under their weight and threatened to give way, so that the militia commanders on the ground looked anxiously to their line managers for guidance and electrified the fencing anyway, for safety, causing many Porphyrants to fall among the feet of their combrogi.

And the King was sensitive to the feelings of his people and sacrificed the new Báb Osama Muhammad, who had served his purpose unto the Kingdom, and was only ever a number five anyway.

"Arrest that man", he commanded.

"Let him be taken to Swansea Castle and put in chains there for the rest of his days. So shall he further serve the destiny of our New Dawn".

Rebekka kneaded the love handle of her King that was near to her, in wordless gratitude, for despite the elevation of her current position, she still had in many respects the mentality of a shop girl, and had feared that she would be one day brought to account for her murder of the estate agent cunt.

King Quintus now found his way back to the point he had intended.

"There is good news", he said. "And bad news. Also more bad news. Which would you have first?".

The crowd seemed divided in their opinion, and the King decided for them.

"You shall have the bad news first", he declared, and there was silence in the valleys.

"Some of you here were present at the Tournament Final", he said, "and all of you have anyway heard of the sudden weakness in my arm that nearly gave victory to Sam Sara".

The crowd murmured softly as they remembered this great occasion.

"So much has happened since that day", Quintus continued. "I am so happy. So proud. But I am dying".

The valley gasped.

"Not now, nor even imminently, for I am still strong, and have the love and support of my Queen, my family, and my people".

"Huzzah, Huzzah", came the shouts again from the compounds.

"But the paint that I wear on my face, that I have worn for as many years as I remember, turns out to be mainly lead, and to have leached through my body and into my vital organs, that are much delapidated as a result, and this has caused the occasional weakness in my arm, that you have seen, and will sooner or later cause me to die".

There was now wailing in the compounds as the King continued.

"Furthermore, I have been frustrated in my desire to sire an heir to the throne of Porphyra with my lovely Queen Rebekka by some more bad news".

Again the woman's shout was heard in the compounds "fat kraut", and again a single shot rang out, and again the militiaman missed his target. As Muff watched the red hat fall downwards, though she could not see the body beneath, she wondered if it belonged to Sam Sara, who had never recovered to himself since his humiliation in the last two games of the Tournament Final.

"She has taken infection from some crystal misplaced inside her, and may never conceive a child, by me or any other man".

"Won't stop her trying", came the shout from the compounds, "fat kraut", and another shot rang out. As Muff saw the red hat fall downwards and though she could not see the body beneath, she wondered this time if it were her own.

King Quintus now proclaimed, among the wailing of the crowd, "but there is good news". He pointed suddenly at Myfanwy. "I lay with this woman, and she has borne me a boy child, and she brings him here today as my rightful heir and as your future King".

There was now a complete silence in the land, and it was not the rose pink quietness of togetherness, nor the ice blue whisper of understanding, rather a vacuum that was cold, sour and yellow, and sucked all thought and feeling from the world and left it only selfish and therefore evil.

"Bring me my child", he commanded.

His nephew Jeb stepped forward, drew from his tracksuit bottoms the lucky squash ball and hurled it upwards into the sky. Myfanwy seemed to lose consciousness for a moment as with everyone else she tracked the course of the small black ball above them. When she came to, she was running towards the eyehole in the mountain tabletop and stood now above the torrent of seaweed that raged below. She felt hands scrabbling at her arms and legs, pulling her back from the edge of the shaft, and as she now clasped her boy child to her and kissed him for the first time, she made with him an eternal bond, and so nearly yielded to the hands behind her, just to hold her precious son a moment longer. But then she saw before her, opposite, the glinting eye of Queen Rebekka, beckoning the boy into the New Dawn, and she now calmly took the bone handles of the King's Ear, holding them firmly to secure her throw, and launched the bag into the void below.

She watched it tumble away from her, and even as her heart near exploded with the grief of the moment, yet everything in her relaxed, for she knew that by her own sacrifice she had saved her son for Idristan.

Deep below her, just above the red river, she caught a flash of yellow and green in the turning handbag, and she knew that her son had opened his eyes and was watching her now, and saying goodbye.

She raised herself at the lip of the hole, held her arms aloft and screamed at the universe, and the sound held such rage, grief and also defiance, that it was unbearable to the people in the compounds, who now covered their eyes and ears and wept in spite of themselves.

Myfanwy Muff Maboob now saw herself spinning back down into reality, and her eyes fixed into the rotation of the small black rubber ball, and caught hold of the wonky yellow-green dots so their spin slowed, and the ball fell neatly into her left hand where it felt unnatural, for she was normally right-handed, and she squeezed it once, not at all hard, and it broke open by a small hole in the join, and all the air inside now came out.

And Myfanwy fell to the ground in a coma of unknowing, for it was not safe for her to contemplate the destiny of her son.

So her friends came to her now, Jeb and Mickey Henshaw, and Heidi Hyson and Nicky de la Chwyth, and lifted her onto a stretcher made of heather, and carried her away from that evil place.

And none stood in their way, for their eyes were full of reproach, and the Porphyrants were full of self-loathing, if only from the selfishness of their own regard, and turned from the rescue party with shame.

In this way was made a passage through the crowd, and Myfanwy was carried through it and so eventually reached the safety of the chapel.

Chaplet 90

Fat Kraut

When I woke up I was in his bed. I love this boat, with its dark walls and small furniture, like the chapels Mum and Dad took me to when we went back home. 'Cept for the funny things on the wall, chains and weird rubber thingummies, instead of Jesus.

There was something glinting on the low wooden table by the bed and I remember that he took the gold ring out of his ear before we made love. Looks like three rings, actually, from here, though I don't feel like lifting my head to look properly and my eyes are a bit blurry anyway. Is there such a thing as triple vision, I wonder? Ha-ha, maybe we made love three times and he took out a ring from somewhere else on his body every time.

No, I remember now, it was only once, but lovely, and I just wanted it to go on for ever, and it was over far too soon. 'Cept he explained that it did go on for ever, in the real world, the world that was hidden from us by convention, and by science.

Which he'd said before, I remember now, earlier on, because he got very intense with me, and tried to explain the nature of the universe, which I kind of got, because we've done some of that stuff at College, World Religions, with Mr Sara, who's very fit and apparently a monster tabla player, whatever that is. And it's kind of what Dad once tried to explain to me about music, and also that awful bloke Cornelius who took over teaching me piano from Jeb, but he was very stiff and pompous, so what he said about beauty didn't quite jel. Is it gel or jel?

I wonder what my hair looks like? It must have dried off now. Shit, my head's sore, that's quite a big lump I can feel. Must have bashed it on the boat on the way over the side.
He was so sweet, getting down to rescue me in the mud and then helping me wash it all off, and lending me those funny pantaloons. They were so big on me, even though he seems so long and tall and skinny compared with me and my big hips. I suppose it's all a question of proportion.

Timing, he said. It's all a question of timing. Ha-ha, that's when he started to pull the pantaloons down over my bum, that was so sexy, thank you God, I'll always remember that feeling. But I got the point he was making, I think, about the universe, that if we had the intelligence and the courage to understand, we would know that everything is happening all at once, and is both **punctual** and eternal, because this is what being is, and there is **only** one time. And by punctual he didn't mean turning up **on** time, which wasn't his strong point, I remember now, because wasn't there a meeting we had for a squash game and **he** was late, but when was that?

Surely that was after the boat love? I'll have to work that one out in a minute, when my head clears.

What he meant, anyway, I think, if I have it right, is that because we cannot get our heads round the idea, and also the consequences, of an infinite stream of being, we have invented a world full of separate things, each with a beginning and an end, for our own convenience. And it's true what he said, I remember from College, that different cultures implement this materialism to a greater or lesser extent. The Aborigines, for example, are more in the ancient stream than in the modern supermarket aisle, and navigate more by song and dream than by trolley. I like the way he put that, it makes sense, even though they've changed a lot since his time, the Aborigines, and I think they probably get a lot of booze from the supermarkets these days, because it's so much cheaper.

I brought him some wine, I remember now, and that was really expensive, because I don't know anything about the stuff really, because we all drink Baileys and Red Bull, me and my mates, and I wanted to impress him, because he's so posh, and wise, or old, anyway. That's how I ended up in that fancy off-licence. He is quite old, I know that, older than my Dad, and I know it's not right, but I don't care because I love him. I'm sure that empty bottle was by the bed, or on the table. He must have cleared up, bless.

Anyway, that's the point, isn't it, that once you know that the material world is relative, because it's different in different places to different people, then you can see it's an invention, our invention. It's just our way of organising experience. Not that it's any less real. Things are separate, aren't they, all with beginnings and ends, in space and time? We all live and die.

But that's just one small part of it, one narrow way of looking at it, that's what he said, that's what I remember. The infinite stream, the real medium of being is still flowing, beneath all our simple materialistic surface bullshit, even though we don't most of us have the capacity to live there. But, and this is when he grabbed my arm and began speaking into my ear, and I could feel his fierce blue eyes just boring into my skull, I remember, he said human experience takes its richness and intensity from the infinite stream of being. There is no meaning in the momentary and materialist here and now, except as an organisation, a bureaucracy, he said, of experience, and if we have love, and beauty, and feeling, in the here and now, it is only because we are simultaneously multiplied and extended into an eternal now. There is only one time, he said, and we can have more or less of it in our lives as we choose, for we can live safe and rational, as chopped-up dessicated pieces of stuff, or dangerous and dizzy, in the stream of the one time.

And I still didn't quite get it, about the one time, and he started talking about a halfway place where there are different layers of experience, so that one tiny moment of experience in the here and now can be understood as a much longer and deeper experience elsewhere in time, but he also said that this would be happening elsewhere and also simultaneously and everywhere, so it didn't really make anything clearer for me. Do you agree that this is a beautiful moment, he asked me, and I just wanted to turn and kiss him but he wouldn't let me and made me carry on looking forward. Yes, yes, I said, and he asked me to describe it, the feeling I had, and I couldn't and he asked me why, and I said because it was too beautiful to say. And he said I was right but it was too beautiful to say because it was really happening not just now but in the past and in the future and for a very short time and for all eternity, because this is what now really is, this is why now is so full and rich and inexpressible, because there's so much of it. That's why we can't ever say it fully. And I asked him if what was happening now had already happened before and would it happen again in the future, and he sighed and said that our past and our future are not behind and in front of us but are different dimensions, different layers of the same thing, because everything is really happening at once.

And I asked him if it was like the layers in web design, because I did some of that as well in College, though I never got very far with it because of my bad typing. Ironic really, that pompous twat Cornelius slagging me off for my piano-playing and saying it sounded like I was typing, when I was actually bloody accurate on the piano and hopelessly random with the keyboard and mouse. Why is that? Why should I choose to be scientific when it's time to be emotional, and emotional when it's time to be scientific? Dad always had a go at me at dinner, I remember now, because if Mum did spaghetti I wanted potatoes and if she did potatoes I wanted spaghetti. It's a power game really, I can see that now, but why would I want to play a power game with myself?

But I knew the web thing would impress him, interest him anyway, because Jeb told me his Uncle did some web design, as well as the counselling, and the aromatherapy, and the witchcraft. And he asked me if I knew what a div was, and I remember wanting to say that I thought he was a real div when I first saw him on the squash court, with those daft pantaloons, and the earring, and those barmy shots. But I didn't say it. I was still trying to impress him.

He turned out to be a lot better on court than he looked at first, quite tricky, and much better than Jeb, thank God, who never once gave me a decent game. That was ironic too, come to think of it, that Mum and Dad got so aerated about Jeb and made me change teacher. Because I know Jeb fancied me and was always trying it on, but I never fancied him at all and I never would have let him touch me, even though he was a good mate, and I wish Mum and Dad had trusted me. Because it was that new teacher Cornelius who told me I couldn't play music. Cunt.

He was right, though, because I could tell the difference between my playing and say, what my Dad did, with Steve and Mickey, the Maboob Mob. Because my stuff was just notes, just technical exercises really, but theirs was, well it was beauty, it was music. And I felt really bad about that, about having to stop, not really for me, but for Dad, because I felt he'd been counting on me, like, to do something creative, something he felt he couldn't do himself, and I don't quite get that either, 'cos he's brilliant, everyone can hear that. Everyone 'cept him, probably. And when he said what he did,

Cornelius, it was like they both relaxed, Mum and Dad, well, slumped, more like, and said right that's what we wanted but it's not going to happen after all, as we sort of knew all along, so we might as well just settle back into something more realistic. And I felt bad and depressed, not just because they gave up on me, but because they kind of gave up on themselves, and it turns out Dad's cutting back on the playing now and going into jazz education. That really depressed me.

And then suddenly, what was worse, it was all about them and their plans in life, and I had to be there all the time, shopping and cooking and cleaning, because Mum was suddenly too busy planning Dad's new career in education, and I think she'd been waiting for this chance for a long time, to make him respectable, bring him back into the fold. Sheepify him, like. I suppose even Buddhists prefer their money regular. But it was like me and my plans didn't matter any more, because suddenly I didn't have any because someone found out I couldn't play real music after all, so all my hands were fit for, overnight, like, was helping.

So I needed to get out of the house, and I thought it wouldn't hurt to pick up my old squash racquet and bash the ball round the court a bit, and I didn't tell Mum and Dad I was doing the squash with Jeb because they would have started on at me all over again, and I'm certainly not going to tell them what that led to, Jeb introducing me to his Uncle Quintus who lived in the houseboat on the river at the bottom of the squash club field, and who invited me for a drink even after I'd whopped his arse on court, and me bringing the wine and then slipping on the deck and falling overboard and then ending up with his mad pantaloons halfway down my bum and him whispering sweet nothingness in my ear. I wasn't going to tell Mum and Dad about that ever, not with Jeb's other Uncle, Mickey, in the band and all, and I wasn't going to tell lovely Quintus that I thought he was a div.

His idea of one was different, anyway. I remember he told me that a div was a container, and you could have lots of divs on a page, and divs within other divs, each with its own style and also affected by the divs outside it. Sort of a Russian Doll effect, I remember he said, and this was another way of looking at experience, as having one meaning in one place and time and simultaneous meanings in many other places and times. And he said the meanings were never different, always just the same, only more so.

And I still didn't quite get it, and then he turned me round and lay me back on the bed and pulled the rest of his pantaloons off my bum, and raised my legs in the air and took out his earring, I remember, and as his body came down on mine, he said again "there is only one time", and then he entered me, and this time I think I finally understood, and thank you God, I'll always remember that feeling.

Blimey, my head is sore. And I still feel a bit dizzy. Or is that the rocking of the boat? What is that? Blimey, he keeps a crystal under the pillow. You could split your head open on that. Oh, I remember now. There was another squash game, that we arranged for a few days afterwards. That's when he was late. And he was very distant with me as well, which threw me, after the love we'd made together before, and I didn't play well, couldn't move properly, 'cos I felt rejected and uncertain of my footing, and I got stranded in the front then had to make a dash for the back and play off the back-wall and though I hit the thing in the end I mistimed it awfully and bashed into the wall, and then I remember the ball just going straight up parallel with the back wall, nowhere near the front, and then it came spinning down and I kept my eye on the yellow dots just like my old coach Osama used to tell me, and then my own head went all spinny and I must have passed out, but I remember catching the ball.

It's still here. I can feel it in my left hand now. It's so round and willing and pliable. Just needs warming up a little. It's me, really, it's what I can be for Quintus for ever, if he'll let me. Maybe that's what he meant, and if some people can't find this stream thingummy with music, like Dad does, or with magic, like Quintus does, then they can find it with love. Maybe that's what I can do.

He's brought me back here, anyway, to look after me. That's something. He was only distant with me because he was preoccupied. Thinking about work, perhaps. You've got to leave him his space, girl. And it'll all work out right in the end. So you've had a bash on the head, you're back in his bed again, aren't you?

Hello. Hello? Is that you, darling? Is that the kettle? I'd love a cup of tea. I'm feeling better now. Forget the tea, come and talk to me, darling. I've missed your voice. You and Jeb sound quite similar, you know, you have these funny little hiccups and inflexions in your patterns. It's very sexy. When you do it, anyway. Jeb just sounds like a div.

Then my cup of tea walks in and it's a woman. Not Quintus. A woman. In her other hand she has a thermometer and she sits on the bed. Sticks it in my mouth. Don't speak, she says. Listen. I'm Rebekka. I'm a nurse. She leans over to the table and picks out two of the gold rings and slots them easily back into her ears. Quintus is my lover, she says. We don't stay together much. I can't abide this place. It's so dark and creepy. But he fucks me good so I come back. He was worried about your head so he brought you here and called me. He's gone on a trip. She takes the thermometer out of my mouth and reads it. Good, she says. You're better. You can go home now. She pulls back the bedclothes and sure enough I'm still wearing my boring squash kit, not the magic pantaloons of love. She takes the squash ball from my hand. I am limp and loose, cannot resist. Pwyffthh, she says, squeezing the ball and echoing the sound of escaping air, this one is fucked good too. I will cut it into pieces and use it for my sculpture. She points at the rubber thingummies on the wall. Pwyffthh, she says again. It is only hobby, jah? First we must earn living.

I take the ball back and tell her. I think you'll find this is Quintus's lucky ball.

Pwyffthh, she says. Whatever. He told me what happened, you know. How you played together and then you brought wine here and jumped into the mud and dressed in his clothes and seduced him, and now you have ideas in your head. Ideas about him. That's why he brings you here now, and me, I told you. He is worried about your head.

I tell her, that's a lie. Of course it is, she says. Quintus has failed you. Just like the piano has failed you. He told me all about that too.

She looks at me with sympathy, I think, and it is an odd effect, because her face is fat and opaque, and her eyes lazy and cruel, and the kindness sits there like a turd.

She says. Forget music and love. Do something useful for a change. Learn to type. Whatever. Just fuck off and leave Quintus and me alone.

I push her out of the way and make a dash for the toilet. I retch violently for a while but nothing comes up. I am caught between Quintus's words, Quintus's love, Quintus's stream of being, that I know to be right and true, and the oppressive concrete reality of the here and now. I cannot join them together.

As I look down into the toilet I see the stream of reddish brown water that swirls beneath the boat, and Quintus's lovely wise face hovers in it for a moment. Now it begins to spin and dissolve, is replaced by the iron jaw of the nurse Rebekka. My head spins now as well, and I hear beautiful music, but only briefly, for it too dissolves, and I feel myself sliding away into nothingness, and I know now that it is better for me, or at least safer and easier, to be a determined something, however small and unfulfilled, than to risk dissolving completely, at least for the time being, until I get myself straight again, so I take hold of myself and hurl my small broken ball down through the funnel of the bowl into the red mud below, for I know that even though Rebekka is totally wrong about the universe, in absolute terms, she is right about me, for the time being.

And I will probably do what she says and be a secretary, for the time being, because in any case, whatever the rights and wrongs, she has Quintus, for the time being.

And she's not having me for a sculpture.

Fat kraut.

THE MABOOB MOB

the third book

Chaplet 91

A Stained Tearglass

When I awoke from my coma, in the Idristan village chapel, I was weak and trembly, for a number of reasons. I also felt religious.

Understandable, you may say; I had not eaten any meat for the years of my unknowing, and I had, I soon remembered, thrown my newborn son, in an act of desperate faith, into a river of red slime.

I was lightheaded; I was tragic: I was vegetarian. All the preconditions of religious belief were present.

A single tear ran down my cheek and slowed on my flesh, slowed into a dream of the nature of being. And the tear was a single drop of my human essence, that multiplied until it became a river, and flowed into an ocean, and then distilled itself back into a single drop. And the ocean was also a commingling of infinite other drops, and this was also the nature of its distilled essence.

And in this dream I suddenly saw that there were no beginnings and ends, just an infinite and continuous flow of essences out into the world and back into themselves.

Then I heard the harsh words of Queen Rebekka and again saw her face, fat and twisted with hate, as she fought with me above the eyehole in the mountain top, and now I remembered her words.

"You could have everything you want", she had screamed. "You fucking lala bint. Just give Quintus his son".

And then afterwards, when it was too late, when he had gone away down, as I passed out, I heard her say,

"What are you going to do now, write your fucking memoirs?".

And in my dream now I saw that was probably what I wanted to do, write down in some way or another, any way I could really, how the essence flows out of everything and then back into itself.

Then my dream wandered off, as I thought of the different people, and different ways they had of telling me the same thing. Quintus said it one way, and Plato, whom I came to know through my Academy work, said it another way, with his Forms, and his Reality that was shadows of these essences projected onto a cave wall, which was prescient, as they didn't even have tellies back then, leave alone Grideoblogs.

And I realized that no-one ever learned anything much from anyone wise and sensible, because the people who had taught me stuff were mostly evil or barmy.

I shall miss Iestyn. His was a simple soul. That's why I'm weepy, I think. It's the idea of the simple soul, an essence that is fully formed, complete in itself, and therefore incapable of change. Sure, it must also flow out and become an ocean before it can become completely itself again; but this is merely activity, a change of state rather than of nature.

All these beginnings and ends along the way are important and real, they really happen, but only in the course of our becoming.

And if I'm weepy now, and religious, it's because when I think of becoming as the creation of an essence that has already also been formed, I feel small, and helpless, and predetermined. Suddenly God seems like a very good idea.

But I'm feeling maudlin today. Lightheaded. Not enough meat, and then what I did with my son.

The idea of writing stuff down makes me suddenly cheerful. Odd that I should have this from that evil cunt Rebekka. Which is just what I was saying earlier.

But I realize that there won't be any happy endings, much as I'd like there to be, simply because all that linear stuff, all the drama of things happening and being bad and then becoming good, is just on the surface; it's just activity.

What I want to write down, what I want to describe, is what I said before, it's how the single drop, the essence of ourselves, the soul, flows out and becomes an ocean and in so doing becomes itself.

And now I feel much more cheerful, and not so keen on God; self-reliant, almost. Because now I can see, if I choose to look in a certain way, that my essence is not pre-formed, but determined in my own becoming.

I'm waking from my dream now, and feeling uncomfortable, annoyed. I can hear music again, and though the playing is beautiful, for I recognise the sweet-sour vibrato of my soulmate Nicky de la Chwyth, and though I once loved this tune, I now loathe its message. It is 'Cry me a river', and I am suddenly filled with horror that my own metaphor of being should have started with a single tear, and I fling back the rough blankets of my pew coma and leap out into the chapel, for my soul is now free of sadness, and full of the joy and energy of becoming.

I seized the ingeniously engineered car jack that Nicky played, tearing it from his lips at the climax of the bridge passage, and threw it straight out through the stained glass window of the nave, and in that moment our idea of God was for ever shattered, and music in our village of Idristan was never heard for eleven years more.

Chaplet 92

Quiet Roundabout

I woke up with the idea that I was going to write down everything; but it didn't happen.

For one thing, I understood now that that there is no end to everything, so writing it down is an unrealistic goal. There are any number of long possible expansions of each tiny moment of the life I have chosen, and any number of possible words to describe them. Don't go there, girl. It should be enough just to pull the thread of liquid out of the ocean and turn it back towards its genetic drop, so that everything can start over.

Also, I realized as I began to write, I'm not very funny on my own. I'm too earnest to be entertaining. That's why I got my Dad Len to tell most of the story. He's a funny guy. He's used to finding new angles on an old tune, used to spinning a line so it feels like it's going in a new direction even though you've seen it fall in the same spot a thousand times before. It's what he does; he's a musician.

And I always planned to leave the last word for my Mum, Heidi, because of her light touch. She's got the knack of making the tragic trivial. It's a good trick for a Buddhist.

But something else happened anyway, that changed my writing, when I started to die.

It was a gradual thing at first; the roundabout just seemed slower, so that I now had to wait around in nothingness for a long time before another meaning showed up. Which is an odd sensation because once, not even that long ago, I seem to remember meanings whizzing in upon me from all angles and in every moment, and I seem to remember being overwhelmed, almost, by the multiplicity and intensity of being. It's much quieter now. But I don't like it. I like even less the fact that the meanings, when they bother to turn up at all, are faded, washed-out, as though they've been round a few times too many in the same mind, which after all they have, and I can barely grasp them as they pass, nor retain their imprint in me when they have gone away by.

I feel myself slipping away, and am suddenly desperate. How much or how little to excavate, and in whose voice - these questions now seem artistic, irrelevant.

There is a real danger that I may not now reach my starting point at all. Then I will really die, rather than merely fade away into my new beginning.

Just as I decide to begin to write for home, Nicky appears in full evening dress.

"Come on, my love", he says. "We're taking you out for a dinner. You've a lot to catch up on".

Chaplet 93

Ground Work

Everything feels better after a good meal, and I didn't get one at Miskers that night. But I enjoyed seeing all my friends again, after what I discovered had been four years of coma. I learned that I had been kept alive by the ministrations of Nicky, Jeb and Mickey, along with my Mum and Dad and the other Heidi, and Elektra, a young child I hadn't met yet, for they had each taken their turn to smear my lips with lamb butter as I lay dreaming.

There was lamb butter aplenty upon the new Miskers menu, along with honey, lamb bacon, and sloke, dulse and laverbread in every possible form and presentation, savoury and sweet. People liked to eat differently now, at least these people, in their bulky, gleaming wheelchairs, and their red hats edged with blue.

We were all wearing red hats too, I noticed. They were made of jersey, and lay sodden on our heads. It had been a long walk in the rain from the Red Hat Enclosure where Mickey had parked the hearse.

"Everyone wears them, who isn't a Barehead, one of Queen Rebekka's coterie", explained Nicky de la Chwyth.

"The penalty for not is death", said Jeb, "Unless you're a visitor like them". He gestured out around the restaurant, and I remembered his stumpy finger again.

"They get given blue caps for underneath, so if the Red Hat falls off, in the wind, say, they get another chance".

"If ours come off", said Nicky, "the crime is impersonation of a Barehead".

"And the penalty is death", said Jeb again.

I nodded, checking that my hat was securely on. There was so much to take in. I didn't like the new way of eating. The menus were as large as hospital screens; the waiters lurked behind them like consultants with news of cancer.

"Pancetta d'agneau with a sloke jus and her spray of heather miel", I read aloud. "What on earth is that?".

"Lamb bacon, honey, and laverbread", said my Mum. "Your favourite, darling".

But it wasn't as I remembered it at all, not great lovely hunks of baby lamb smothered in honey and cooking juices all bedded down in a sexy mermaid gloop. It came now as tiny portions, overworked and tasteless, not as food, but as emblems of food.

"It's all flown in, see", explained Heidi Hyson. "First it's flown out, then they do this to it". She made a quick, careful face as she pointed down at her plate, for the waiters were still watching, and they were bareheaded. "Then it's flown in again", she finished.

The plates were huge and bore a strange crest of crystals in the shape of the letter R.

R for Rebekka.

"Costs an arm and a leg, as well", said my Dad Len. "By the time it gets back here".

I remarked that many of the diners were missing arms and legs, beneath their red hats edged with blue.

"They're all New Englanders", said Jeb. "They come over for the gastronomy now, as well as the dry land".

I laughed at the idea of Cymru being thought of as dry land.

"When they paved over the country they forced the aquatic life into a corner and it developed into a cod monster. Quintus saw them. He told us all about them", said Len. My Mum pinched his arm at this mention of my lapsed lover, and gave him her own version of a savage cod monster face.

"King Quintus is dead", said the other Heidi gently, and squeezed my arm in sisterhood.

"So is the Nutter King", said my Dad, who was determined to get all his bad news off his chest as soon as he could.

"He died peacefully in the harmonium", said the other Heidi. "The Nutter King, I mean. One day when we were going through some old Billie Holiday songs, suddenly we noticed that there was no snoring, and then Jeb couldn't get the pedals down any more, and we found him in there dead, slumped over the innards, like".

"Poor old sod", said Mickey. "But his daughter's lovely. Elektra. She just turned up on the doorstep. We still don't know who the mother is. But she's the spit of her Dad. Got the ears and everything. Loves jazz, an' all".

"She likes you", said my Mum. "She's been looking after you really special".

How did Quintus die, I wondered?

"Crystal cut to the penis", said my Mum briskly. "We always warn against inappropriate use on the packaging, but people don't read the small print, do they? He had lead poisoning, anyway, do you remember, love? He was always going to die. But the septicaemia got him first".

So the Maboob Emporium was still going then, with the crystals and everything?

"Oh yes, darling, said my Mum. "It's mostly what we live off now. There's no more teaching for the boys, and no gigs".

"Anyway, I saw the cod monsters myself", said Jeb. "And they were scary, I can tell you. What happened next was that the monsoons came, because there was global warming anyway, even before the Groodles, but it was just incredible after them, and the whole of the country was under rain for most of the year, and there was no drainage, because there was no soil, except in the Heritage Sites, only concrete, so now most of New England is under water".

"They got the Groodles up onto stilts", said Mickey. "Otherwise it would have been electric eels, as well as monster cod".

"You couldn't make it up", said the other Heidi. "It's like a film".

Yes, I remarked. A remake of Jaws with Death in Venice.

"And it's unusual to see a whole person from over there

now", said Jeb. "They're all foodies now, of course. Not posh, just very sentimental about the past. That's why we see so many of them over here, because they think our food is part of their ancient history. And they're all missing arms and legs, and other dangly bits, all gone over the side, to the cod. All in wheelchairs". He waved his finger stump around the restaurant again.

At the next table a New England visitor began to argue with his waiter.

"Don't call me mate. I'm not your fucking mate, mate. I've just come over for a quiet family dinner, me and my wife and my lovely daughter, so keep your fucking eyes off them. Don't you even think about touching them, you Welsh cunt!", the fat man shouted, first struggling to his feet, then collapsing back into his wheelchair under the weight of his own sentiment. No, I thought, they're not posh.

I heard some high-pitched laughter and my eyes found a group of Bareheads at a raised table in the corner of the restaurant. It was, I remembered, where Quintus and Rebekka and Dai Jefferies and the Nutter King had played their Enochian chess while I waited below, on the day of the Tournament Final. Where Iestyn had died.

I walked over to the table and found I knew most of the diners. Richard Henshaw was among them, and Victor Oguike, and Cornelius Coltrane Brewster, and Spiff Abrahams.

"Who dat dere?", shouted Victor as I approached, and winked at me, also letting out an explosive fart. I was absurdly pleased to see him.

They rose and greeted me effusively, as their friend, and explained that Cornelius and Spiff had moved to Porphyra permanently, to take over the running of the Academy.

"It was a brilliant idea", said Spiff. "But poorly executed. It needed a great mind to make it work. One like mine".

"We couldn't keep the old boys on any longer, not in charge, and not after the Nutter King finally passed, though I loved his mother and father, as God is my witness", said Cornelius.

"But they are still very useful around the place, in maintenance, and on the door, and so on. Mickey, Steve, and your father Len. And I'm sure you've still enough to live on, haven't you, dear?"

As the conversation set off again I crawled under the table to look for bloodstains. The wood had been bleached, but I found a long reddish-brown mark where Iestyn had bled away, and I rubbed my hands over it and wept, and remembered the red river below the mountain, wherein I had cast my boy child. In the distance above me I heard a bleating noise.

"And of course the whole world changed after Bip-Bop, I know it did, and I know I created it, but funnily enough I never realized at the time how important I was, and how much I was changing the world…".

Spiff was in full flow. I could tell from the tone of his voice and the twitch in his trousers. I fished his long miserable cock out of the corduroy, for old times' sake, and because I was still peckish, and gave it a tonguing. His voice never changed.

"I've always been at the cutting edge; the cutting edge of my own artistic vision", he finished.

"Oh, hello", he said as I emerged. "It's you again. Where have you been?".

"The food here is terrible", I replied.

"Oh. We rather like it", said Richard Henshaw.

"It's certainly expensive enough", said Cornelius, "even on expenses".

"It's got fuck-all to do with real food", I said, "the receipts are fake".

Spiff looked anxious.

"Will that affect the claiming procedure?", he asked Cornelius.

"No. The recipes are all wrong", I said.

I was annoyed now. It was such a simple thing to get wrong.

"I have them all in my head, you see", I told them.

"From the old times. I know how it should look, how it should taste. Not like this".

I pointed to the grotesque food wreckage on the dinner plates.

"Then, my dear", said Cornelius, "you must write them down. Describe them for us. And for yourself, and for your countrymen. Do you have the words to describe them, Myfanwy?".

"I shall not use my words to describe, but to understand them", I replied.

It had stopped raining when we left the restaurant, and I

dragged my friends down on to the beach for a walk in the moonlight.

After a while we sat on the rocks where I once waited for Quintus, near where he gave me my child, and as we watched the red-hatted diners bobbing up and down in their amphibious wheelchairs on their journey back to their boatels in Mumbles Bay, we were enchanted by the glinting play of the light on metal and water, and though we heard no music, we were happy.

Chaplet 94

Hokum Slokum

"This is bullshit", said Jamal, the beautiful young kitchen porter who had just joined the Miskers staff. He had been left in the restaurant by a weird and violent dreadlocked woman claiming to be his mother, although everyone doubted that.

"Just you make sure you look after 'im", she said, and disappeared for ever.

Timmy Gordon looked covetously at the lithe buttocks of the youth bent over the deep stainless titanium sink.

"Oh I'd look after him well enough", he said to himself, "given half a chance".

He felt old jealous eyes on him and waved over to his senior sous-chef, Len Maboob. He was turning into a real clinger, thought Timmy. Another lifestyle gay, he mused, as he worked patiently with the dulse and lambtail terrine. Got tired of his big new Harley and wanted something new and more exciting to ride. From biker to batty boy in one easy step. Another weekend willy warrior. He had pureed the seaweed and mixed it with enough sheep hoof gelatine to make a savoury jelly.

Still, Len talked a good romance, even it was mostly hokum. Typical musician. Hokum-slokum, he hummed to himself. This was Len's favourite, he thought fondly, as he poured the jelly carefully over the lambtail nuggets.

The only thing was, for all of Len's knowledge, and cooking skills, as well, that he'd developed with Myfanwy while she wrote that amazing book, that she called simply Idristan, and that was now the Bible of Traditional Cookery, not just because of the local recipes, or receipts as she called them, but because of its universal relevance to locality, so that it kind of worked everywhere in the world, whatever ingredients you used, because it was more an approach and a collection of methods than just menus, well for all that, the bloke was a crap chef. Couldn't hold more than one thing in his mind at one time, so service was always a nightmare. Christ knows how he used to manage on the piano, with all those notes on the go at once. Stuck with him now, thought Timmy, in more ways than one, and copped another furtive peep at Jamal's arse.

The boy turned from the sink, his eyes flashing. They were a yellowy-green colour, and unusual in such a dark face. Timmy felt suddenly paternal and protective towards his new employee, and at the same time filled with lust for his young flesh. Jesus, he thought. I'm turning Greek. It's a good job they knocked the old Academy on the head when they did, otherwise we'd all be back in the cave with Plato.

Timmy was now filled with grief for the old days, and as he remembered the innocent words of the young waiter Iestyn and the innocent cheeks of tthe young DJ Morgan Oguike, a tear rolled down his face and plopped into the laverbread jelly.

"This is bullshit", said Jamal, again.

"You know what, mate", said Timmy Gordon. "I completely agree with you", and so saying he hurled the terrine into the long mirror of the kitchen wall.

And the kitchen staff were no longer caught in their own reflections, nor bound in their own spells, and were free to recreate themselves.

And they walked until they came to our chapel in the village called Idristan, and I rose with great energy and compassion to make them welcome here, though I was still weak from many years of writing. And among them I saw the large nose and green eyes of Jamal and recognised him as my son, and I knew that though I had once cast him from me into an unknowable river, I had finally saved him, and he was now returned to my side.

And as he spoke to me of his travels in the East, of his apprenticeships in tribes with cooks, musicians and jesters, I heard in his voice also the nineteen divisions of his grandfather's octave, and I forgave his father.

And as we talked and talked, and remade and rediscovered our bond, the boys banged about in the barn next door, and created an intimate and authentic restaurant in the old style, and fit and proper for the serving of real food to real people, and they also made a minstrel gallery.

And Jamal then took me there to see what had been made, and while I sat at the best new table, all my friends gathered in the gallery, and they had instruments of many sorts and dimensions, for Nicky de la Chwyth had never stopped his engineering, though I had forbade them all from playing for eleven years or more.

And they were silent now, as they gathered before and above me, and looked at me with love and respect, for I am their Muse, and also with pain and regret, for they felt me fading from them now. And they had a question in their eyes, and as I nodded my head graciously in my answer, they began to play.

And I do not know if the music was good. Jeb struggled as ever at the harmonium, with his stumpy finger and lack of taste and restraint; Mickey had become half-mad by the combination in his body of the Ketamine thirteen eight with the infant memories of his father's nineteen; My Dad Len had gone slushy in his old age, and all we heard from the piano was big romantic chords, no matter what else was going on. And Steve was well rusty on his double bass, and blistered up in the first number. I don't know if it was that good, really. But Heidi, the other one, Heidi Hyson, not my Mum, was in good voice, I think, and still did a good Hoya Hoya, though I couldn't tell the German strands from the Native American ones any more. Now she just sounded Welsh. Or maybe Jewish. I couldn't tell any more. And I knew I didn't have enough time left to work it out.

It all started fading then, in the middle of the third number, a modal thing in six, or seven maybe. I can't remember the tune now, and I won't hear it again anyway, when it comes back after the solos. If they ever find their way back. They're a long way out now, at the moment, it seems to me. How will they ever get back? All the sounds are fading now, going into a cool grey mist, and all I can hear now is some beautiful clear pizzicato bass notes, and I know that's my son Jamal, because he's a virtuoso, you know, I heard Steve say so; then there's Nicky's haunting high melody that I hear weaving through the middle of the sound and finding its way up into the top, above everyone else. And a girl's voice suddenly spirals upwards, and for a moment I think it might be mine, might be the voice I had inside me but could never let sing, and then I know that it belongs to Elektra, who is a true daughter of Idristan, and the three sounds merge together and arch around the others and give them shape and meaning, and I know that I can rest.

And that's the last thing I see now, a grey shape retreating into the distance, with a flash of green inside that I know is my boy child, and that's me over here, and over there is my Maboob Mob, and I know I've been part of them always while being alone among them for so long, and as I lie in my Mum's arms she rings her little bell, and I close my eyes for the last time and then I can only hear the music very faintly, just a last high harmony and a last low thud, and Heidi, my Mum's words as she says goodbye.

"I'll finish your story for you, love. I'll take you home".

Chaplet 95

Starting Over

I rang the bell over and over again. I knew Len might think it was the phone and wake up. Deep down he still thinks he's a musician, poor love.

I don't mind this cooking jag he's on, though I don't like him taking over my kitchen all of a sudden, like he's just discovered he's a King. Typical man.

I am worried about him, though. I think something happened while he was over on that course in Wales.

Ironic, really, all those Summer Schools he taught on, for all those years, and those so-called Orange Badges he used to laugh about, the students that weren't really there to learn, but to change their lives, get rid of a career, or a husband. Or a wife.

We used to laugh about them together, but we both knew he was shagging them. I think he still wants me, still needs me, though. We've been through a lot together, and I understand him. And there's Myfanwy to think about.

So what happens? He loses his main teaching job at the

Royal English, which is a scandal, and it still makes me mad when I think of the way the boys were treated, and the gigs dry up, like everything does when you get older, which he never anticipated, when I saw it coming a long time ago, and then he finds he's ended up as an Unofficial Orange Badge Counsellor, fondler in chief to the all-comer Summer fuckups. And he discovers cooking, goes on a course, and becomes an Orange Badge himself! Ironic, as I say.

I don't think it's a woman tutor, though. I think it's a bloke. He's been walking funny since he got back. Oh well. I expect we'll get through, somehow.

Myfanwy's the important one at the moment, anyway. She needs all my support, what with her new job.

It was touch and go for her, poor love, after the knockback with the music, and that other business afterwards that I never got to the bottom of. There was a bloke involved somewhere in that, of course, I know that, but I don't think it was Jeb.

It was something to do with him, though, him or his family, and all a little too close for comfort with his Uncle Mickey being in the band, so I never wanted to know all the details at the time, which I still feel badly about.

But young girls fall in love. That's what they do. Then they get hurt. That's what happens.

She did fall hard, though, and it was uphill keeping her going through secretarial college, day after day, when all she wanted was to sleep and cry. She was like the walking dead for a while.

I should be used to that, mind, with her Dad. They're a pair of dreamers, those two. I don't know what I'm doing with either of them, really. If I could get as far away in my meditation as they do just over breakfast, I'd be the Big Boss of all the Buddhists. If they wanted one.

Anyway, we got her all trained up, I got her all trained up, shall we say, because Len was away with the fairies as usual, and in more ways than one, as I'm now starting to realize, and we've got her a nice new job, as it happens through her last piano teacher, the one after Jeb. Cornelius Coltrane Brewster, his name is, and I don't mind him, even if he was nasty to Muff about her music. But he was very good about taking her on. Probably felt guilty about firing Len and the boys, which is what he did, effectively, I think they call it constructive dismissal, because cleaning the toilets isn't the same as an OBE, whatever anyone tells you.

I don't much care for the Head of Jazz there, though, that Spiff Abrahams fellow, and Myfanwy has to deal with him a lot. Very arrogant for such a young man. Only just finished his lessons with my Len, and hardly a proper gig under his belt, and already thinks he's a fucking genius. Typical man. Anyway, it all worked out OK for our Myfanwy, fingers crossed, which is what counts in the end, isn't it? You stop worrying so much about yourself if you're a parent, don't you? So long as it all works out for your kids.

I'd be happier if she was still at home with us as well, instead of all on her own in that caravan. She'll get cold enough in there come the winter. That's independence for you.

I'll drop in later today, I think. Take Myfanwy in some of her Nan's Welsh Cakes, and see if I can get her to take an hour off for lunch.

She works too hard, I think. It's unusual work as well. Very modern. They showed me into the Principal's office last time. It's lovely, you know, very grand. They all want to be down on the lower corridor, apparently. What was that word she used? Oh yes, coveted. I like that.

Anyway, I happened to catch sight of Myfanwy under his desk. I know it was her because I saw the heels of the Italian shoes I bought her last Christmas, and they're unique, I've never seen them anywhere else. What was she doing down there, I kept asking myself?

So I do worry about our girl, and I shall keep going in to see her, no matter how much she tries to put me off, just to let her know I'm watching her back.

I did try to raise the subject, but I didn't get very far.

"Oh yes, Mum", she says. "There's always a lot of ground work to be done".

All very modern, like I say. Not like it used to be in my day.

Maybe it will be next time round.

Nick Weldon is the author of a number of poems, songs and translations, and also of the play 'Laura-Mae and the Olivardies', broadcast on Radio Four.

•

Nick is the son of writer Fay Weldon and folk singer and actor Colyn Davies, and himself has two grown-up sons, Max and Felix.

•

Nick is well known as a jazz pianist and teacher and also plays the double bass in several orchestras. He writes longhand, for the sake of the rhythm.

•

Nick lives in a Shoefactory in Rushden, Northamptonshire with his partner, singer Andra Sparks.

•

Idristan is his first novel.

•

For more information, visit the website
www.nickweldon.com

Printed in the United Kingdom by
Lightning Source UK Ltd., Milton Keynes
138615UK00001B/56/P